THE ROAD
TO
ST. CECELIA'S

Jean Gillespie

PublishAmerica
Baltimore

ISBN: 1-60703-017-9
PUBLISHED BY PUBLISHAMERICA, LLLP
www.publishamerica.com
Baltimore

Printed in the United States of America

⌘

This book is dedicated to Barbara Mayer Good (1940-2007) who was taken from us much too soon.

Acknowledgments

I would like to thank the Sisters of the Visitation at Mount de Chantal Academy in Wheeling, West Virginia, for their permission to base St. Cecelia's Academy on the Mount. Appreciation is also extended to the faculty and staff who supported this project. This is a work of complete fiction manufactured in the author's mind. It is my sincere hope that no one will take offense at the portrayal of certain characters.

S usan Foster sat at the red light at the intersection of James and Collingwood crying her eyes out. She was in a state of shock. *Mon Dieu! Mon Dieu!* was the only phrase she could muster.

The rain beat down on the car roof with a vengeance, splattering the windshield until it became as blurry as Susan's eyes. The blare of a horn from the impatient driver behind jolted her back to reality. She floored the gas pedal and sped across James Street to South Collingwood. Thank God there wasn't a car in front of her. She'd have rear ended it for sure.

Calm down, she ordered herself. She did, pulling over to the side of the road to catch her breath. She glanced over at the small sheet of paper on the passenger seat, gave a sigh and picked it up. *If this is a dream, let me wake up.* It wasn't. She didn't.

When Susan felt calm enough to re-read the sheet of paper she'd pilfered from her mother's private papers, she reached over to the passenger seat and picked up the fragile piece of paper. It was brittle with age, so Susan unfolded it slowly, trying her best to keep it intact. She succeeded, except for a rip at the bottom of the center fold. Too excited to care, she shone her small flashlight on the open page.

Acte de Naissance
Nom: Suzette Fontaine
Dat de Naissance: Juin 3, 1975
Nom de Mère: Anna Fauberge
Nom de Père: Jacques Fontaine
Ville de Naissance: Dijon, France

No matter what language it was written in, French or English, *Juin* 3 or June 3, 1975 was Susan Foster's birth date. But who was Suzette Fontaine? She was tempted to turn the car around and drive back across James Street and down North Collingwood to her mother's. But her pride wouldn't permit such a rash move, at least not tonight. She'd wait till tomorrow when she'd had the benefit of a good night's sleep to calm her down. Tomorrow was Saturday. Her mother would be at home all day. She'd phone the minute she got to Karen's on South Midler and arrange to see her at lunch time.

Anna Foster, Susan's mother, had always been an enigma to her daughter. She'd raised Susan by herself. Her husband, Susan's father, had died when Susan was a baby. Anna claimed to have no living relatives. From the time Susan was a little girl she'd been curious about the lack of family connections. All the other kids had grandparents, aunts, uncles, cousins. Some even had great-grandparents. Susan's curiosity clearly annoyed her mother who answered all questions regarding her mysterious background by doing what she did best, shrugging her shoulders and keeping her mouth shut. Susan's effervescent personality was at odds with her mother's aloofness and bode ill for any sort of mother-daughter closeness.

By the time Susan left for college, she was no closer to finding out about her mother's background than she'd been in kindergarten. She never got a satisfactory answer, so she gave up asking. The last time she'd asked Anna why she never referred to her family or its roots, she was told in no uncertain terms that since the past had never done anything for her she was banking on the future.

Anna ran a small, successful accounting firm which grossed most of its revenue from handling the monthly payrolls for several companies in Syracuse and the surrounding area. She assumed that Susan would major in business in college, acquire an MBA and become a partner in what she referred to as the family firm. Susan guessed that was what her mother meant by banking on the future. But Susan had other ideas. She had no interest in business. The day after her mother left her in her dorm room at NYU, she changed the business major her mother had forced her to declare to French history and literature.

Anna hit the roof when informed of the switch in majors over long distance. It was the strongest burst of emotion Susan had ever encountered from her mother. Her voice changed completely, the tone, intonation, pronunciation, and speed of delivery were practically incomprehensible. If she hadn't known it was her mother on the other end of the line, Susan would have sworn she was speaking French. But she knew that was impossible. Now she wasn't so sure.

Susan folded the document back into quarters. It had been folded up for so long that it almost sprang back to that shape automatically. If a paper could take on a personality of its own, this one had. It was in such a rush to get back to its undisturbed shape with the writing hidden from view that Susan was convinced it hadn't wanted to be opened and read in the first place.

Susan restarted the car. A few minutes later, she pulled into her friend's driveway on South Midler. The front porch light and another at a side door welcomed her arrival. Karen had told her they'd leave the lights on a timer in case she got in late. Their friendly glow brought a smile to Susan's face. She was already beginning to feel better. The sensation of shock over the newly found birth certificate was subsiding and becoming one of curiosity. She removed her small overnight bag from the trunk and retrieved the door key from its hiding place under a flower pot. Once inside, she was thankful she had the house to herself. She needed time to think. Had Karen been at home, they'd have stayed up all night, conjuring up all sorts of scenarios to explain the mysterious birth certificate.

There was a note on the kitchen table thanking Susan for spending the weekend there to watch over the house, making it appear inhabited and a poor risk for any would-be robbers. While Susan waited for the kettle to boil for a late night cup of tea, she phoned her mother. The answering machine picked up before the first ring.

"Mom. Let's get together for lunch tomorrow. I'll be there by noon." She didn't ask her mother to call back. She knew she wouldn't.

Anna Foster rarely answered the phone. She claimed that talking on the phone made her nervous. She'd always made sure, even in the early days of her business, that there was enough in the budget to cover the salary of a receptionist. Anna Foster was a hard worker. She'd tackle any kind of job except when it required talking. Over the years, she'd turned down numerous offers to speak to civic groups and school classes. On more than one occasion, she'd sent Susan as her proxy when she was the recipient of an award from the business community.

Susan sat on Karen's couch and sipped her tea slowly. *Suzette Fontaine! What a beautiful name. If I really were French, that's the name I'd want.*

Susan's love for France, its language and history had been a part of her since childhood. When she placed her dolls in their tiny chairs around her miniature table, the names she assigned them were always French : Gigi, Marcella, Madeleine and Pierre. They were the brother and sisters she'd never had.

"Where did you hear those names?" her mother would ask.

"I don't remember," Susan answered honestly.

"Are you sure?"

"Yes. I'm sure." But she never told her mother that those were also the names of her imaginary friends. In her young mind their faces were very real to her. It was as if those names had always been a part of her. Until this evening's discovery, she'd thought they were figments of her childhood imagination. Now she wasn't so sure.

When Susan signed up for French in high school, her mother argued that Spanish would be more beneficial. But Susan's choice prevailed. And a wise one it was. The teacher was amazed at the speed with which she learned the language.

"You sound like a native, Susan," Madame Mandigo had insisted. "Are you sure you haven't spoken French before?" Susan assured her that only if she'd lived a previous life.

"Lived a previous life," Susan said out loud. "Now I'm beginning to wonder. Anna Foster has some explaining to do."

She thought back to earlier in the evening when she'd asked her mother if she could look at some old photograph albums, the ones she kept in a cupboard in her bedroom.

"No! No you can't!" her mother had stated emphatically. "It would take ages to find them, and then it would leave a mess. More trouble than it's worth. Nothing in them you need to see." Susan hadn't argued. But she took the opportunity of sneaking into her mother's bedroom to look for the albums she'd never been allowed to see when her mother went down to the basement to unload the dryer. Feeling like a thief, Susan opened the cupboard doors. Various file folders and a few photograph albums were stacked neatly on the shelves. This was the most accessible assortment of family records she could imagine. She quickly removed one photo album and leafed through it. It turned out to be the album her mother had assembled of her high school senior year, an assortment of photographs, invitations, graduation announcements, and programs. When she replaced it, a piece of carefully folded paper fell from the album onto the floor. Quickly, Susan knelt down to pick it up. For reasons she couldn't explain, she stuffed it into the back pocket of her jeans. A few minutes later she opened it up in the bathroom. She was so outraged over the contents of the strange document that she left the house without even saying good-night to her mother. Tomorrow's confrontation couldn't come soon enough.

⌘

Susan awoke in a stupor after a dream-plagued night. It took her a few minutes to figure out where she was. The dreams had been pleasant enough, small children laughing and playing games: petite Marcella, chubby little Gigi, a sullen Madeleine and boisterous Pierre, Susan's imaginary friends who'd entered her life in childhood and never left. But were they imaginary? Now she wasn't so sure.

After a leisurely breakfast, Susan washed and dried the few dishes she'd used. The drenching rain that had pelted down half the night ceased as suddenly as it had begun. Gray skies had given way to bright blue. It was a beautiful April morning, so Susan decided to walk the few short blocks to her mother's house. She rarely stayed there on her infrequent visits to Syracuse. That didn't bother her mother. Anna preferred solitude and considered it an inconvenience to have to entertain someone, even if the intruder were her daughter, and, if she were to be believed, her only living relative.

Susan stopped at a neighborhood deli to purchase sandwiches, a ready-made salad for two and two slices of apple pie. Her mother always insisted on going out for lunch. But that wouldn't happen today. Susan had decided to confront her mother in the privacy of her own home.

Just for spite, Susan almost rang her mother's front doorbell. But she thought better of it and walked up the driveway to the back door. For reasons Susan had never been able to fathom, Anna Foster never used her front door. A neatly printed sign in the porch window at the side of the door read PLEASE USE REAR ENTRY. As a teenager, Susan had taken great delight in ringing the front doorbell to announce her arrival. It was worth it to see the look of disgust on her mother's face when she walked into the glassed-in porch and saw her daughter standing at the door laughing. But she never opened it. She would stand behind the door and direct her daughter to the back of the house. In all her years growing up in that house, Susan couldn't remember a single time she'd entered or left through the front door. Today, for the first time, Susan wondered if her mother was hiding from someone. Anything was possible.

Anna was in the back yard arranging tulips in a concrete urn.

"They look great, Mom."

"Thank you. And thanks for not ringing the front door bell."

"No bother at all. I knew it would upset you. But what do you do in winter?"

"What do you mean?"

"Don't tell me you still put on boots and all your winter gear to walk around to the front door to get the mail?"

"Of course I do. Sometimes I almost freeze. You know what Syracuse winters are like."

"But the mailbox is on the wall just outside the front door. Wouldn't it make more sense to open the front door and reach into the box to get your mail?"

"Why do you have to be so argumentative, Susan? Why can't you just accept the fact that the front door of this house is never used?"

"Because it's stupid!"

"It's civilized!"

Susan shut up. Anyone who could come up with the rules Anna Foster did was not open to criticism, so Susan changed the subject.

"I've brought lunch," she said, holding up the deli bags.

"Why didn't you go to that new deli on James Street? It's got a much better selection. Did you get soup?"

"No. Didn't want to risk spilling it."

"You know I never eat lunch without soup. Let's drive over to the Marriot. We can eat your sandwiches later."

"No. I need to talk to you about something important."

"Don't tell me your stock broker is finally going to make an honest woman of you. It's about time."

"No, Mom. I'm not getting married."

"Good. In this day and age there's no good reason for a woman with a career to get married. Look at me. I've done just fine on my own."

"Are you saying that you're glad my father died and left you alone with a daughter to raise?"

"Why do you always have to twist everything I say completely out of shape? I'm just letting you know that I don't care if you ever get married. Don't rush into wedlock on my account."

"Then why all the snide comments about making an honest woman of me?"

"I'm just joking. Can't you see that?"

"No. Your accusatory tone doesn't sound like you're joking."

"How many times do I have to tell you that I can't help the tone of my voice?"

"Come on, Mom. Lighten up for once. Aren't you getting anxious to hear the patter of little feet running around the house?"

" No! One pair of those was enough for a lifetime."

"Geez, Mom. You really know how to make a girl feel wanted."

Anna didn't respond. She just led the way through the back door into the kitchen. Susan followed. She took the opportunity of her mother's washing her hands in the bathroom to set the table and put the kettle on the stove. They ate in silence.

"I do have to admit these sandwiches were pretty tasty. When I mentioned the new deli, I was just trying to let you know there is a second choice available now. I wasn't criticizing you. Sometimes I have difficulty saying things the correct way."

You can say that again, thought Susan.

"Now," continued her mother. "What's the important subject you want to discuss?"

"Promise not to get angry?"

"About what?"

"Something I found last night."

"Depends on what you found. Why all the secrecy?"

"Secrecy! I'm the one who should be asking you that. Anyway, when you went down to the basement last night, I decided to snoop."

"Where? Why? I don't understand."

"I wanted to look through your old photograph albums that you insist on hiding from me in the bedroom cupboard."

"I'm not hiding anything."

"Then why have I never seen this before?"

Susan retrieved the *acte de naissance* from her purse and unfolded it on the table.

"Whose birth certificate is this?"

"It's called a *acte de naissance* in France."

"How do you know that? I didn't know you knew French?"

Her mother shrugged her shoulders in reply.

"The date of birth on this *acte* is the same as mine. Why?"

"Because it is yours."

Susan stared at her mother in disbelief. Anna continued.

"Your real name is Suzette Fontaine, and you were born in Dijon, France. I will tell you my story without any emotion because you were dishonest about prying into my affairs."

"Since when has going into a cupboard in your own family home to look for photograph albums been labeled dishonest and prying?"

"This is no longer your home. You made that quite clear when you went off to college. Sometimes I think that educating you was the dumbest thing I've ever done. You've looked down on me ever since."

"That's not true."

"Do you want me to continue my story or not?"

"Of course I do."

"I had a love affair with a man named Jacques Fontaine."

"The French journalist?"

"*Oui*. Jacques Fontaine is your father."

"What happened?"

"I got pregnant. But we never married."

"Why? Was he already married?"

"No. But he was not about to stay in Dijon, France and settle into married life."

"He lives and writes in Vietnam, doesn't he?"

"*Oui*. He was fascinated with the old Indochine. I knew he would want to settle there after the Vietnam War."

"Did he know you were pregnant?"

"No. I never told him.

"Why?"

"I did not wish to tie him down."

"You could have gone to Vietnam with him."

"Why? I had no desire to do so."

"Did he keep in touch?"

"For a while, but I never answered his letters or returned his phone calls. He needed his independence. A distant relative sponsored my entry into the United States. A cousin in Dijon gave me enough money to set up my own business here. It was easier for Europeans to come here then than it is now. Perhaps you will now understand my tirades over all this illegal immigration."

"Don't try to change the subject, Mom. But why Syracuse, New York of all places?"

"A family in Dijon had lived here years ago. They told me so much about it that I felt it was the only place I could go with my little daughter."

"How old was I when we came here?"

"Almost four years old. I'll never forget how you cried and cried the day we left our apartment for the last time. Your little playmates lined up to wave goodbye. It was very sad."

"And let me guess," Susan interrupted. "Their names were Gigi, Marcella, Madeleine and Pierre."

Anna nodded her head in reply. She remained silent for a few seconds before continuing.

"There were times when I thought the emigration papers would never go through. During the three years we waited, I studied English day and night. Mainly pronunciation. I needed to be able to pass myself off as an American."

"Why?"

"I thought it would make it easier for me in the business world. I was right."

"You certainly succeeded in the language department. I never once suspected you were anything but American."

"But, in spite of everything I tried to do to erase my past, you were the constant reminder of France. When you began to study French in high school, I was scared to death I'd slip up and go back to my French. The back of the camel, or however the saying goes in English, was broken when you decided to major in French in college."

"But why all the secrecy?"

"It was what I wanted. I wanted a new life, an American life. But God punished me."

"How?"

"Through you. You were a constant reminder of all that had gone wrong. I am so ashamed"

"No. No, *maman*. That's not true." Susan longed to run to her mother and embrace her but thought better of it. There were now tears in Anna'a eyes as she continued her story.

"It is the second *acte* I am so ashamed of. Let me see it?"

"What second *acte*? I found only one."

"*Mon Dieu*! I am so stupid."

Anna rose to her feet and walked into her bedroom. She returned a few minutes later with another sheet of folded paper which she opened up and spread out on the table.

"You might as well know it all."

The second *acte* was dated March 4, 1965. The name of the child was Solange Dupré. Susan studied it carefully.

"Who is Solange Dupré, *maman*? More to the point, where is Solange Dupré?"

"Maybe still in Dijon. I had a wild affair as a teenager with a not-so-nice boy in our neighborhood. I put the child, a little girl, up for adoption."

"You're telling me that I have a sister?"

"At least a half-one."

"No wonder you were so anxious to leave the country. You were quite the little slut, *maman*!"

"Susan!"

"Sorry. I mean *je le regrette*. Does this mean we can speak French now?"

"If you'd like."

Susan's head was swimming. Several things about her mother were now beginning to make sense, mainly her phobias about answering the phone or making speeches.

"Now I understand. You've always been afraid to speak on the phone in case your accent came across."

"Of course. Anyone who has ever learned a new language finds it impossible to use it fluently on the phone. It is a dead give-away. You are unable to use body language or hesitate before answering. That's why my office has never been without a receptionist."

"And you always sent me to accept your awards."

"*Oui*. I would never have been able to keep from lapsing into French, at least an accent of some sort."

"Remember when you read to me when I was a little girl?"

"*Oui*."

"That's the only time your voice was different. That's where I picked up my intonation."

"French was your first language. There was nothing I could do to make you forget it completely."

"I did have a previous life. Madame Mandigo was right."

"Are you very angry with me?"

"Of course I am. What an utterly ridiculous deception."

"But you must try to understand how things were for me; the shame of putting a child up for adoption, the birth of a second one out-of-

17

wedlock. People were always whispering about us. I was a desperate woman. I wanted to protect you."

Susan rose to her feet.

"Where are you going?"

"As far away from you as I can get."

"I don't blame you."

"How did you come up with the name Susan Foster?"

"It was easy. I took the first two letters of your real first and last names and came up with two common American ones beginning with them. Susan Foster. *Viola*! It sounded right at the time. What do you plan to do with all this information?"

"Find someone important."

"He's still in Vietnam."

"Not him! I am going to find Solange."

Susan stomped out of the kitchen, through the center hall and out the front door.

⌘

Anna sat at the kitchen table and poured out all the tears she'd held in for years. She detested herself for having built a life based on lies for Susan and herself. But it wasn't over. She'd done it again. Solange Dupré was not Susan's half-sister. She was not even Anna's daughter. It had all happened so many years ago. But she was afraid if she tried to explain it all to Susan, she'd screw it up. She didn't have a way with words in either French or English. There had to be another way. She knew that Susan would head for France at the first opportunity to check out the veracity of her mother's confessions. There was nothing she could do to prevent that.

Late into the evening, Anna sat at her desk with a pile of documents in front of her. She placed three of them, Susan's original *acte de naissance* with the raised seal, the *passeporte* mother and daughter had used for entry into the United States, and the original copy of Susan's American naturalization papers in a thick padded envelope. Susan would need those if she applied for a French passport. *Not if,* Anna laughed to herself. *When* was closer to the truth. She stapled a business card with the address of the French consulate in Washington, D.C. to a personal letter of apology to her daughter.

Anna kept telling herself that she had done her best to raise Susan as an American. But it hadn't worked. There were childhood images in the form of imaginary friends which would be forever imprinted on Susan's brain She'd been an idiot not to explain her past to Susan years ago, downright selfish, since it concerned Susan as much as herself.

Anna sealed the envelope and addressed it to Susan's office at the translation center. She'd send it Fed Ex. That way, Susan would have to sign for it. She'd open it immediately, thinking it was a document which required an immediate translation. Anna would have notification of delivery if Susan decided to ignore her.

Anna made herself a cup of tea and turned on the evening news. But she couldn't concentrate. Her thoughts kept returning to the France of her youth. Anna and her best friend, Annemarie Marceau, had laughed and partied their way through their teens until their sins caught up with them during the swinging sixties. Tight mini-skirts and sweaters accessorized with the trademark white go-go boots were the only clothes they owned. They ran with a fast crowd. Booze and drugs were the order of the day. Anna had managed to pull herself together long enough to earn a certificate in accounting from a local business college. She was able to maintain a balance between her studies and the freewheeling lifestyle enjoyed by her peers. But it took the death of Annemarie's loser of a boyfriend from a drug overdose to jolt them back to reality.

At the funeral, Annemarie sobbed her heart out, but not entirely from grief. She'd found out the previous day that she was pregnant. An abortion was out of the question. It was still against the law in France. And a back-street one was too risky, at least Anna thought so. Annemarie didn't agree, but she wasn't thinking straight. The sudden death of the father of her child and the thought of raising that child on her own were too much for Annemarie's drug-riddled mind to deal with. It fell to Anna to take charge.

The day after Annemarie broke the news of her pregnancy to Anna, a postcard arrived from their friend, Isabelle. Anna took that as an omen. Whenever they were in trouble, they went to Isabelle. She'd gone to school with them. It always amazed Anna that the three of them had become so close. Isabelle was quiet and sweet. She exhibited none of the wild, self-destructive tendencies of the other two. They knew she was religious, but it had blown their minds when she revealed her intention of entering the religious life.

"*Mon Dieu*," was all Anna and Annemarie could utter. It was difficult for them to imagine themselves being close friends with a nun, those women who dressed in long black habits and wimples. They'd seen lots of nuns, been taught by them at school, but having one as an actual friend, one who'd listened to all their dirty little secrets, was incomprehensible. Isabelle couldn't be serious. But she was. The day after she left high school, she packed her bags and traveled to a convent not far from the Swiss border. Anna and Annemarie joked that now they could sin all they wanted. Isabelle was their ticket to redemption. She could spend her days and nights on her knees praying for their souls.

It took Annemarie's unwanted pregnancy to wipe the smirks from both their faces. Anna decided to pay Isabelle a visit. She'd know what to do. Isabelle was kind. She would help Annemarie.

"I always knew you two would come to a bad end," sighed Isabelle.

"I didn't come here for you to gloat, and I have not come to a bad end," snarled Anna.

"I'm not gloating. I'm furious with myself for not trying harder to sober up the two of you. At least you have an accounting certificate. You can get a job. We need to concentrate on Annemarie."

"That's what I keep saying."

"What does she want to do?"

"She wants to get rid of it."

"That is the worst sin she could commit. God will forgive the drinking, the drugs and even the sex, but he will not forgive taking the life of an innocent unborn child."

"That's easy for you to say. You're not the one having it."

Isabelle didn't answer. She was deep in thought.

"I'm sorry, Isabelle. That was a rotten thing to say. I'm just jealous."

"Jealous? Of what?"

"The success you've made of your life compared to the mess Annemarie and I have made of ours."

Isabelle laughed.

"What's so funny?"

"You. Listen to yourself. You are only twenty years old."

"But I'm a complete fuck-up."

"No, you're not. You have done a wonderful thing for your friend who is in trouble. God will not abandon you. He loves those who take care of the less fortunate."

"Does that mean I have to sign on here for life?"

"Of course not. You don't have to sign up for the religious life to be a good person in the eyes of God."

"Stop with the compliments, Isabelle. You're giving me a swelled head."

"Tell me, Anna, why did you come here? Surely not just to cry on my shoulder. Self-pity isn't your style, is it?"

"No, of course it isn't. I came for advice. What should Annemarie do?"

"Would she come here?"

"You mean stay in the convent with you?"

"No, of course not. I could find a family for her to stay with until she has the baby."

"How difficult would that be?"

"Not too. There are many families in the parish who do good deeds."

"You are wonderful, Isabelle."

Isabelle ignored the compliment.

"But there is one stipulation."

"Only one? We will pull our resources and pay the family."

"No. It is not about money. It is adoption. The baby must be adopted by a good Catholic family who will raise the child as its own."

"You must be kidding. Annemarie will never give up her baby once she's agreed to carry to full term."

"Then don't bring her here."

Two weeks later, Annemarie, carrying only a small suitcase, arrived at the home of the Dupré family in Sauret near the Swiss border. In return for help with the household chores, Annemarie had a place to stay until her confinement. Monsieur and Madame Dupré had been unsuccessful in their attempts to conceive a child. A private adoption was arranged. But, in her sixth month, Annemarie confided to Isabelle that she had no intention of relinquishing her parental rights. She wanted her baby.

Isabelle did not comment.

Towards the end of her eighth month, Isabelle invited Annemarie to the convent for tea. The two chatted amiably about their childhoods in Dijon. It was like old times. But, no matter how much sugar Annemarie stirred into her tea, it still tasted bitter. Annemarie was too polite to comment. Isabelle had been so kind to her in her time of need that the least she could do was drink the disgusting brew.

On her long walk back to the Dupré's, the cramps began. By the time she reached the house, she was hemorrhaging. She knew her labor had begun. Madame Dupré would know what to do. But the lady of the house was not at home. In desperation, Annemarie telephoned for Isabelle at the convent.

"Come quickly. Get the doctor, Isabelle. The baby is coming."

"We'll be there as quickly as possible."

Isabelle was alone when she arrived at Annemarie's bedside. No doctor ever appeared. Isabelle delivered the baby. Then, she calmly held Annemarie's hand until she bled to death. *This is God's will,* sighed Isabelle. *Such sinners must be punished.*

⌘

The week after Solange's birth and Annemarie's death, Isabelle sat at the small desk in her tiny, cell-like room. She wrote two letters. The first was addressed to Annemarie's family.

Madame et Monsieur Marceau,

It is with a heavy heart that I write to inform you of the death of your beloved daughter, Annemarie, in a tragic automobile accident last evening. The crash occurred only a few miles from the convent where I reside. Since Annemarie had visited me a few days before, I was asked by the village coroner to identify the body. The funeral will take place here in Sauret in the village cemetery tomorrow morning. It is our custom here to bury the victims of accidents as quickly as possible to help alleviate the suffering of the family. I decided to contact you in writing. A telephone call at this time would have been too impersonal.

Your servant in the Lord,
Isabelle Duchamps

The second letter was to Anna.

My Dear Anna,

Our beloved Annemarie was called home to God a few hours after delivering a beautiful baby girl. The doctor in attendance did all he could to save Annemarie's life, but God's will prevailed. I held her hand throughout the ordeal, so you can take comfort in knowing that she did not leave this world without a loved one by her side. We laid her to rest in the Sauret village cemetery. Madame and Monsieur Dupré have named the child Solange. She is beautiful. The Duprés will be wonderful parents.

Because of the delicate circumstances surrounding Annemarie's death and Solange's birth, it was necessary to create a fictitious story for Annemarie's family. They believe their daughter died in a car accident. Do not tell them the truth. Decent people do not need to carry the burden of a sinful daughter on their shoulders. They know nothing of their little granddaughter's existence. I am depending on you to keep her birth a secret.

Your loving friend and servant in the Lord,
Isabelle

Isabelle mailed the letter to Annemarie's family first. Three days later, she mailed the one to Anna. By the time Anna contacted the Marceaus, they would have had enough time to get over the initial shock of their daughter's death in a car accident. Anna would not want to intensify their grief by telling them the truth. She was right. By the time Anna received hers, Madame Marceau had already phoned to thank Isabelle for taking care of the arrangements for their daughter's funeral.

"You were always such a wonderful friend to our Annemarie, a true angel of mercy," gushed Madame Marceau. "Your parents were so blessed. Do my husband and I need to come to Sauret to finalize any matters?"

"No. There is no need," Isabelle reassured them. "I have taken care of everything. Perhaps later, to visit Annemarie's grave."

"Her father and I will send a donation to your convent, Isabelle. You are right, as usual. It would be much too painful to visit now."

Isabelle was smiling when she replaced the receiver. Her greatest fear had been that the Marceaus would rush to Sauret and discover the true circumstances of Annemarie's death.

The local villagers were appalled that someone in their midst had died in childbirth. Such deaths were unheard of nowadays. But they all agreed that if such a tragedy had to befall someone in their village, the willingness of the Duprés to adopt the little foundling they'd named Solange made the tragedy more bearable. But the unspoken question on everyone's mind was why a nun from the local convent had been the only person present during the birth. Isabelle stated emphatically during the compulsory inquest that she had tried in vain to reach the village doctor. That satisfied the villagers. If you couldn't trust a nun from the village convent, who could you trust?

At home in Dijon, Anna was not quite so accepting of Isabelle's explanation of Annemarie's death, especially the one to her parents. She thought it was preposterous. Anna's grief over the death of her best friend in the entire world was soon replaced by hostility towards Isabelle.

"Have you lost your fucking mind?" she screamed over the phone. "And what kind of a doctor loses a young, healthy woman in childbirth nowadays? There is something wrong with this entire scenario. Give me the doctor's name. I need to talk to him."

"There was no doctor."

"Then why did you say there was? And why wasn't there a doctor in attendance? Are you telling me you didn't get in touch with him?"

"His phone line was busy. Why would you think I didn't try to reach him?"

When Anna realized she wasn't going to get any further information, at least some she could believe, she hung up on Isabelle. Isabelle was furious. *How dare that sinful woman hang up on a servant of God!* She vowed to take care of Anna at a later date.

Another person not buying into Isabelle's *tried in vain to reach the doctor* statement was Henri Villiers, the good doctor himself. He'd been in his office the entire afternoon of Annemarie's confinement. It had been a quiet afternoon. He couldn't understand why no one had rung for his services. And why would a woman in labor call a nun for assistance instead of a doctor? And why wouldn't the nun in question have sent someone to find him if unable to reach him by phone? This was Sauret, not Paris. You could spit from one end of the village to the other. None of it made sense. But Henri decided to let the matter rest. He'd always found Isabelle somewhat sinister; didn't fancy having her as an enemy. The reality was that the mother was dead. Nothing could bring her back. And the child was in excellent hands. The Duprés would provide a more secure life for the child than a single mother with no visible means of support.

It didn't take long for the villagers of Sauret to return to normal. The conversations in the local cafe soon moved from Annemarie's death to spring planting. Isabelle knelt before the altar in the convent's chapel each evening and thanked God for giving her the power to punish a sinner and save an innocent.

At home in Dijon, Anna was determined to find out the true cause of Annemarie's untimely death. "That crazy bitch, Isabelle, with all her talk about punishing sinners! How could I have been so stupid? I know she did something to cause Annemarie's death."

Two weeks after receiving Isabelle's letter, Anna reread it for the umpteenth time. There was only one thing to do. She needed to talk to Jacques. He'd know what to do. She took a taxi across town and marched into her brother's office at the local newspaper.

"To what do I owe this unexpected pleasure, sister dear?"

Anna thrust Isabelle's letter into Jacques' hand.

"Read this," she ordered. "It's unbelievable."

"Who's it from?"

"Isabelle."

"Ah. My old flame. Does she miss me?"

"Don't joke."

"Oh, my God. Did Annemarie have her baby already?"

"Yes, but….." Anna's voice broke. Jacques got up from his desk and walked to where she was standing. "What's wrong, Anna?" he asked, putting his arms around her and pulling her close.

"Annemarie is dead."

"Don't be ridiculous, Anna." But he picked up the letter and read it.

"Merciful God. That stupid bitch. She could go to jail for this. Let's get out of here. We've got to figure out what to do. We can't let her get away with this."

"Isn't it a little late to do something? Annemarie is dead. She's not coming back."

"I'm not stupid, Anna," said Jacques, pulling her into the hall.

"Where are we going?"

"I don't know. But we've got to sit down and calmly figure out what to do."

Anna and Jacques found a secluded table at the back of a small café.

"Should we tell her parents the truth, Jacques?"

"No. At least not right away. We need to talk to Isabelle first, face to face."

"Right. I can go this weekend. I'll leave on Friday, right after work."

"No. I'll go," said Jacques. "She'll talk to me. Tell me the truth. She damned well better."

"Don't be silly, Jacques. She hardly knows you."

"That's what you think. Isabelle and I go back a long way. She's far from the shrinking little violet you and Annemarie thought she was."

"What are you talking about?"

"Isabelle and me. You and Annemarie were too busy enjoying yourselves to notice how cozy Isabelle and I had become."

"I don't believe you. Isabelle was never interested in boys."

"She was in this one."

"Are you trying to tell me that the two of you were intimate?"

Jacques smiled. " What a quaint way of putting it. Let's just say that I know Isabelle Duchamps better than anyone else in the entire universe."

"But she's always been so holier than thou. I can't believe she was......."

"Playing around rather than praying around?" interrupted Jacques.

Anna was too stunned to answer.

"Come on, little sister, even religious zealots have hormones."

"I guess so! But Isabelle Duchamps?"

"*Oui.* Even Isabelle Duchamps. Therefore, I feel the most qualified to question Isabelle about the circumstances of Annemarie's death. I think I'll leave tomorrow. I can hardly wait to see her."

"I'll bet you can't."

"I'll phone her tonight. Let her know I'm coming."

"What if she won't talk?"

"I have my ways," he said with a sly wink. "She'll tell me everything."

"You're disgusting!"

"Merely human."

"But Isabelle is a nun."

"So?"

"Would you do that?"

"That depends on Isabelle. I'll let you know when I return."

"You know what you are, Jacques Fontaine?"

"A good journalist?"

"*Oui.* But you are an amoral human being. I don't know why I put up with you."

"I'm your brother. You have to."

Before they went their separate ways, Jacques promised to phone Anna as soon as he'd made arrangements to meet Isabelle in Sauret.

"All right. But don't phone too late. You know how early *maman* goes to bed."

"Why do you think I don't live there anymore?"

"So you can stay up late writing, of course."

"Yeah. Right!

⌘

On the morning after her conversation with Jacques, the receptionist at Anna's office notified her just before ten that she had a personal phone call. She stressed the word personal as if she were issuing a reprimand.

"It must be an emergency," said Anna. "I'll keep it short. Don't worry."

"Hello. Anna Fontaine here."

"Oh, Anna. I am sorry to bother you at your office, but I must speak with you. This is Michelle, Michelle Dupré."

"Is the baby all right?"

"*Oui*. She is fine, although I am certain she misses her mother. I can just tell. There is something sad and questioning in her eyes when I look into them." The woman began to sob.

"Oh, Madame Durpré, I am so sorry."

"Please call me Michelle. I have need of your friendship."

"Of course, Michelle. I'll help you any way I can. What do you want me to do?"

"Meet me. We must talk."

"I can come to Sauret at the weekend."

"No. You must not come here."

"Why?"

"The evil one will be watching."

"The evil one?"

"Isabelle."

"Why do you call her evil?"

"When we meet, I will tell you."

"Just tell me when and where, Michelle. It's the least I can do."

"There is a little village between Sauret and Dijon. I think it is called Vison."

"I know it well. Could we meet there? How about tomorrow afternoon? My office is closed then."

"*Parfait*."

"There is a café in the station," continued Anna. "How about three o'clock?"

"I'll see you then. And thank you, Anna. This means so much to me."

"Me too," sighed Anna. "*A bientôt!*"

Anna replaced the receiver under the watchful eye of the nosy receptionist who looked at her as if awaiting a full explanation of the call. But Anna ignored her. She was too busy thinking about how to get in touch with Jacques to tell him to hold off traveling to Sauret until after her meeting with Michelle to pay any attention to the older woman. She decided against phoning him from the office. That call could wait until her lunch hour. She didn't want to risk anyone's overhearing her suspicions about Annemarie's death in Sauret. Dijon was a small town in many ways. It thrived on gossip.

The two hours between ten o'clock and noon dragged. They seemed endless. Anna thought that twelve o'clock would never come. When it finally did, she put on her coat and walked out into the street to find a telephone kiosk where she could talk to Jacques in privacy. While she waited for him to answer on his private line, she prayed that he hadn't already left for Sauret. When he finally answered, Anna let out a long sigh of relief.

"Thank God you're still in the office."

"Why? You're lucky you caught me. I was just on my way out the door."

"I got a call from Michelle Dupre."

"The woman who has Annemarie's baby?"

"Yes. She sounded frantic."

"Why?"

"She'll tell me that tomorrow. We are going to meet in Vosin at three o'clock."

"Why not Sauret?"

"Your girlfriend, Isabelle. Michelle referred to her as the evil one."

"*Mon dieu.* This doesn't look good. You still think I should go to Sauret to talk to Isabelle?"

"Yes. But not today. Wait until after I meet with Michelle tomorrow afternoon. Have you phoned Isabelle to tell her you're coming ?"

"Yes. I said I'd be there tonight. She'll be disappointed at the delay."

"I'll bet."

"Said she's horny as hell."

"Lucky you! Just as long as you get all the information we need about Annemarie's death. Personally, I don't give a damn how you get it."

"I'll do my best."

"I'm sure you will."

⌘

Michelle Dupré was waiting on the station platform when Anna got off the train in Vosin. She was pushing a small baby pram. The two women embraced.

"You brought her with you," beamed Anna, looking at the small bundle swaddled against the damp, windy weather. "I can't wait to hold her."

"Wait till we get inside," laughed Michelle. "It's freezing out here."

Once inside, Michelle removed the infant from the pram and placed her in Anna's arms.

"Well? What do you think, *Tatie Anna?* Say something."

"I think she is the most beautiful baby I have ever seen. And I think you are the most wonderful person in the entire universe for taking such good care of her. How can I ever thank you?"

"By listening to me. Oh, Anna, my heart is so heavy. Annemarie was such a strong, healthy young woman that her death in childbirth is highly suspicious, at least to me."

"And to me," replied Anna. "How could such a thing happen? You were there. You must explain the circumstances to me."

"That's just it. I was not there. I was in Mernar, the closest town to Sauret. When I returned home, it was all over."

"But Isabelle was there, wasn't she?"

"She was. The witch! But let me explain from the beginning," said Michelle, taking a long sip of her coffee. She took a few minutes to swallow before continuing. "Where to begin? I guess the beginning. Right?"

"Right," agreed Anna.

"A few weeks ago, Annemarie told me she was having second thoughts about giving up her child. This did not surprise me."

"Why?"

"From the very beginning of her stay with us, it was clear that Isabelle was the one in favor of her giving up the baby. For some crazy reason, she was determined that my husband and I would adopt Annemarie's baby the minute it was born. I never could understand what Isabelle's interest in the affair was since both Gaston and I were in agreement from day one about not interfering if Annemarie changed her mind about the adoption and decided to keep her baby. Annemarie was aware of our feelings. But she made me promise from early on never to mention any of this to Isabelle. I never understood why Annemarie refused to confront the woman. After all, they'd known each other for years. They grew up together."

"Well, it's obvious from the letter I received from Isabelle telling me about Annemarie's death that she's totally unraveled. Annemarie must have suspected something was not quite right with her. Thinks she's a servant of God. She's always had a Joan of Arc complex. Annemarie and I used to tease her about it. We thought it was only a phase. Evidently it wasn't. I think Annemarie sensed she had gone over the edge and was afraid to confront her."

"One day," continued Michelle, "unknown to Annemarie, I made the mistake of telling Isabelle that Gaston and I would have no objections if Annemarie decided to keep her baby."

"How did she react? What did she say?"

"Nothing. It was scary. She just stared at me. I could almost see the wheels turning inside her head. It was as if something inside her had exploded. A few weeks later, she phoned to ask me if I could drive to Mernar the following Tuesday instead of the usual Thursday to pick up some supplies for the convent. I agreed. Since I would be gone for the day, she invited Annemarie to visit her at the convent. Neither of us thought anything was amiss. On Tuesday I offered to drive Annemarie to the convent on my way out of town. She refused. Said she would walk since it was a decent day and she needed the exercise. When I returned around six in the evening, Isabelle greeted me at the front door. She was sobbing. 'She is gone, Michelle. Our Annemarie is gone.'"

"Gone?" I asked. "Gone where? What are you talking about? Where did she go? Home to Dijon?"

"No, you idiot," she screamed at me. "She has gone to be with our heavenly father."

It was only then that I saw the blood stains on Isabelle's hands. I ran to Annemarie's room. She was lying on the bed with her hands folded across her chest. She was already cold.

"What did you do?"

My first question was, "Where is Dr. Villiers?"

"He is not here. I could not reach him. This is God's will." Then she reached into a wicker basket at the side of the bed and lifted out the baby and handed it to me. In the calmest voice I've ever heard, she said, "Here is your gift from God, Michelle. You are the mother of a baby girl."

"Apart from the doctor's not being there, did you find anything else disturbing?"

"Not until she pointed to the bed and said, 'At least that pile of filth will not interfere with your little daughter. The sooner we bury it, the better.'"

"My God!"

"I know, Anna. I was too shocked to speak. But I am sure Isabelle murdered her."

"How?"

"Poison. I am convinced that she used some of the herbs or pesticides she uses in the convent garden to induce Annemarie's labor. She is in charge of the garden and the greenhouse there. She chose a Tuesday because Gaston works late that night at his brother's garage. All she had to do was get me out of town and invite Annemarie to the convent where she could poison her. Oh God! I feel so guilty. I should never have told Isabelle that Gaston and I were willing to let Annemarie keep her child. I feel like a murderer."

"Get that thought right out of your head. You had no way of knowing how insane Isabelle really is. She enjoys playing God."

"That must be one of the reasons why she has still not taken her final vows," said Michelle.

"You may be right. She keeps telling me that the mother superior does not like her. I think that because of the delay in permitting her to become a fully fledged sister in the order she decided to prove her worthiness by being an angel of mercy to Annemarie and you and Gaston. She set up her own rules."

"But why?"

"I keep telling you. She has always enjoyed playing God. Do you think we can bring charges against her?"

"I hope we can. The entire series of events leading to Annemarie's death were premeditated. She made sure I was out of town when she induced Annemarie's labor."

"Have you talked to the doctor, heard his side of the story about why he couldn't be reached?"

"I haven't spoken to him personally. The word in the village is that he himself can't figure that one out. He claims he was home all day. But why did she have to do this? Nothing can bring Annemarie back."

"I keep telling you, Michelle, Isabelle likes to get her own way. She was furious with Annemarie for having second thoughts about the adoption."

"Should we go to the police?"

"No. Absolutely not. At least,not yet. She'll be watching you and your husband. She has decided that you and Gaston will raise this child as your own. If you make waves, you, your husband and this beautiful little baby could become her next victims."

Michelle shivered. "*Mon Dieu.* You are right, Anna."

"Let's be sensible, Michelle. Annemarie isn't coming back. Solange needs a good home. You and Gaston are the perfect couple to raise her. Continue on with your life. We will stay in touch."

"What about Isabelle?"

"Stay out of her way. She won't bother you as long as she sees you going along with her plan to raise Solange in a good Catholic home."

"Do we have a way of checking up on her?"

"Oh, yes. He'll be there tomorrow."

"Who?"

"Jacques Fontaine."

"The journalist?"

"*Oui.* The journalist, Jacques Fontaine, is my brother. He is also Isabelle's lover. Does that surprise you?"

"Nothing surprises me about that one," sighed Michelle.

Before Michelle and Solange boarded the train for their return trip to Sauret, Michelle handed Anna a large brown envelope.

"What's this?"

"Solange's birth certificate, two copies with the official seal. One is for Annemarie's family if they ever find out about their little granddaughter. The other is for you in case anything ever happens to me."

"Don't even think such a thing," said Anna. "Isabelle wouldn't hurt you."

"She might if she thinks her plan of blessing a barren couple with a child has been interfered with."

"What are you talking about?"

Michelle opened her coat. She didn't have to reply. Her swollen belly said it all.

The two women did not meet again for several years.

$$\mathbb{H}$$

At four a.m., Anna crawled into bed. Reliving the ordeal of Annemarie's death and Solange's birth had left her emotionally and physically drained. She knew she needed to phone Jacques but was too exhausted to do so. She'd phone before she went to the office. Although there was an eleven hour time difference, she knew he often stayed in the press room late into the evening. She'd take her chances. In her current state, she didn't think she could garner enough strength to explain the recent turn of events with Susan in either French or English. Better to wait till she'd had a chance to rest and refresh her brain. Even if sleep eluded her, she was convinced she would feel better in the morning. She fell into a deep sleep the minute her head touched the pillow.

Anna awoke to the sound of a ringing noise which she couldn't identify at first. It didn't sound like the alarm. Was that the phone? It was. She jumped out of bed and ran into the living room to answer it. As she lifted the receiver, she was aware of daylight entering the room around the edges of the closed drapes.

"Hello. Who is it?"

"Me."

When Anna didn't reply, the voice continued in its heavy Glasgow brogue. "It's me. Molly Murdoch." She had to bite her tongue to keep from saying, "Your secretary, remember?" But she daren't. It didn't do to use Glaswegian humor with the Yanks, especially one as reserved as Anna Foster.

"Oh, Molly. My goodness! What time is it?"

"Half nineish."

"What?"

"I mean nine thirty."

Molly laughed to herself. She'd lived in America for three years and still couldn't understand why those silly Yanks couldn't figure out how to decipher figures of speech different from their own.

"Mrs. Foster, are you still there?"

"Yes, Molly. Thank you for calling. I must have overslept. You know how it is."

Molly didn't believe her for a minute. In the two and a half years she'd worked for Anna Foster, she'd never known the woman to be late for work. Anna Foster never overslept. No matter how early Molly tried to make it into the office in the morning, her workaholic boss was there before her.

When Anna didn't continue the conversation, Molly asked, "When will you be in? There's been a few calls. I told them you were in meetings and to call back later."

"Good. Good. Listen, Molly, do you think you can handle everything in the office until this afternoon? I don't think I can make it in until around one. Could you wait till then to take your lunch break?"

"Not a problem. I've got a piece with me. I'll eat at my desk if I have to."

"A piece? A piece of what?"

"My lunch."

"Another Glasgow term?"

"Aye."

"Honestly, Molly. If we ever decide to go into publishing, you'll be able to write a Glasgow dictionary."

"Who'd use it?"

"Tourists, silly. People are always going to Scotland."

"But not to Glasgow. They're aye hung up on Edinburgh. They consider Glasgow the darker side of the continent."

"We'll have a chat about that at another time. I've got to get going. And thank you, Molly. I really do appreciate it. I apologize for not phoning earlier to let you know I wouldn't be in this morning. "

"Is everything all right, Mrs. Foster? You sound a wee bit frazzled."

"Everything's fine, Molly. Well, actually it's not. I've received a bit of bad news. I need this morning to make a few calls."

"Well, don't worry about the office. Everything's under control."

"Just make sure you answer that stack of mail that came in on Friday."

"Yes ma'am."

"And, Molly, thank you again. I don't know what I'd do without you."

"Don't give it another thought," said Molly, but she almost dropped the phone. In all the time she'd been employed at Foster Accounting, she'd never received a compliment.

"Something's up, wi' her," sighed Molly. "Something's no' right." She hoped it didn't have anything to do with the strange woman who'd turned up at the office on Friday just as she was closing up for the weekend.

Molly was accustomed to people turning up at closing time on Fridays. It was usually a regular client desperate for an answer to a payroll or tax question. But this woman was not a regular client. Molly had never set eyes on her before. She sounded European, but Molly was clueless when it came to identifying specific accents. If you weren't from Scotland or America, she was lost. They'd had their share of foreign clients during the time Molly had been employed by Mrs. Foster. But this woman wasn't one of them. She was a real oddity in looks and extremely pushy, demanding to see Anna Foster herself. But Molly had been equally as pushy when it came to getting rid of her. When she'd asked where she could find Madame Foster, Molly lied and said she was out of town for the weekend. When she'd asked, correction, demanded the home address of Madame Foster, Molly lied again. Told her she was the hired help not the best friend of Mrs. Foster. Anna knew darned well where Anna Foster lived. It was only two blocks from her own house; but she wasn't about to turn over the address to this impertinent foreigner. A gut feeling told her that Anna Foster would not be pleased to see this woman.

Molly had been too busy over the weekend to think about the unwelcome guest on Friday. But the failure of her boss to turn up for work this morning and her nervous responses to Molly's questions were worrisome. Was it possible that Friday's mysterious guest had found out where Mrs. Foster lived and was holding her hostage? Maybe she was being ridiculous, but, if Mrs. Foster didn't turn up by one o'clock, she was definitely going round to her house to check. "Trust no one; suspect everyone," Molly said out loud. That was the Murdoch family motto. It had stood the family in good stead in their rough home territory in Glasgow. It was beginning to look as if it needed to be applied in America as well.

Molly looked up at the clock. It was already ten fifteen. She'd better get busy if she intended to finish answering the mail by the time her boss came in at one. With a shrug of her shoulders, she swiveled her chair towards her desk and tried to concentrate on the stack of folders in front of her.

⌘

Anna was appalled that she'd slept so late. It was a point of pride with her that she didn't need to use an alarm clock. But she wasn't in the habit of going to bed at four in the morning. Her plans for the rest of the day were already forming in her mind while she started the coffee. The first thing she had to do was phone Jacques in his office in Vietnam. That was the only number she could find for him. If he wasn't there, she had no idea how long it would take her to locate him. It would be almost nine at night there, but chances were he'd still be at his desk finishing up his feature of the day and sending it out over the wires just in time for the morning papers in Europe. He was fastidious to the point of paranoia when it came to his deadlines. He swore that if a story arrived early, it might be tossed out in favor of another late-breaking news item. So, night after night, he sat at his desk and pressed the send button on his Fax machines at precisely the time he knew was the best for getting his story into the *Times, the Paris Journal and the Geneva Times.* If his articles appeared in those revered dailies, the lesser wires picked them up by nightfall.

"*Viola!*" Jacques' voice sang out as he pressed send and listened to his articles zipping their way westward. That changed to "*Merde.* Who wants me at this hour?" when the phone rang. He was on the brink of ignoring the ringing but thought better of it.

"Sorry. The newsroom is closed for the day. This is a recording."

"The hell it is," laughed Anna.

"Anna, is that you? Why didn't you say so?"

"You didn't give me the chance. Trying to skip out early, eh?"

"On the contrary! I needed to stay late to get an article to Paris for the morning papers. I didn't want to be disturbed."

"Sounds important!"

"Everything I do is important."

"Oh, excuse me, your highness. But, if you don't want to be disturbed by your admiring public, you should get one of those devices that shows the number of the party calling."

"I know. Call forwarding. I just keep forgetting to do it. But what's up? You didn't phone halfway around the world to talk about my phone habits. I was going to call you at the office later tonight. Catch you before you'd begun your daily grind."

"About anything important?"

"A trip to San Francisco."

"Any particular reason?"

"The main one is the blasted heat here. The humidity's a bummer. I must be getting old. Those things never bothered me before."

"Why San Francisco?"

"I need to do some research there. I really need to go to Monterey, and I thought you might like to meet up with me. Can you pry yourself loose for a week?"

"Yes. I think so."

"Didn't have to twist your arm this time. You must be horny."

"You are disgusting."

"How is Henri?"

"He's fine."

"Has he given up on making an honest woman of you?"

"No. And he may be closer to that goal than he thinks."

"How so? You don't sound too happy about it."

"We are close to the end of our charade, Jacques," said Anna.

"Correction, Anna. It's always been your charade. Sounds like Susan found out what she should have been told years ago."

"I'll tell you when I see you."

"Have you heard from the Duprés recently?"

"A couple of times. They are in touch with Solange and her family but won't reveal her whereabouts."

"I can't blame them. That girl and her family have suffered enough."

"Can you believe Solange's kids are now ten and twelve? And Solange is forty now. How time flies."

"Even when you're not having fun."

"You can say that again."

There was silence for a few seconds before Jacques asked hesitantly, "Does Susan know the whole truth?"

"No. At least, not yet."

"Why?"

Anna let out a long audible sigh as she searched for the answer to that question.

"Are you still there, Anna?"

"Yes. I guess it's because I want her to go on thinking I'm her mother, even if it's just for a little while longer. I want to postpone the hatred and loathing she'll feel when she finds out the truth. It's like standing under a sky covered in black clouds just waiting for them to burst open and pour down torrents of rain. I shiver just thinking about how Susan will react."

"You're exaggerating."

"No, I'm not. I'm just waiting to receive my just desserts."

"In that case, they will be awe and gratitude."

"But not love."

"That's already there, Anna. Take my word for it."

"If you say so."

"I do say so. I just wish I were right there to comfort you."

"You can do that in San Francisco."

"Where is Susan?"

"Back in New York. She's determined to start looking for Solange. I have a packet of information ready to send her today. It will send her to Dijon to begin the search. She can digest our wretched life stories one part at a time."

"If you want it that way, I'll go along with it. After all you have done for me, Anna, it's the least I can do. E-mail me your arrival plans. I'll phone you at Henri's."

"*Bonsoir*, Jacques."

"*Bonsoir.*"

Anna hung up. Just the sound of Jacques' voice had comforted her. The clock said eleven. She'd better get busy if she were going to make it into the office by one. But before she left the house, she needed to phone Henri in San Francisco. Once again Anna picked up the phone.

"Hello. Dr. Villiers speaking."

"Good. You're still at home. I was afraid you'd have left for the day. What are you doing at home at this hour?"

"This is the day I don't have to be there until one. Is something wrong, Anna? You sound anxious."

"Not really. I mean nothing is wrong, but you're right. I am feeling anxious, very anxious."

"Has something happened?"

"Susan found her *acte* a couple of days ago. It wasn't difficult for her to figure out it was hers."

"Did you tell her everything?"

"No."

"Oh, Anna. You promised."

"I know. But I just couldn't."

"What does she know?"

"She knows that Jacques is her father. I would have told her everything, but she was very angry. The more I told her, the angrier she got, so I just clammed up."

"What else does she know besides the fact that Jacques is her father?"

"Solange. She knows all about Solange."

"Good."

"Not so good. She thinks Solange is her half-sister."

"Why did you let her think that?"

"Because she thinks I'm both her and Solange's mother."

"How did she react?"

"She called me a slut."

Henri started to laugh.

"You think that's funny?"

"Hysterical. When she finds out the truth, she will apologize. I miss you, Anna. When will I see you again?"

"Would tomorrow be too soon?"

"Tomorrow? Are you serious?"

"Yes. I spoke with Jacques this morning. He's flying to San Francisco tomorrow. He wants to meet me there. Henri, are you still on the line?"

"Of course. But I'm in a state of shock. I have missed you so much, Anna. How long can you stay?"

"A couple......."

"No! No! That's not good enough. We need more than a couple of days together."

"Let me finish, Henri. I was going to say a couple of weeks."

"A couple of weeks? I don't believe it. How is this possible?"

"Molly Murdoch."

"Molly Murdoch?"

"My assistant. I'm going to speak with her this afternoon. I'm sure she can handle everything. She does already."

"This is music to my ears, Anna."

"I'll call back with my flight information."

"Leave it on my voice mail if I'm not here. I'll pick you up at the Airport."

"Can you get time off?"

"Tomorrow is my day off. I'm yours for the entire day, and night, I might add. I love you so much, Anna."

"I love you, Henri."

For several minutes after their conversation ended, Henri walked around his study with the phone in his hand. He knew he should get ready to leave for the clinic, but the voices of the past began and paralyzed his movements. Still clutching the phone, he sank into a large leather easy chair and stared into space.

Henri Villiers and his wife, Lili, had lived in the village of Sauret for only a few months in 1965 when Annemarie Marceau died giving birth to Solange. Had Henri been notified about the young woman's labor, she would have most certainly survived the delivery. Thank God Michelle and Gaston Dupré had been on hand to care for the newborn little girl. Isabelle Duchamps had sworn on the Bible that she had tried in vain to contact him on the day of Anne Marie's confinement. Henri knew that was a lie. Lili did too. But, because of her status as Henri's spouse, her testimony about her husband's being in his home office on that tragic afternoon was not taken seriously. The inquest's result was the complete exoneration of Isabelle Duchamps from any blame in the unfortunate death of Annemarie Marceau. The word of a nun in the tiny village of Sauret was sacrosanct. Lili and Henri were out outraged over the verdict but managed to control their emotions, at least outside their own home. Henri needed the financial security of his job in Sauret to get on his feet. His medical school fees had left him almost penniless, and Lili had a good position as a teacher in the village primary school.

Henri stared at the black and white portrait of Lili which sat on the table next to his chair. If the two of them hadn't been so practical and remained in Sauret, Lili would be with him now in the flesh rather than a fading photograph in a tarnished frame. Henri sighed but couldn't resist a smile when he looked at the photograph next to Lili's. It was a photograph of David, their son, taken when David was in his teens.

The ringing of the phone brought Henri back to reality.

"Hello. Dr. Villiers here."

"Dad. Are you all right?"

"Yes. I am fine. I'm just running a little late."

"That's not like you."

"Anna phoned."

"How is she?"

"You'll find out soon enough. She's flying out here for a couple of weeks."

"Ask her to marry you."

"I already have. Several times. You know that."

"Make her say yes this time."

"How do I do that?"

"You're French for God's sake. It should be a cinch."

"I promise I'll try. See you in about half an hour."

"Hurry. I'm starving. I need to go to lunch."

Henri pressed the END button on his phone. He was smiling by the time he left the house. David always made him smile. He was a wonderful son. He was also a good doctor. Henri couldn't ask for a better partner in his family medicine practice at the Villiers Clinic. If Lili were here, she would be smiling too. She would be so proud of David.

Susan sat on the living room couch with her legs tucked up under her and ignored the ringing of the phone. She knew it wouldn't be her mother. She'd already made the obligatory call to say she'd arrived safe and sound in Manhattan. Anna hadn't even referred to their conversation of the previous day. She'd retreated into her cocoon of aloofness. Whoever was phoning would call back if it were important. Then she'd answer. It rang just seconds later. Susan picked up.

"Susan here."

"Did you just get in?" Scott's voice came over the line.

"I got back this afternoon."

"Why didn't you phone? We could have worked out together."

"Too much on my mind to work out, physically that is."

"I'll bet you didn't run once when you were in Syracuse."

"That's right. It was great."

"Not a good attitude."

"Afraid I'll turn into a slacker?"

"Worse. A blimp. You know how you tend to pack on the pounds when you slow down."

"Wouldn't want to be seen with me a size larger?"

"Definitely not! And I mean that."

When Susan didn't answer, Scott continued. "Are you there? Are you listening to me?"

"Yeah. I just have a lot on my mind."

"Like what?"

"Nothing you'd be interested in."

"Well, just as long as you don't forget about next weekend."

"What's so important about next weekend?"

"The big bash my folks are throwing for Claire's birthday. How could you forget?"

Very easily, Susan chuckled to herself. Scott's mother spent her entire life organizing social extravaganzas. Each one ended with an invitation to the next.

"Susan, are you listening to me?"

"Yeah. Of course I am. And I haven't forgotten about your sister's birthday."

"That's good because she might not be here for the next one."

"Why? Is she terminal?"

"That's not funny, Susan. She'll be in college next year. Might not be able to make it home for the big day."

Susan smiled to herself. *Way to go, Claire!* . Her parents were too full of themselves to realize that their youngest child had opted for a California college to escape their clutches. Mom and Dad were too immersed in their own lifestyle to realize that any of their offspring could possibly harbor serious thoughts of living a different one. They were terrified about Claire's move to California. Susan had visions of the entire Johnson clan lined up at La Guardia with balloons and posters to welcome Claire home at Christmas. Anna Foster might have a shady past, but she was not a control freak. Susan made a mental note to thank her mother for that the next time they spoke.

"Susan, are you there?"

"Yeah. I told you I was."

"Then answer the question. Will you?"

"Will I what?"

"Buy Claire's birthday present. I'm too tied up at work."

"And I'm not?"

"Well, it's just that you always seem to be able to come up with time for frivolous activities."

"Like shopping for your sister's birthday gift?"

"Exactly!"

Susan was too exhausted to argue.

"Of course, I'll do it. Any suggestions?"

"Just make it something nice. Really nice. And expensive. You know how my folks are about appearances."

Do I ever, thought Susan, but she was too chicken to say that to Scott. "I'll do my best," she replied.

"Thanks, Susan. I'll square up with you at the weekend. And, while you're at it, could you pick out a good card for Jack. His birthday is on Tuesday."

"Shit, Scott. He's your friend. And it's too late to get a card to him by Tuesday. Send an e-card."

"It takes me forever to do that. Would you do it?"

"Why not? Give me his email address."

"Hang on a minute."

During the brief time it took Scott to look up Jack's email address, Susan thought up an excuse for not being available to see him on Friday evening. She had so many important matters swimming around in her head that his whining was getting on her nerves.

"Here's the address. Do you have a pen?"

"Of course."

"How about working out together Friday after work? We could spend the night at your place and then drive out to Long Island early Saturday afternoon."

"I'd love to. But I've got extra translations to work on. I'm way behind," Susan lied. The thought of spending Friday evening on a treadmill had lost its luster.

"Pick me up around one on Saturday for the party."

"Will do. Bye for now."

"I love you, Scott."

"Just don't forget the present and Jack's email card."

Without a love you, good-bye or drop dead Scott hung up.

"And a good evening to you too, Scott."

Her friend, Jenna, was right. Scott Johnson was a jerk. Why had it taken her two years to see his true colors? But she'd keep up the charade of caring about him, at least, for the near future. She simply didn't have the energy for a break-up at this point in time. She needed to put all her efforts into absorbing the shock of the information on her French *acte* and figuring out how to go about locating her sister.

Anna's packet containing the materials Susan needed to apply for her French passport arrived at her office on Tuesday morning. By the afternoon, she'd filled out the application and Faxed it to the French Consulate in Washington, D.C. Too impatient to wait for a written reply to her question of how long it would take to process the passport, she phoned the Consulate on Wednesday to find out the answer.

"Three or four weeks," the receptionist answered.

"What if I come in person?"

"Three or four hours. Do you want to make an appointment? You sound impatient."

"I am."

"The earliest appointment we have is on Monday afternoon at one. How would that be?"

"Perfect."

The receptionist took down Susan's name and told her to be there promptly at one on the following Monday. She sounded American, but Susan found her Gallic efficiency encouraging.

Five long days until Monday, sighed Susan. *I'll be a nervous wreck by then.* But an overload of translations due to a colleague's illness made the rest of the week fly by, and, when she wasn't at work, her lunch hours and early evenings were taken up with shopping for the perfect birthday gift for Claire. Her devotion to the gift quest proved to her that she wasn't as ready to give up on her relationship with Scott as she'd thought. Besides, she really liked Claire, admired her spunk in choosing a California college instead of one on the East Coast. Claire was a bit of a spoiled brat, but Susan had always suspected that underneath the designer trappings beat the heart of an intelligent, sensitive young woman. The girl needed some breathing space, time away from her socialite parents. Scott was ambivalent and visibly annoyed that Susan wasted time pondering such mundane matters.

Shopping was definitely not one of Susan's favorite pastimes, so she was thrilled when taking a short cut through the linen department in Macy's to find an entire aisle devoted to college dorm room decor. An animated group of teenage girls was going through the stacks of sheets, blankets, comforters and towels. Joining the group, Susan asked them if they'd be pleased to get those items as a gift.

"Are you kidding?" laughed one. "I'd be overjoyed. These things are not cheap." Her friends nodded their agreement. Susan spent the next half hour selecting two sets of sheets and pillow cases and a comforter with matching shams. The items had a penguin motif. Since Claire had a collection of stuffed penguins, Susan knew she'd be thrilled. On her way to the cash register, another display of items decorated with penguins caught her eye, blanket-sized towels this time. Susan couldn't resist. She added two to her already overloaded arms. When the register tape rang up at almost four hundred dollars, Susan let out an audible gasp, but she was feeling too pleased with her purchases to cancel the order. The Johnson's penchant for over-spending must be catching up with her, but she knew Scott would reimburse her for half. That took the edge off her extravagance.

Susan relaxed over a cappuccino in the store's café while waiting for her purchases to be gift-wrapped. She was feeling rather smug about their appropriateness. Just the right thing for a girl heading for the dorm scene. Scott would be proud. But a little voice, that of her best friend, Jenna, went off inside her head like an alarm. *Get a grip, Susan. Why are you always so worried about what Scott thinks of you?*

⌘

The chances of finding a parking place outside Susan's apartment were slim to none, so Susan waited outside in the rain for Scott to arrive on Saturday afternoon. She placed the two beautifully wrapped boxes in the trunk of the car then slipped into the passenger seat next to him. He kissed her briefly on the forehead then asked brusquely, "You didn't forget Jack's card, did you?"

Before she could answer, he gave her a frown and said, "Careful, Susan. You're getting the interior all wet. Watch it."

"For God's sakes, Scott. You're like a fussy old woman."

"You would be too if you'd paid what I did for this baby. Well, did you send Jack a card or not?"

"What do you think? And don't you want to know what I bought for your sister?"

"Not really. Just as long as it reeks of extravagance. It was expensive, wasn't it? Please say yes."

"Yes. Yes. Yes. Believe me. It was. There are several parts to the gift. And each part was very expensive."

"Good."

During the drive out to Long Island, the silence was almost unbearable until Scott turned on the radio.

"What do you think?"

"About what?"

"The radio."

"How much is there to say about a radio?"

"You obviously weren't paying attention when I told you about this system. It's satellite. I can get over a hundred channels."

"I hope not all at the one time."

"Very funny."

The rest of the trip consisted of heavy metal music and Scott's never-ending monologue about the advantages of his satellite radio system. The only good thing about the din of the music was that it blocked out Scott's voice.

"Scott," Susan interrupted, screaming to be heard over the cacophony. "We haven't seen each other in over a week and all you can find to talk about is your damned satellite radio. I find that insulting."

"You've got to admit it's exciting. I can get over a...."

"I know," Susan interrupted again. "You can get over a zillion channels. How proud you must be!"

Failing to take in Susan's sarcasm, Scott answered, "Of course, I'm proud. And you need to lighten up, Susan. You're much too serous."

"You haven't even asked me what I bought for Claire or how much it cost."

"I told you. I don't want to know; just as long as it's expensive."

"Why is the expensive part so important to you?"

"I don't want to let my mother down. She's not like yours. She enjoys fine things."

"And mine doesn't?"

"Well, she doesn't seem to. Look at that dinky little house she has in Syracuse. It's not exactly in an upscale area."

Susan was livid but kept her mouth shut. Much more of Scott's impertinence and she'd jump out of the car onto the highway. The breaking up thoughts started up once again, but, before she could concentrate on them, he pulled into his parents' driveway.

Fred, the professional decorator Mrs. Johnson used for all her soirées, had been hired to turn the house into a glitzy birthday wonderland. "Hello, Susan. Nice to see you again," he sang out as he minced past her on his way into the dining room. "What do you think, Susan? Is it birthdayish enough?"

"Yes, Fred. It certainly is. You've outdone yourself," replied Susan, surveying the garishly decorated living room. But, just as with Scott in the car, her sarcasm went right over his head.

"Thank you, dear. It's nice to know that Scott's young lady has such good taste."

Once Fred had disappeared into the dining room, Susan walked up to the champagne fountain that had been assembled in the middle of the living room and filled herself a glass. The fountain was on four levels with champagne gushing from tulip-shaped spouts on each one. It looked hideous, but the bubbly tasted great. It was just what Susan needed to calm her nerves. The entire room resembled the set of an old black and white movie. Susan stole a glance at the lavish spiral staircase in the hallway and half expected to see Gloria Swanson or Tullulah Bankhead descend the stairs in a sequined gown with flowing train. Her reverie was interrupted by Scott's mom blowing her famous air kisses in her direction. Louise Johnson's trademark greeting was a source of pride to her socialite brood. Susan thought it was ridiculous, another affectation which she could never imagine her own mother attempting.

"Talk to you later, Sweetie," Mrs. Johnson called out from the other side of the room. "So much to do. Can't talk now. Do make yourself at home." That was exactly where Susan wished she were, at home in her own apartment, stretched out in sweats either reading a book or watching a movie. Anywhere but here. Scott was ensconced in an armchair on the back porch, phonying it up with his Dad's wine and cheese set of professional moochers. She spotted Karen, Scott's sister-in-law, sitting by herself at the far end of the living room and headed in that direction.

"Hi, Susan. I was hoping you'd be here. So far, you're the only guest I recognize. I can't understand where Louise finds these people. Sometimes I think she has a recycling mill in the basement."

"I know what you mean," agreed Susan. "Especially for a teenager's birthday party. Does Claire know any of these people?

"Probably not. But remember, teenagers don't give lavish gifts. That's the reason for the two parties."

"The two parties?"

"Yes," said Karen. "They're hosting a dance at the country club this evening for Claire's friends. Can you believe it?"

Susan rolled her eyes in answer.

"At least you don't have to spend every holiday with them. It gets downright gruesome after the first two or three years."

"Why don't you or Tommy put your foot down?"

"I did last year. We spent Thanksgiving at home, just us and the kids."

"How was it?"

"Great. But Louise almost took to her bed. Phoned us at least a half dozen times during the day. It was ludicrous, so ludicrous, in fact, that Tommy has informed me we will be here this Thanksgiving. My advice to you, Susan, that is, if you marry Scott, is either resign yourself to all holidays here or move to another planet."

"I refuse to move away from New York because of Louise Johnson."

"Suit yourself. But don't say I didn't warn you."

The conversation was cut short by the arrival of Claire who hugged Susan exuberantly. The hug seemed genuine. *I'll not worry about Claire until she starts blowing those damned air kisses,* thought Susan.

"Happy birthday, kid," laughed Susan. "Have you opened any presents yet?"

"I sure have. I opened yours, and I love all those penguin decorated sheets and towels. You are a genius, Susan. From now on I want Scott to let you choose all my gifts. He never has a clue!"

The short conversation came to an abrupt end when Susan felt a heavy hand on her shoulder. She turned around to face a scowling Scott. "Can I see you outside for a minute, Susan?"

"Sounds serious," laughed Claire. "You'd better go."

Susan followed Scott out to his car.

"Get in. We need to talk. You have embarrassed me and my family in front of our guests."

Susan opened the passenger side door of the car and got in. "Take me home. I can't take any more of your rotten attitude towards me."

"Okay. If that's the way you feel, let's go." Scott started up the car and backed out of the driveway. They drove in silence until they reached the highway. Then, he lit into her with a vengeance. "What were you thinking? How could you insult my sister by giving her sheets and towels for a birthday gift? I've never been more embarrassed in my life than the moment Claire opened that first box and pulled out a towel."

"Claire loved the gift."

"She doesn't know any better. She's just a kid."

"Oh, grow up for God's sake. Claire made the best decision of her life when she decided to go off to California in the fall. She'll need all that stuff for her dorm. Why was it such a bad present?"

"Why? I'll tell you why. It sends the message that my folks can't afford to buy her the basics. Claire thanked you so profusely because she's such a polite kid."

"Her brother certainly isn't!"

They drove the final twenty minutes into the City in silence. When they pulled up at Susan's apartment, Scott was appalled that she didn't want him to spend the night.

"You're too sensitive, Susan. You know what your problem is?"

"I have a feeling I'm going to find out."

"You're damned right. Somebody has to tell you. Your main problem, just one of many, is that you can't take criticism."

Susan didn't dignify his accusation with an answer. She got out of the car and slammed the door. Scott drove off, leaving her standing on the sidewalk. Later in the evening he plagued her with phone calls which Susan let her voice mail pick up. She decided not to tell him that she was going to D.C. on Monday. The truth was that she had lost all interest in continuing her relationship with Scott Johnson. He had finally made an honest woman of her.

⌘

On Monday morning, Susan took a taxi to Penn Station and caught the eight o'clock train to D.C. She'd brought along the Sunday *New York Times* crossword, her weekly nemesis, with every intention of working on it to pass the time. But she couldn't concentrate. After what seemed an eternity, the train pulled into Union Station at ten forty-five. It was hard to believe the journey had been only two hours and forty-five minutes. It felt more like forty-five hours and two minutes. Susan was exhausted, but she decided to take the Metro instead of a taxi to the French Consulate She couldn't risk being stuck in traffic and missing her one o'clock appointment. She didn't start to relax until she got off the Metro at Foggy Bottom and walked into Georgetown where she had plenty of time to look around some shops and eat a leisurely lunch at a trendy restaurant before heading to Reservoir Road where the French Consulate was located.

The hustle and bustle of Washington was similar to New York but with one major difference. Washingtonians had that smug, self-satisfied demeanor of government employees who spend their entire day working towards the greater good of the country. New Yorkers, on the other hand, wore the arrogantly smug expressions of entrepreneurs out to make their own personal fortunes. But Susan knew that the well-dressed workers in both cities probably dragged their weary bones home on the subway each night to their appallingly small basement apartments while those fortunate enough to own a car and a home in the suburbs sat in traffic for hours at the end of each day, contemplating their exorbitant mortgages. But the residents of both cities had one thing in common. They clung steadfastly to the belief that life anywhere else in the country was a vast wasteland. Susan suddenly appreciated her mother's largesse. Anna had insisted on purchasing Susan's large loft in Manhattan outright when she'd decided to settle in the Big Apple.

Susan was so deep in thought that she walked past the entrance to the Consulate and had to backtrack for almost five minutes. But she entered the building with ten minutes to spare and took the elevator to the appointed floor.

An unsmiling receptionist directed Susan to a waiting room where she was surprised to find she was the room's only occupant. Surely she wasn't the only person applying for a French passport today. But she didn't have to wonder for long. She'd no sooner sat down than the grim-faced woman appeared at the door and grunted, "Please come with me." Susan obeyed and found herself in the office of a woman who at least smiled.

"Don't let Madame Defarge scare you. She takes her job a little too seriously."

"Is that really her name?"

"No. But we all call her that for obvious reasons. Please sit down."

The woman behind the desk leafed through some papers on her desk. "Everything seems to be in order," she said, pulling a red French passport out of a folder. "Do you have any questions?"

"Just one. Does everyone who applies for a French passport receive such individualized treatment?"

"No. Of course not. That would be impossible. The personal attention happens only when the applicant is known to the Consulate."

"Why would I be known to the Consulate?"

"Monsieur Chabot will explain that to you. I'm sure it's nothing to worry about," she replied, placing the passport back in the folder.

"Is that my passport you put back in the folder?"

"Yes. Don't worry. You'll have it in your hand when you leave the building after Monsieur Chabot speaks with you. He'll be here in a few minutes."

"Is there a problem?" asked Susan, starting to panic.

The woman didn't answer. She rose from her chair behind the desk and walked out of the room, closing the door behind her. While waiting for Monsieur Chabot to appear, Susan began to have second thoughts about applying for the passport. *Had her mother left France under a cloud of suspicion? Had she committed a crime?* That would go a long way towards explaining her mother's metamorphosis from French to American and her denial of all things Gallic. *You're being ridiculous,* she told herself. *If there was any problem, she'd never have sent you all the info you needed to obtain your French passport. Pull yourself together.*

Before Susan's mind could continue farther on its flights of fancy, Monsieur Chabot appeared on the scene.

"*Bonjour, Mademoiselle.*"

"*Bonjour, Monsieur.*"

When Monsieur Chabot sat down at the desk and started to leaf through some papers he removed from a drawer, Susan couldn't help but blurt out, "Am I in some sort of trouble?"

"No. Not at all. But there is a matter I need to discuss with you?"

"About what? Is there a problem?"

"That's what I was going to ask you?"

"About what?"

"A small mystery."

"Look. All I did was apply for a French passport the minute I discovered my real identity and country of birth. There's no mystery involved."

"Are you sure that's all?"

"Yes. My story is quite simple. I grew up never realizing that I was born in Dijon, France. When I accidentally found my French *acte*, I confronted my mother with the evidence. She explained the background of my birth and then sent me all the necessary documents to apply for a French passport."

"Calm down. Do not excite yourself."

"But I don't understand what this is all about?"

"It's a rather odd story."

"I know. My mother is a little odd."

"No. No. Not that story. Not your mother."

"Then what?"

"The fact is that at least twice a year for the past several, this office has received periodic calls asking if we have a Suzette Fontaine registered as a French citizen. That is the name on your *acte*, *n'est pas?*"

"Yes. Is it a man or woman who calls?"

"A woman with a very husky voice. The huskiness is more pronounced since she is obviously trying to disguise her real voice."

"Can't you trace the call?"

"She doesn't stay on the line long enough. It's such an odd story that three of us who have worked here since the calls began have often wondered who this Suzette Fontaine is. You must understand that when your passport application and documentation were received we were more than curious, especially since you are applying for your first French passport at the age of thirty."

"That's because I didn't know I was French until two weeks ago."

"That is strange. The clerk who spoke with you on the phone said that you spoke flawless French, like a native."

"I majored in French in college and studied at the Sorbonne. I work for a private translation company in New York City."

"And you want me to believe you didn't know you were French?"

"Exactly! It's the truth. I have no reason to lie."

"Why didn't your mother tell you the details of your birth until two weeks ago?"

"Because I was illegitimate. She wanted to make a fresh start in the United States."

"It sounds like she made a success of it. Do you know your father?"

"Yes. I mean I know who he is. He is Jacques Fontaine, the French journalist. He lives in Vietnam. Perhaps I am not the Suzette Fontaine your mysterious caller is trying to locate."

"Perhaps not. But the possibility exists that someone is trying to find you. But don't look so worried. We do not reveal the names of passport holders to people who call here out of the blue. We do a background check on the caller first. In this case, we have not been able to do so since the caller refuses to identify herself."

"What do you tell her?"

"Up until now, the truth, that we cannot help her."

"How does she react?"

"She becomes irrational and starts to use four letter words."

"Sounds sinister."

"Perhaps. Or it could be nothing to worry about. You may not be the Suzette Fontaine she is looking for, but please be careful."

"Are you trying to scare me?"

"Not at all. I don't think you need to walk around looking over your shoulder every few minutes. Just be a little more aware of what's going on around you. And perhaps you could ask your mother if she knows of someone who might be looking for you."

"No. And don't you dare contact my mother. She has enough to deal with. She is a single woman who runs a successful business in upstate New York. She has enough on her plate without worrying about her daughter being stalked. Promise me you won't bother her."

"You have my word."

Monsieur Chabot walked Susan to the elevator where he handed her a business card. "Here. Take my card. If you are the person this woman is looking for, and, if she finds you, please let me know. We are all curious, and it is the mission of this office to protect all French citizens residing in the United States."

"But you must never contact my mother."

"I am a man of my word."

"Thank you. Let's hope she never finds me."

Throughout her session with Monsieur Chabot, Susan had remained calm, but the minute she entered the empty elevator, her self confidence began to crumble. Her only thought was to catch the Metro back to Union Station as soon as possible and board the first train headed for New York. Washington had lost its magic for the time being.

Susan selected a half-empty compartment on the return trip to New York. She needed some peace and quiet to think and sort out the information Monsieur Chabot had shared with her. She leaned back and closed her eyes while she went over their meeting. The question of the mysterious female caller didn't interest her as much as her attitude towards her mother. She felt herself becoming protective of the woman she'd been at odds with most of her life. She needed to find out the truth about Anna's and her own past. She needed to get to France as soon as possible. She had to find Solange. She was convinced that finding Solange would help clear up the mystery of her mother's move to the United States. Anna Foster was a strange woman, but Susan was convinced there was no way she would willingly have offered up a child for adoption.

⌘

Jenna stretched out on her bed and stared up at the ceiling. It was great being able to lie in bed after the alarm went off on a Saturday morning. But, even on weekends she usually got up the minute it went off and made herself a cup of coffee. Force of habit. She must have been really tired this morning because she had turned off the alarm and gone right back to sleep. A quick glance at the clock on her bedside table told her it was already nine a.m. She hadn't slept this long on a Saturday for weeks. There just didn't seem to be any need to get up. A counselor from a family services organization had spoken to her middle school students last week about the signs of depression. A lack of desire to get out of bed was listed as one of the classic symptoms of clinical depression. *Oh God,* Jenna prayed silently, *please don't let me become one of those classic symptoms.*

The phone rang. Jenna reached for her bedside cordless but thought better of it. She got up slowly and walked into the living room, sat down on the couch and picked up the phone on the coffee table.

"Hi. Jenna here."

"Good morning. It's me, Susan. I was just about to hang up. What took you so long to answer? Were you in the bathroom?"

Jenna ignored the question.

"Susan, do you think I could be clinically depressed?"

"You? I don't think so. Clinically depressing to those who try to keep up with your strange ideas but definitely not clinically depressed."

"Don't joke, Susan. I'm serious."

"What brought this on?"

"Well, last week a counselor spoke to the kids about the symptoms of depression. One of them was not wanting to get out of bed."

"So?"

"So, this morning I didn't get up when the alarm went off at six. I fell back into a deep sleep and didn't wake up until nine."

"It's Saturday. Why would you get up at six? More to the point, why would you have your alarm set for six on a Saturday?"

"To make sure I keep my body rhythms on an even keel."

"That's the most ridiculous thing I've ever heard. You're supposed to catch up on your rest on the weekends. That's why they were invented."

"I'm scared."

"Of what?"

"Being clinically depressed."

"Jenna, you are the least likely candidate for depression that I know. Neurotic, yes. You are so neurotic that you drive all your friends nuts.

You're lucky you have any left. Promise me you won't go around for the next few weeks asking everyone you meet if they think you're depressed."

"Would I do that?"

"Yeah. You would."

"What makes you think that?"

"Your track record. Remember when a counselor from the eating disorder clinic talked to the kids last semester?"

"Vaguely."

"Vaguely, my ass. The following week you called to inform me you were bulimic."

"The way I was barfing up everything I ate scared me to death. I had all the classic symptoms of bulimia."

"You had the flu like everyone else in Manhattan and the surrounding areas."

"Well, maybe I did over-react, but that's a one-time example."

"No, it isn't."

"Yes, it is."

"I think you have a very short memory, Jenna."

"Why do you say that?"

"Phase Two of your eating disorder paranoia. If I recall events correctly, when you were recovering from the flu and had next-to-no appetite, you were convinced you were anorexic."

"You're right. I remember that. It was scary."

"It was ridiculous."

"Just because I'm chubby no one took me seriously."

"You said it. I didn't."

"For your information, I am trying to lose a few pounds. Do you think…."

"Shut up, Jenna. I called to ask if you could meet me for lunch at one o'clock."

"Where's Scott?"

"I have absolutely no idea where he is."

"And it sounds like you don't even care."

"You catch on fast, Jenna."

"Not really. You've sounded that way about Scott for several months now."

"You've never said anything before."

"Of course not. Every time I open my mouth I'm accused of being neurotic and having a much too vivid imagination for my own good. I'm sick and tired of getting a long lecture from you whenever I offer an opinion."

"On what?"

"On anything."

There was silence. Then the two of them exploded in laughter.

"Well, at least you're not as neurotic as Morag."

"That's not much of a compliment. What's Morag's latest neurosis?"

"She phoned me in the middle of the night last week to inform me that she and Ian are convinced that their Wee Alistair has a psychosis."

"For God's sakes. The kid's only three. What's the problem this time?"

"It seems that there are certain pictures that send him into a frenzy when he looks at them."

"You mean photographs?"

"No. Pictures hanging on the walls of hotels and museums. Evidently, he'll look at a certain picture and scream."

"You would too if you were dragged around as many art museums as that poor kid."

"I agree. But Morag's been on the internet researching this problem. She swears there's an acknowledged syndrome where some kids become overly stimulated by certain visuals and can't control their emotions."

"And what is this syndrome called?"

"I can't remember. It was the middle of the night when she called. I was too tired to take it all in. You know Morag. If it's ten a.m. in Paris, it must be ten a.m. in the States."

"They were probably looking at Munch's *The Scream* when all this happened. What do they intend to do?"

"Take him to a psychologist if it continues."

"Poor Alistair!"

"I doubt that will ever happen. They'll be on to something else next week and tell me they don't remember the picture incident if I ask about it."

"Morag can be such an idiot!" laughed Jenna.

"I know, but she really had you going freshman year when she said she was related to the Loch Ness monster."

"You've got to admit she sounded convincing, and she kept it up for an entire semester."

"Only because she knew you believed her. Anyway, can you meet me for lunch at one?"

"Sure. I think I can get my act together by then. Where?"

"How about Herbie's, that new place on Fifth Avenue. I think that's what it's called."

"I've already been there. The food's great."

"I thought you were anorexic."

"No. Just depressed. But I'd better get going if we're going to meet at one."

By noon Jenna was strolling around Times Square. It was a beautiful sunny morning. A great day for a walk. Before she realized it, she found herself across the street from Macy's Department Store. A large banner flapping in the breeze announced a shoe sale.

Why not?" thought Jenna. *There's nothing like a sale at Macy's to get the weekend going.* She didn't even bother to cross with the light at the corner. She darted into the traffic to the sound of horns and hands sticking out of windows with the middle finger extended. But Jenna just laughed. She was too exhilarated to care.

It had been ages since Jenna had ventured anywhere near a shoe sale at Macy's. She remembered why as soon as she stepped off the escalator at the shoe department. The entire floor was littered with shoes discarded by bargain-crazed customers searching for the best deal in their sizes. Jenna's heart sank. She couldn't figure out where to begin looking for a pair in her size. But her eyes fell on a tiered shelf with an untouched display of black leather brogues. They were ugly as sin but would be great in winter.

It didn't take long for the clerk to find the mate of the shoe Jenna held aloft in her right hand. She'd appeared like magic, asked her size, disappeared and reappeared in what seemed like only a few seconds, holding a box with the shoe Jenna had requested.

"I don't know how you can stay sane in this mess," commented Jenna, trying on the shoes. "What do you think?" she asked the bored looking clerk.

"What do I think?" the young woman said with a sneer. "I think you look like you just escaped from the Russian army. That's what I think."

"But everyone's wearing them nowadays. They're actually quite fashionable. Those three inch heels you're swaying around in will kill your back."

"Better killing my back than my chances of catching a man. Well, do you want them or not?"

"Be honest. How do you think they look?"

"I've already told you. But, if you like them, take them," she said with a shrug.

"I will," said Jenna defiantly. "Wrap them up."

By the time Jenna met Susan at the restaurant, she was starved.

"You're always starving," laughed Susan.

"I forgot to eat breakfast," said Jenna.

"Oh no. Now you're probably going to worry about being anorexic again."

"I doubt it. I'm hungry enough to eat a horse."

Over their salads, Susan got right to the point.

"Can you take two weeks off school?"

"Right now?"

"Yes."

"Of course not."

"Too bad. I was going to ask you to accompany me to Paris next week."

Jenna dropped her fork into her salad.

"Are you serious?"

"Never more so."

"But why now? Why can't we wait till summer vacation?"

"It's an emergency. I'm taking a leave of absence from the translation company."

"Why?"

"To find someone."

"Who?"

"Solange. My half-sister."

By now, Jenna's mouth was wide open. She was too shocked to speak.

Susan spent the next half hour recounting the facts of the past two weeks from the discovery of her birth certificate to the trip to Washington to pick up her French passport. The only detail she didn't include was the mystery phone calls. As neurotic as Jenna tended to be, Susan was afraid she'd go off on all sorts of tangents with that information.

"Well, do you want to go with me?"

"Of course. But just one question. You said your mother has given you information on areas of Dijon where someone might know the whereabouts of Solange. Right?"

"Right? But what's the question?"

"Does that mean I don't get to tour Paris?"

"Of course not. I promise we'll spend two days in Paris before taking a train to Dijon. After all, it is my favorite city."

"In the entire world?"

"Don't know. I haven't been in all the cities of the world."

"But you're way ahead of me."

"Well, will you go or not?"

"Yes. Yes. I got my passport five years ago and have never used it."

"There's no time like the present."

"True. And I've always dreamed of being one of those people who walks into the principal's office and says, no, I mean announces, with a cavalier wave of the hand, 'By the way. I'll be taking two weeks off to go to Paris.'"

"Well, now your dream has come true. How long have you been teaching there?"

"Eight years. And, in all that time, I've rarely taken a sick or personal day. I only seem to get sick on official days off."

"I'll get the tickets on Air France. You can reimburse me."

"You're not going to shop around for the best deal?"

"No. It's too late for that. Besides, all my frequent flyer miles are on Air France."

"Why did you decide to ask me to tag along?"

"To carry the bags!"

"And I was hoping you were going to say, 'Comic relief!'"

"Well, that's what it will be if you dare take those ugly new shoes to Paris."

"All the guide books say that you should take comfortable shoes for walking."

"There's a difference between comfortable shoes and storm-trooper uglies. I'll bet our troops in Iraq have gone into battle wearing lighter footwear."

"Okay. I'll leave them home. I wouldn't want to embarrass you, O sophisticated one."

"Do what you want. But, unless you wear them every day, they'll add to the baggage we'll be dragging around on public transport. Besides, they'll kill your chances of finding a man."

"That's exactly what the sales clerk said."

"She's right. No self-respecting Frenchman would be seen with a girl in such unfeminine shoes. Take my word for it."

"I will."

They left the restaurant and went their separate ways at the corner of Fifth and Madison. .

"I'll call as soon as I buy the tickets. You aren't upset about my comments on your new shoes, are you?"

"No. I'm too excited about the trip to Paris to give a damn about your snide remarks."

⌘

The waiting area at their gate in JFK was teeming with teenage travelers. Susan had planned the trip without remembering this was one of the busiest times of the year to fly to Paris. Spring break! The annual assault of the American high school French classes on the City of Light. Kids were stretched out all over the filthy floor, laughing and giggling. The noise was deafening. But it wasn't just the kids creating the din. Susan would never understand why people talking on cell phones had to be so loud. Within seconds, she'd learned more of the private life of the woman sitting next to her than she cared to, and the middle-aged man seated across from her wasn't much better. He hadn't shut up since he sat down. She'd thought he wasn't quite all there when he started talking to himself until she'd noticed one of those ridiculous ear pieces attached to his right lobe. "It's called a blue tooth, Susan, Get with the program," Jenna informed her.

"The world has gone mad, Jenna. This is ridiculous. I should have remembered that March and April are the worst times to travel to Paris. We'll be up all night listening to those kids on the plane."

"That's because you've been to Paris so many times. I don't care how noisy it is. Oh, my God, Susan. Don't look now, but the hottest looking guy I've ever seen is smiling at me."

"He's probably a molester."

"No. I think he's in charge of one of the groups. He must be a French teacher."

"Same thing."

"He's walking over to the Starbucks' kiosk. I'm going over there."

"For God's sakes, Jenna. Act your age."

"I am. Desperate! I'll be thirty next month."

Before Susan could answer, Jenna disappeared into the crowd. Susan opened her *Paris Match* magazine but couldn't concentrate. She reached into her purse and took out her French passport. When they arrived at Charles de Gaulle in the morning, she planned to use it for the first time, go through the European Union line. She'd explain that maneuver to Jenna on the way over. Susan leaned back and closed her eyes.

A sudden sound in front of her made her open her eyes. She found herself face to face with the man Jenna had shadowed to the coffee kiosk. He was holding a cup of coffee in each hand.

"*Êtes-vous Susan?*"

"*Oui. Mais, qui êtes-vous?*"

"Georges."

"Wait a minute. What started all this? Why are you talking to me?"

"Jenna, your friend, when I asked her who you were."

"What did she say?" asked an irate Susan, switching to English.

"Only that you were a Francophile on your way to France to do some personal research."

"And you thought you'd dazzle me with your French. Is that your usual pick-up ploy? I'll kill Jenna when she gets back here."

"Really?"

"Yeah, really. But I'm allowed. She's my best friend. A little high strung, but my best friend.

Georges' face turned scarlet.

"What's wrong?"

"The pick-up ploy remark. I assure you I was only trying to make conversation. I grew up half in the States and half in France. I just wanted someone to converse with, someone who knew more than a few phrases of the language. Sorry to have bothered you," he added, turning and starting to walk away. Then he turned around abruptly and handed Susan one of the cups of coffee. "Here. I almost forgot. This one is for you. One cream. No sugar. Just the way you like it."

A chastened and embarrassed Susan took the paper cup from his outstretched hand.

"*Merci. Merci beaucoup.* I am truly sorry. I thought you were a teacher with one of those noisy and annoying groups over there."

"I am. Well, not exactly. I made the arrangements for three of the groups. Got a free round trip ticket to Paris for my efforts."

"You're a travel agent?"

"No," he laughed.

"What's so funny?"

"Me being a travel agent. I did it as a favor for a friend. It drove me nuts arranging the itineraries for only three high school groups. I'd be a basket case if I did that for a living."

Susan laughed in spite of herself.

"What *do you do?*"

"I thought you weren't interested."

"Let's just say you've piqued my curiosity."

"I'm an architect."

"You are? I've never met one of you before in person."

"This must be your lucky day. And I assure you we are not a noisy group."

"How about annoying?"

"I'll have to leave that answer up to you. What do you do?"

"Translations."

"English to French?"

"Mostly French to English. A majority of the companies I work for won't even try to read French. The French seem more capable in the English to French department."

"Either that or they won't admit to not being able to do the translation."

"You could be right. I've often visualized a group of translators working frantically all night, translating English business documents into French. Anything to keep the Americans from finding out they need help translating. I've discovered in this business that if there's one sin Americans are punished for on a regular basis it's their honesty in admitting they don't know something, especially when it comes to languages."

"I never thought of it that way," said Georges.

A nervous Jenna appeared in front of them, clutching her passport and boarding pass. "Come on, you two. It's time to board."

"Calm down, Jenna," laughed Georges. "The plane won't leave without us."

With a wave, Georges disappeared into the crowd.

"He is so hot, Susan. I think he likes you."

"For God's sakes, Jenna. You're acting like the high school kids you've been talking to. And why did you send that guy over to talk to me?"

"Oh, lighten up, Susan. We're on vacation. What's happened to your sense of humor? Georges seems very nice."

"Okay, I give up. You're right, Jenna. I am a bit of a tight ass."

"You said it. I didn't."

"But why did you send him over to talk to me?"

"Easy. He asked me who the cute girl with the big tits was, sitting all by herself."

"He did not!"

"Well, not the part about the tits, but he said he'd seen us come in and sit down. He clearly wasn't interested in me, so I told him your name, the way you like your coffee, and...."

"And?"

"And the rest is history, Susan. You've obviously been out of the loop too long with that dork, Scott. I think it's time you got your groove back, as they say in the movies. Relax. Have fun!"

Susan glared at her friend.

"Now what's wrong?"

"Don't make me sorry I brought you along."

"No way, Susan. I'd never do that."

They finally entered the plane and found their seats. They were in a middle row of five seats, Susan in one aisle seat, Jenna in the other. Three exuberant high school students were between them. Before the plane took off, Jenna was acting as goofy as her traveling companions. Susan asked the flight attendant if there was any possibility of being moved to another seat, preferably one surrounded by adults.

"I'll do my best," replied the attendant. "But we're full. Maybe we can find another of their group who'd like to join them."

Susan sighed. She might as well stay where she was. She didn't feel like moving to a seat next to another group of rowdy teenagers further back. They might be even worse that her current companions. *Just suck it up, Susan. Jenna's right. I am a tight ass.*

A voice instructed all passengers to turn their attention to the overhead screen and the safety instructions. Susan stretched out, resigned to spending the next eight hours with her current neighbors. But just before the beverage cart reached their row, Susan felt a hand on her shoulder. She spun around to warn the kid behind her to knock it off, but found herself face to face with Georges.

"Why don't you come back to the next cabin and sit next to me? Maggie here has a wild crush on the boy sitting beside you."

"I do not," said a nose-ringed teen, slapping Georges on the back.

"What's in it for me?" asked Susan. "Another spike-haired, nose-ringed hoodlum to annoy me for the next eight hours? If so, I'd just as soon stay put."

"No, ma'am," replied Maggie. "You'll be stuck between two stiffs, Mr. Bonnard and Miss Stephens, our ancient librarian. No nose rings. No spiked hair. Just complete and utter boredom."

"Thanks for the compliment, Maggie," laughed Georges.

When Susan didn't make a move to stand up, Maggie shook her arm. "Please, Miss. Please let me sit here."

"Yeah," yelled the kid next to Susan. "Please let her sit here."

Susan laughed in spite of herself before rising to her feet and following Georges to the next cabin. Miss Stephens, who couldn't have been a day over twenty-five, was in the window seat reading a magazine. Susan squeezed into the middle seat. Georges took the aisle.

"I've got to admit it, Georges. This is quite an improvement. Thanks for thinking of me."

"I'd say you're welcome, but it was Shelley's idea,' he said with a nod towards Miss Stephens. "She couldn't bear the thought of you flying to Paris next to the rowdiest kids in our group."

Susan thanked Shelley for her consideration but was disappointed that the move hadn't been an act of chivalry on Georges' part. Making a move on her must be the farthest thing from his mind. He didn't even attempt to begin a conversation. Before the meal was served, he'd buried his face in the pages of a notebook filled with technical drawings which didn't make any sense to Susan. The movie was one Susan had seen before, so she covered her eyes with her dark shades and fell asleep.

Susan awoke with a start. "Get your hands off me. Who do you think you are?" She tried to lunge out at the person in the seat next to her, but he was holding her wrists so tightly she couldn't move.

"Calm down! Calm down!. You must have been having a nightmare."

"Oh, my God," said Susan snapping back to reality. "You're right. I was having a dream. I'm so embarrassed. And look what I've done," she said, looking at the open pages of Georges' notebook swimming in a dark liquid. They reeked of whiskey.

"Good thing Shelley was here to grab my glass or we'd all be soaking wet."

Susan turned towards Shelley who was sitting up board straight clutching a glass in each hand. The flight attendant appeared with a wad of paper towels and wiped up the wet pages of the notebook.

"I am so sorry," apologized Susan. "I've ruined your notes."

"That's okay. I can run off another copy when we get to Paris. They're saved on my lap top."

"Thank God. They looked important. Are they"

"Only if you consider a five p.m. deadline tomorrow evening important."

"Oh God! How can I make amends?"

"You could begin by acting a little more civil. You make me feel like Jack the Ripper."

Susan was disappointed. He was supposed to answer her question about making amends with "Have dinner with me."

"I'm sorry."

"You should be. I would ask you to have dinner with me, but you'd accuse me of coming on to you."

"I said I'm sorry."

"Are you coming on to me?"

"No. Of course not. I'm just trying to be civil."

"Well, here's the deal," said Georges. "Tell me why you're going to Paris, and I'll consider asking you out to dinner."

"It's a deal. But I'm simply going to Paris to see the sights and enjoy myself like three fourths of the tourists on this plane."

"And I simply don't believe you."

"Okay. Order me a glass of red wine, and I shall reveal all."

"Why?"

"Why not? I guess I suddenly feel like spilling my guts about the reason for my trip. And my destination is Dijon, not Paris."

"Your friend, Jenna, seems to think it's Paris."

"Well, that's just part of the deal."

"You seem to make a lot of deals."

"Just lately. I promised Jenna that if she'd go with me to France we'd spend two days in the City of Light. She's never been abroad before."

"That explains her exuberance."

"Not really. Jenna's always like that. She's never seen a glass that's half empty."

"Not like you. I imagine all the glasses you see are at least three fourths empty."

"Only recently."

"What happened? I'm guessing it's a man. Am I right?"

"No. Only half right."

"A woman?"

"Certainly not!"

"Do I get to hear the story?"

"It's a long one."

"I have at least six more hours to listen. You have my undivided attention."

It took the better part of an hour for Susan to relate her saga from the discovery of her birth certificate to the admission of her mother that she'd been born in France and that she was going to Dijon to try to unveil some of the mystery surrounding her birth and her mother's life there. She left out the part about Solange. That could wait for another day, if there was going to be one.

"I wouldn't blame you if you didn't believe me."

"It is a little far-fetched, but aren't all mysteries? When are you going to Dijon?"

"On the early afternoon train on Friday."

"I could meet you at the station. I'm traveling on to Dijon this afternoon. I'll be there for a few weeks. I've spent a lot of time there with

71

my grandmother. She lives in an apartment around the university area."

"That's the area where I lived as a young child. That's all my mother has told me. She wants me to see where I lived, but she hasn't given me any names to contact."

"No relatives?"

"Nothing. She swears that they're all dead and buried."

"I'll bet my grandmother could help you out. She remembers everyone who ever lived in that area, and since your father is a well-known journalist, she'll know who he is."

"But he lives in Vietnam."

"Then she'll definitely know all about him. People in France often pay more attention to their successful ex-pats than the ones at home. Gives them a link to France's glory days, especially if they're connected to a former colony like Indochine. So, do you want me to meet you at the Dijon station on Friday?"

"Yes. Definitely."

⌘

They landed in Paris a little before seven-thirty in the morning. Susan felt a tingle of delight as she followed Georges into one of the passport lines set aside for those carrying European Union passports.

"Looks like it may turn out to be a sunny day in Paris," yawned Georges. "Lucky for us. You know how bleak Paris can be in April."

"Tell me about it. It's not the first pair of shoes I've ruined running through puddles in April."

"Ditto. It's like all four seasons in one day, except I never seemed to remember that until I was caught *sans parapluie* and other rain gear between classes."

"You studied in Paris?"

"Architecture. Three years after N.Y.U. How about you?"

Before Susan could answer, the passport checker's voice rang out, "Next!"

"Go ahead," said Georges, stepping behind Susan.

Susan handed the unsmiling official her French passport. He stared at the photograph and then at Susan.

"*Vous-êtes Suzette Fontaine, mademoiselle?*"

"*Oui, monsieur. Je suis Suzette Fontaine.*"

The official smiled when he handed Susan her passport. "*Bienvenu à Paris.*"

"*Merci, monsieur,*" replied a smiling Susan, making a hasty retreat in the direction of the baggage claim area.

"*Un moment, mademoiselle,*" the official called after her. Susan turned around.

"*Qu'est-ce que c'est'?*"

"You look just like your father."

"*Merci, monsieur. Merci beaucoup.*"

Susan practically skipped all the way into the baggage hall.

"You're grinning like a Cheshire cat," said Georges with a puzzled look on his face. "What gives?"

"Happiness. That's the first time I've used my French passport and real name."

"That's bizarre, especially since you studied in Paris. Why do you think your mother waited so long to tell you about your background?"

"Who knows? I'm as bewildered as you. But the truth is that this time last month I didn't even know I was French."

"Are you sure you're not making all this up to entertain me while we wait for our baggage?"

"I'm sure." Susan was beginning to warm up to Georges, but she wasn't ready to reveal her entire life story to someone she'd known for less than twenty-four hours.

There was a loud clicking sound as the baggage carousel began to turn.

"Why don't you and Jenna grab your bags and go to Dijon with me this afternoon? I'm surprised you can wait for two days."

"It was the only way I could coax Jenna into coming with me. She's dreamed of seeing Paris her entire life, so I can't just hustle her off to the Gare du Nord and shove her into a train for a two and a half hour train journey. I had to sweeten the pot a little bit."

"I should hope so. But it's closer to three hours than two and a half."

Jenna came bursting into the baggage hall.

"I thought I'd never get through that line. How do I get one of those E.U. Passports?"

"Look on the bright side," laughed Susan. "On the way back, you'll be able to zip right through at JFK."

Once they'd retrieved their suitcases, the three of them walked together to the closest taxi stand.

"Where are you staying in Paris?" asked Georges.

"Hotel Jardin de Plante."

"Ah, near the Botanical Gardens."

"Yes. The price was right and it's near a Metro station. On Friday, we'll take a train from the Gar du Nord to Dijon."

"Where will you stay in Dijon?"

"The Hotel Marisol."

"How did you choose that?"

"Stayed in one in Biarritz once, so it seemed a good choice. And it's got a fairly central location. But I'm not sure where to start my inquiries."

"I told you. My grandmother. She's in her mid eighties but sharp as a tack. She seems to know or at least know about half the population of Dijon. It doesn't sound as if your mother has been very helpful."

"Don't even go there."

"So, I can meet you at the station on Friday and drive you to your hotel. You wouldn't mind?"

"No. She wouldn't mind in the least," interrupted Jenna.

"Jenna, I think I am capable of answering for myself," laughed Susan. "Of course, you can meet us at the station. It will be great having a contact in unfamiliar territory. But you make me feel guilty."

"About what?"

"Being so rude to you on the plane. I am truly sorry."

"Apology accepted. Just don't do it again."

"I promise," laughed Susan.

"Now what?" asked Jenna as soon as Georges made his exit.

"What do you mean?" asked Susan.

"I mean are you going to stand there looking ga-ga eyed all day or can we go to our hotel?"

Susan signalled to the impatient looking taxi driver at the curb that they did indeed desire his services. Once seated in the taxi, Susan turned to Jenna and stated emphatically, "I am not ga-ga over Georges. I hardly know him."

"Bull shit. You need some romance in your life after that pompous ass, Scott."

"Don't remind me."

An hour later the two friends were sound asleep. It was the middle of the afternoon when they awoke to the sound of the phone ringing. Jenna answered.

"Oh, hi, Bob. Wait. Let me ask Susan."

"Susan, are you awake?"

"I am now."

"It's Bob, one of the teachers from our flight. Would you like to meet up with him and the others at the Pompidou Center?"

"When?"

"In about an hour."

"No."

"Oh. Don't be a spoil sport. Come on, Susan. We're only here for two days."

"You go."

"By myself?"

"You'll be fine. I'll walk you to the Metro and make sure you get headed in the right direction. Let me speak to Bob."

Jenna handed the phone to Susan.

"Hi, Bob. You're familiar with Paris, aren't you? Good. I thought so. Just make sure Jenna gets on the right Metro line to come back here. Great. She'll be there."

Susan hung up.

"I feel like a small child," laughed Jenna.

"You're fine. Bob will meet you at the Pompidou stop and make sure you get headed back in the right direction. Just make sure you catch the last run. You wouldn't want to end up spending the night with Bob would you?"

"Now there's a thought," laughed Jenna.

"Well, if you do, call to let me know before I call out the gendarmes."

"But what are you going to do while I'm out enjoying myself?"

"Eat dinner in the little brasserie around the corner and have an early night. I've got a lot of planning to do."

"The Dijon strategy?"

"Exactly. But I promise not to let my personal agenda put a damper on our two days in Paris. We are going to have fun!"

"You bet we are," laughed Jenna.

An hour later Susan waved goodbye to Jenna from the Metro platform and headed towards the little corner brasserie for dinner.

Although Susan enjoyed Jenna's company, she was delighted to have some time on her own to figure out what she'd started to call her Dijon Plan. If Georges' grandmother lived in the area her mother had mentioned and was as sharp mentally as Georges kept insisting, she might be Susan's only hope of finding Solange, her needle in a haystack. Susan didn't believe in fate, but meeting up with Georges would go a long way to making a believer out of her if his grandmother ended up pointing her in the right direction.

Susan was in bed by ten, determined to overcome her jet lag by putting herself on French time. Hopefully, Jenna wouldn't stay out too late or drink too much. Jet lag was bad enough, but jet lag plus a hangover was never fun, especially when you needed to get an early start in the morning.

"Help! Help! Open the door, Susan. Please! For God's sakes, will someone turn on the damn light."

Susan sprang out of bed and opened the door. The dim light from the room's overhead fixture did little to illuminate the hallway, but she did manage to make out the silhouette of a figure she guessed was Jenna, sitting huddled against a wall in tears.

"Jenna? Is that you?"

"Of course, it's me. Who else knows you're here?

"What are you doing sitting out there? Are you blind drunk?"

"No. Only blind. The minute I stepped out of that dog crate of an elevator and took two steps down the hall, the freakin' lights went out. What a great time for a power failure. I couldn't see a thing, so I started calling your name over and over to get your attention."

"I'm sorry. I was sound asleep. But it isn't a power failure. I should have explained about the lights before you left."

"What about the lights?"

"In most French hotels the main hallway lights are on a timer. You have only so many seconds to get to your door or *viola*! You are left in darkness."

"Is that a remnant of the Reign of Terror?"

"Could be."

"I hope you brought the key with you," said Jenna, looking towards their room door."

"The door's open."

"No it isn't. It slammed shut a few seconds ago. You'll need to go back downstairs to get a spare key."

"Why me? You're dressed. I'm practically naked."

"I refuse to try to speak to anyone else on the staff here. If I try to speak French, they look at me as if I just arrived from Mars. And, if I speak English, they shrug their shoulders. They'll never give me a key. You speak their language, Susan, so you are going down there to get a key."

"Dressed like this? I'll get arrested for indecent exposure."

"There's only a middle-aged woman at the reception desk. The place is empty. So get on that damn elevator before I throw you on. And hurry. I have to pee."

Susan pressed the down button. While she waited for the elevator to arrive, she caught a glimpse of herself in the control panel mirror. It was worse than she'd thought. Her bare breasts were clearly visible inside her flimsy white tee shirt which only just reached the top of her thong undies. This was not a pretty sight, so Susan prayed that only the female receptionist would see her.

The ancient elevator took ages to get to the main floor. When the doors opened, Susan stepped out and found herself surrounded by a group of tourists who were only now checking in. But she held her head high and walked through the middle of the line to the accompaniment of wolf whistles and cat calls in a language which, thank God, she could not understand. And the receptionist was not a woman. He was a man who ogled Susan from head to toe while she explained her situation. When she was finished, he took a key from a hook on the wall but insisted it was hotel policy for an employee to accompany all guests asking for a spare key to their room. On the elevator ride up to the fifth floor, his eyes never left her boobs. He was just about to reach out and touch one when the elevator lurched to a halt. The doors opened, but his gaze never wavered.

"Touch one of these and you're a dead man," warned Susan, wriggling past him. It was only when he caught sight of Jenna in the shadows that he dropped his arm to his side. He quickly opened the room door and fled back to the elevator.

Susan lay down on the bed.

"Are you all right?" asked Jenna.

"Jenna! First, I walked around the lobby of a hotel half-naked much to the delight of a bunch of drunken Eastern European Neanderthals. All I needed was a pole to dance around! Then, I was almost manhandled by that sleazy lounge-singer of a desk clerk. And you have the nerve to ask me if I'm all right. Of course, I'm not all right."

"Well, you don't have to yell. I have a splitting headache."

"You're right. I should have told you about the hallway lights before you left. And you didn't know there was a late-night group checking in. And how were you to know that there would be a change of shift and a man would replace the woman at the desk? So, let's say good-night and forget this thing ever happened."

"I can't."

"Why not?"

"I set you up, Susan."

"What do you mean?"

"The reason I wouldn't go back downstairs to get the key was because that wild crew checking in scared me to death and the weirdo behind the desk kept winking at me. Susan, can you hear me? Are you asleep?"

"No, Jenna. I am lying here plotting your imminent assassination."

⌘

Since it was Jenna's first visit to Paris, Susan did not want to disappoint, but the two days of touring around her favorite city were starting to get on her nerves. Jenna was enthralled with everything she saw. The surly Parisians seemed more pleasant than usual. Even the weather cooperated. It didn't rain once. Each evening they dragged themselves back to the hotel where Susan would throw herself across the bed but be unable to enjoy a nap before dinner because of Jenna's trans-Atlantic calls to her mother, extolling the virtues of Notre Dame, the Musée D'Orsay, Montmartre and even the Père Lachaise Cemetery. The Mona Lisa and the other masterpieces in the Louvre failed to excite Susan as in days past. And Versailles, Susan's favorite palace in all France, appeared to have lost its charm. The dusty glass in the Hall of Mirrors was the only thing that made an impression on Susan. Had the mirrors always been in such dire need of a wash and polish with Windex?

They left the ascent to the top of the Eiffel Tower until Friday morning en-route to the Gare du Nord and their journey to Dijon. The train pulled out of the station at two thirty."

"We should be there around five-thirty," said Jenna.

"Do you think we'll ever see Georges again?"

"He said he'd meet us at the station. He sounded sincere."

"You're right, and, if he's not at the station, I'll bet he phones our hotel immediately. What do you think?"

"I think he'll be waiting for us at the station."

"Why?"

"Because he likes you, Susan. Honestly! Sometimes you can be so dense."

"Maybe he was just being nice, passing the time of day."

"I doubt it Susan. Not after the scene you pulled on the plane."

"Don't remind me. I get embarrassed just thinking about it."

"You should," laughed Jenna.

They arrived in Dijon at five-thirty on the dot.

"Georges was right about the length of the train ride," said Susan, as they gathered up their luggage and got ready to exit the train. Jenna kept having to readjust the load in her over-sized duffel bag to keep it from leaning to one side.

"I can't believe you brought two large bags for a ten day trip, Jenna. I told you it would be a pain lugging them all over Kingdom Come, didn't I?"

"Yes, mommy. But how you can stuff everything you need into that little duffel bag is beyond my comprehension."

"Not if you've done it as many times as I have."

"Show off!"

"Not really. Just savvy traveler! Always remember you can wear only one outfit at a time, and no one you meet will have seen it before or is likely to see it a second time."

"I know all that, Susan, but I kept thinking that.....Oh, my God! There's Georges. I told you he likes you."

Susan looked up and saw Georges standing outside the platform barrier waving to them.

"You wave back, Susan," laughed Jenna. "I don't have a free hand."

"You've just added another reason for packing light."

Georges hurried them through the station to a side entrance.

"Hurry. I'm parked illegally. Pierre will never forgive me if I get a ticket."

"Who's Pierre?" asked Jenna.

"My cousin. He loaned me his car. It's tiny, so I don't know if we'll be able to get that humongous bag into the trunk."

"I told you, Jenna," growled Susan.

"Well, I can take a taxi to the hotel. You two go on ahead."

"Don't be ridiculous, Jenna. That would defeat the purpose of coming to meet you."

It took only a few minutes to solve the luggage problem. Susan's small bag fitted perfectly in the compact trunk. Jenna's two behemoths shared the back seat with her. Susan rode up front with Georges.

"How did you know what train we'd be on?" asked Susan.

"Well, when you weren't on the mid-morning or the mid-afternoon one, I gave this one a try."

Jenna leaned over and poked Susan on the shoulder.

"Tired?" asked Georges.

"No," answered Jenna. "At least, I'm not. I'm too excited to be tired."

"I'm exhausted," laughed Susan.

"From what?" asked Jenna.

"Chasing after you. Rescuing you from dark hallways. Making a fool of myself half-naked in the hotel lobby."

"That does sound interesting," laughed Georges. "Sorry I missed it. Looks like you two have been up to all sorts of high jinx. But you'll have to explain it all later. Here we are, ladies. The Hotel Marisol."

"Already?"

"Already."

George helped them carry in their luggage and waited until they were checked in before leaving.

"When will we see you again?" asked Jenna.

"Jenna! Don't be so rude. I'm sure Georges has much more important things to do in Dijon than baby-sit two American strays."

"*Au contraire, mademoiselles,*" said Georges with a low bow. "My grandmother would like you both to join us for dinner this evening."

"That is so sweet," said Jenna. "What do you say, boss?"

"I say yes. But tell your grandmother not to go to any fuss. Are you sure we're not putting her out?"

"Exactly the opposite. She's thrilled about meeting a Fontaine. She is a big fan of your father. She'll probably wear you out with a barrage of questions."

"Which I will not be able to answer, considering I've never met the man."

"And the food will be delicious."

"Just tell us when to be there," said Susan.

"I can come back for you."

"No. Definitely not. We'll take a taxi."

"Are you sure? It's no problem coming back. It's not that far."

"I'm sure. Just write down the address. What time should we be there?"

"Around seven-thirty. Is that all right?"

"Certainly. Seven-thirty it is. See you then."

"Things are looking up," said Susan as they walked slowly to their room, dragging Jenna's bags behind them.

"They certainly are," said Jenna. "A taxi sounds great. For a minute I was afraid you were going to suggest we take a city bus to save money."

"With the exchange rate the way it is, that's what we should be doing. But I figure we can splurge this once. Madame Bonnard would be disappointed that a Fontaine had to take the bus."

"Me too!" agreed Jenna.

The Bonnard apartment was in a block of flats near the university. The minute Susan got out of the taxi, a feeling of *déjà vu* came over her. Sensing Susan's uneasiness, Jenna slipped a hand under her elbow and led her towards the front door.

"Are you okay, Susan? You look like you've seen a ghost. Have you?"

"Of course not. It's just a strange feeling I have about having been here before. I can't explain it."

"Don't even try. This building makes me feel right at home. It's like being back in New York."

"How so?"

"No elevator."

"Well, at least they're only two flights up."

Their knock on the door was answered immediately by Georges.

"Welcome to *Chez Bonnard, mes amies.* Let me introduce you to my grandmother."

A tall slim woman walked towards them, removing a large apron as she did so.

"*Grandmère*, I'd like you to meet Susan and Jenna."

The woman didn't answer. She stared at Susan; her hand flew to her mouth.

"*Grandmère*, are you all right?"

"I'm fine. You must excuse me, Susan. You look very much like someone I used to know many years ago."

"It must be my father. I've never met him."

"So Georges told me. That is too bad. Does he know about you? I mean, does he know you exist?"

"I doubt it. My mother is a very secretive woman. Until a few weeks ago, I didn't know that I existed."

"I don't understand."

"What Susan means, *grandmère*, is that she found her real *acte* in some family files only three weeks ago. Her mother had hidden the details of her birth from her. Susan had no idea her mother was French."

"But how did she disguise her accent?"

"She perfected an American one."

"*Impossible!*"

"Not where my mother was concerned, Madame Bonnard. She claims that desperate circumstances call for desperate measures."

"Amazing! But let's eat before the food gets cold. Georges, lead the way."

The Bonnard dining room was small but cozy. The array of dishes on their plates showed that Madame Bonnard had spent a busy afternoon in the kitchen. Throughout the meal, she kept staring at Susan.

"So you have come to find your father, Susan?"

"No. He doesn't live here anymore. He lives in Vietnam."

"Then why have you come to Dijon?"

"*Grandmère!* That doesn't sound very welcoming."

"I am sorry, Susan. That didn't come out the right way. My English is not so good."

"It's a lot better than my French," laughed Jenna. "And thank you all for speaking English this evening. I was really nervous about not understanding a word tonight."

"Would I do that to you, Jenna?" laughed Susan.

"Yes. In a heartbeat."

"You must remember, *grandmère*, that people visit many places in France, not just Paris."

"I am well aware of that, Georges. I may be old, but I'm not senile yet. I just find it strange that you are in the birthplace of your father but aren't expecting to find him here."

"Perhaps Susan just wants to see what Dijon looks like," said Georges.

"Next you'll be trying to convince me that she's here to buy mustard."

"You're right, Madame Bonnard," said Susan. "I am searching for someone."

"Who?" asked Georges.

"Solange."

"Solange? Who is Solange?"

"My sister. At least my half-sister. My mother gave birth to a baby girl out-of-wedlock in 1965. She put the child up for adoption. Ten years later, I came along."

"And this Solange. Is she also the daughter of Jacques Fontaine ?"

"No. She is not. My mother, by her own admission, had an affair with a rather disreputable boy when she was very young."

"Your mother must be quite a girl!" said Georges.

"Georges! That is no way to talk. You must forgive my grandson, Susan. The 1960's were a crazy time. Sex and drugs all over the place."

"That's what my mother says, but I'm having a difficult time imagining my mother being bad."

"Why?" asked George.

"Because she is so prim and proper. Right, Jenna?"

Jenna nodded her head in response.

The older woman rested her elbows on the table and studied Susan. "*Remarkable! Remarkable!*"

"What's *remarkable?*" asked Georges.

"The resemblance of Susan to her mother."

"You mean you knew my mother?"

"No. But I have seen someone before who looked just like you. I think she lived in the neighborhood. It must have been your mother."

"That's odd."

"Why?"

"Because I look nothing like my mother. She has blond hair and a very fair complexion. Here, let me show you a photograph."

Susan took a picture out of her wallet and handed it to Georges' grandmother. The color drained from the woman's face.

"Are you all right?" asked Georges.

"Yes. I am fine. It is always a shock to see someone you have not seen for many years, even if just in a photograph."

"Speaking of photographs, Susan, you're in for a pleasant surprise. *Grandmère* has a clipping from an old newspaper. It's a photograph of your father. Didn't you say it was from the 1960's?"

"Yes. Georges. It was. But I can't find it. I've looked everywhere. It must have been thrown out accidentally when I was cleaning out some papers at my grandson's insistence. Downsizing, as Georges likes to say."

Georges stared at his grandmother in disbelief.

"Coffee everyone?" asked Madame Bonnard rhetorically.

They sat around the living room enjoying Madame Bonnard's rich, dark coffee. During a lull in the conversation, she turned to Susan and asked, "What is the first name of your mother?"

"Anna. It's Anna."

The elderly woman sat deep in thought before speaking again.

"Anna. Oh my! I think I may be able to help you in your quest ."

"To find Solange?"

"Yes. You see, there were three girls who ran around together at the time you are talking about. It was such an odd time in the '60s. But one of the young girls was very religious. It's all coming back. She entered a convent in a little town near the Swiss border called Sauret."

"How do you know this, *grandmère*?"

"The newspapers. Their names were all mentioned when one of the three girls was killed in an automobile accident while visiting the one in Sauret. It was very tragic."

"What does that have to do with Solange?" asked Susan.

"Maybe nothing, *ma petite*, but I just thought the one who entered the convent there might have some information. Your mother was very close to her. It seems logical that she might have helped your mother with the adoption."

"Tell me again how you knew them?" asked Susan.

"I didn't really know them. I just remember seeing them together on the street and in a local café. They were inseparable."

"Do you know the name of the one who entered the convent?"

"No. I never did know it. She was just someone I was familiar with from seeing her in the neighborhood. Sauret is only an hour and a half by train from here. If you go there, you could talk to her. The convent is small, so she would be easy to identify. You could ask her if she knew what happened to Solange."

"It sounds like a shot in the dark," said Susan.

"But maybe not," said Madame Bonnard. "Nuns frequently arranged private adoptions in those days, so it makes sense that if a young girl needed help she would go the nuns, especially if one was her good friend."

"It's worth a try," said Jenna. "We've come all this way. Another short journey couldn't hurt."

"I agree," said Madame Bonnard.

"What do you think, Jenna?" asked Susan. "Are you up for another train trip?"

"You bet!"

Georges opened a desk drawer and pulled out a train schedule.

"There's an express train to Sauret at one o'clock every afternoon. You could talk to the people at the convent and catch the seven o'clock back to Dijon. But why don't you wait until Monday? Let me show you around Dijon this weekend. I can drive you to the station on Monday. What do you say?"

"It does sound like fun. I've never been in Dijon before," said Susan.

"I hope I'm not sending you on, how do you say in English, the wild chase of the goose," said Madame Bonnard.

"It doesn't matter if it does turn out to be a wild goose chase," said Susan. "It's all we've got to go on."

"Then you won't be upset with me if your visit to Sauret turns out to be a waste of time?"

"Don't give it a second thought," said Jenna. "Susan and I like to see new places, so it will not be a waste of time either way."

Georges insisted on driving Susan and Jenna back to their hotel. As soon as they left the apartment, Madame Bonnard walked into her bedroom and removed a newspaper clipping from the top drawer of her dresser. It was a photograph beginning to yellow with age. But the faces of the two subjects were crystal clear. Madame Bonnard was still staring at the photograph when Georges returned.

"Where are you, *grandmère*?"

"In here, Georges. In here."

"Okay. Good night."

"Can you come in here a minute, Georges?"

"Of course. Are you all right?"

"I keep telling you I'm fine. I just want you to see something."

Madame Bonnard handed her grandson the newspaper photograph.

"*Grandmère*! You lied. Why? Why did you tell Susan you couldn't find the photograph?"

"Look at it closely."

"I am. What is it I'm supposed to see?"

"The young woman's face."

"Very pretty. She hasn't changed much over the years. I'd still be able to recognize her from the photograph Susan showed us at dinner."

"Does she look anything like Susan?"

"No. But lots of offspring don't resemble their parents."

"Read the description of the photograph. Out loud, please."

"It says, 'The opening of the new theater was attended by Dijon's popular up-and-coming young journalist, Jacques Fontaine, accompanied by his sister, Anna.' What are you getting at, *grandmère*?"

"Don't you see, George! When I told Susan that she looked like her mother, that wasn't the woman I was talking about. The woman named Anna is Jacques Fontaine's sister. She can't be Susan's mother. That's why I lied about losing the photograph."

"Why would her mother or whoever she really is lie to Susan?"

"I don't know. Maybe she kidnapped her. That would explain the flight to America. I have a bad feeling about all this. Something sinister must be involved in this girl's background."

"I think you've had too much wine, *grandmère*."

"Perhaps. But don't forget I told you this if and when Susan finds out the truth."

"I won't. But, *grandmère*, what do you think of Susan, as a regular person, I mean?"

"You mean as a girlfriend?"

"Of course."

"I liked her very much."

"Then you approve?"

"As long as her parents don't turn out to be brother and sister!"

⌘

Georges lay awake for a long time thinking about Susan. It must be dreadful to have never met her father and half-sister. He simply refused to believe that Susan's parents were siblings. The idea was too preposterous to bear thinking about. There had to be a simple explanation. He looked at the clock. It was almost midnight. *If it weren't so late, I'd try to phone Anna, Susan's mother, in Syracuse and ask her for an explanation.* It suddenly hit him. *What's the matter with me? It's only seven o'clock on the East Coast.*

Georges swung his legs over the side of the bed and jumped to his feet. In the dark, he knocked over a stool.

"What's wrong, Georges? Are you all right?"

"Of course. It's so dark in here that I bumped into a stool on my way to the desk. Go back to sleep, *grandmère*"

"Might I suggest, young man, that you turn on the light for your midnight romps and quit scaring old ladies out of their wits, at least, this old lady."

"Sorry, *grandmère*. It won't happen again."

"Good. "*Alors, bonsoir, mon petit.*"

George opened his laptop and paced up and down while he waited impatiently for it to boot up.

"Finally!" he growled, clicking into the internet.

A search of the American white pages was useless. Anna Foster's personal number was unlisted. What was it the woman did for a living? Was she a lawyer? Accountant! *That's it. She's an accountant. Owns her own business.* The yellow pages produced a long list of accounting firms. *Let's hope it's listed under her name.* It took several minutes before George was able to yell out loud, "Success!" There it was: Foster Accounting. *Damn! It's probably closed already.* But Georges keyed in the number anyway. *Come on! Let someone be there! Please!* After the sixth ring, a heavily accented message provided the information that Foster Accounting's hours of operation were nine to five, Monday thru Friday. However, if the caller felt he had a question of supreme importance, he could call the following 315 area code number. George scribbled down the number so fast that he prayed he'd gotten it correctly. He hung up and took several deep breaths before keying it in. The voice on the message had pronounced the words *supreme importance* in such formidable tones that Georges had thought twice about calling.

"Good evening. Foster Accounting answering service. How may I help you?"

"I don't suppose you can give me Mrs. Foster's home phone number, can you? I'd be ever so grateful."

"Regardless, I'm still not going to give it to you."

"Who am I speaking with?"

"Shouldn't I be the one asking that question?"

"Sorry. It's just that I'm calling from France. It's almost midnight here."

"Frae France? Away you go! Is this some sort of a joke?"

"I assure you it's no joke."

"But we don't have any clients in France."

"I'm not a client. I'm a friend of Susan's."

"Scott?"

"Georges."

"Well, Georgie boy, this is your lucky day, or, should I say, night."

"Why lucky?"

"Susan is currently in France."

"I know that."

"Then why are you calling here?"

"I need to speak with her mother."

There was silence on the other end.

"She's gone to San Francisco for a few days."

"May I please have her number there?"

"Hmm! I don't know if she'd appreciate me handing out that number to every Tom, Dick or Harry."

"For God's sakes! I'm not just any Tom, Dick or Harry."

"I know. I know. You're Georges. You already told me that."

"Come on. Please give me her number. It's very important that I speak with her."

"Don't get your shorts in a twist. I'm looking for it on the computer."

"Thank you. Thank you."

"Here we go," said the voice, rattling off the number. "Got it?"

"Yes."

"It's only about four o'clock on the West Coast, so, if Mrs. Foster isn't there, you've got lots of time to phone without waking her up."

"If I stay up all night."

"Hey! It's your call. You're the cheeky monkey who initiated all this. No me!"

"And just who are you?"

"I don't need to tell you who I am."

"Then how can I thank you?"

"Just say it plain and simple."

"But a thank you always sounds more sincere if you attach a name to it."

A giggle came over the line. "Aye. You're dead right. Makes it sound that much more personal. I agree. The name's Molly, Molly Murdoch. I work for Mrs. Foster."

"And where in God's name do you come from? That's quite a brogue."

"Thank you. I'll take that as a compliment. Glad you like it."

"I bet you're Irish?"

"Bite your tongue! I'm a Glaswegian, born and bred."

"Well, Mrs. Foster is certainly getting her money's worth out of you."

"What do you mean?"

"I mean she doesn't have to buy a guard dog for protection. You're saving her a bundle."

"Very funny, Georges. But I'll have you know I am Mrs. Foster's personal assistant, and I am in charge of the office while she's in San Francisco."

"Well, if and when I get to speak with Mrs. Foster, I will certainly tell her that you are doing an excellent job. I hope you don't look as ferocious as you sound."

"Ha! Ha!"

"Any messages for Mrs. Foster when I reach her?"

"As a matter of fact, yes. Tell her that some loony woman with a strange accent keeps coming into the office. I can't get rid of her."

"Well, if you think her accent is strange, it must be."

"Ha! Ha! On second thought, Georges, don't tell her about the strange woman with the foreign accent. I don't think it's worth mentioning. She'll just worry for nothing."

"Are you sure, Molly?"

"Aye. I am definitely sure. Now, good night, Georges.

"Good night, Molly, and thanks again for the number."

Georges sat on the edge of his bed staring at the phone. He couldn't decide if he were being ridiculous, overly cautious or downright paranoid. This time last week he hadn't even known Susan Foster existed. Now he was making international phone calls on her behalf without being quite sure why he was doing so. But deep down he already knew the answer. Love. He was falling in love with this strange young woman who had insulted him in the airport and again on the plane. But he had to admit that as outrageous as her behavior had been and as absurd as her life story was he was completely smitten with her.

He started to key in the number he'd been given for Susan's mother in San Francisco but pressed the end button before completion. He couldn't just say, "Hello. I'm calling about your daughter, Susan Foster. Is it true that her father is your brother?" Of course not. That was no way to begin a conversation, especially when he didn't even know the woman. He sat on the bed for several minutes trying to think up a better approach. After he pressed redial, he felt courageous enough to complete his mission.

"Hello," a male voice answered in a distinct French accent.

"Hello. May I please speak with Anna Foster?"

"May I tell her who's calling?"

"Of course. My name is George Bonnard. I'm calling from France. It's about Susan, her daughter."

"Is something wrong? Has something happened to Susan?"

"No. She's fine. I just need to ask her mother a few questions."

"Hold on one moment. Anna, it's for you. A young man from France. It's about Susan."

"Oh, my God," came a woman's voice over the line. "Is Susan all right?"

"She's fine."

"There must be something wrong. Why are you calling at this hour?"

"I thought it was early evening in San Francisco?"

"I mean in France. I repeat, why are you phoning at this ungodly hour?"

"I'm sorry if I alarmed you, but you must believe me. Susan is all right. I just dropped her and her friend, Jenna, at their hotel."

"In Paris?"

"Dijon."

Georges was aware of the woman taking a long breath.

"Well, what do you want? Speak up."

"My name is Georges."

"Okay, Georges. What can I do for you?"

"I'm not exactly sure. I guess I just wanted you to know that Susan is determined to find her half-sister."

"Solange."

"Yes. Anyway, she came to Dijon looking for her or at least to find out some information about her whereabouts."

"I doubt that she'll find out anything."

"But she already has. On Monday, she and her friend, Jenna, are taking the train to Sauret."

"You must be joking. I told Susan nothing of Sauret."

"You can blame me for revealing that piece of information. My eighty year old grandmother still lives in the university district of Dijon. We had dinner with her this evening."

"I don't understand. How did you and your grandmother get involved with my daughter?"

"Susan and I met on the plane. I sat next to her on the flight to Paris. When she said she was going to Dijon to look for someone, I told her my grandmother might be able to help."

"What is your grandmother's name?"

"Bonnard. Francoise Bonnard."

"I am not familiar with that name. I do not know her."

"My grandmother thought that Susan reminded her of someone who lived in her neighborhood in the 60's. Susan showed her a photograph of you. It seemed to shock my grandmother. She said she remembered you, a blond-haired girl and two others running around together. When Susan told her you had given birth to a little girl who'd been put up for adoption, my grandmother advised her to go to the convent in Sauret for information."

"Why?"

"I think you know why, Madame Foster."

"Because of Isabelle?"

"Isabelle? Is that the name of the member of your trio who entered the convent in Sauret? My grandmother couldn't recall her name. She may never have known it."

"Then how did she know she'd gone to the convent in Sauret?"

"As the saying goes, 'the word on the street'."

"But why does she think going to Sauret will help Susan locate Solange?"

"Oh, come now, Madame Foster. Wasn't that where you had the baby and arranged for the adoption? My grandmother says that most adoptions were handled by the nuns in those days."

"Young man, this is none of your business. And your grandmother sounds like a meddling old busy-body. What do you hope to accomplish by pursuing this?"

Georges ignored both the insults and the question.

"Will Susan find information about Solange in Sauret or not?"

"Why should I answer that?"

"Because you have too many secrets. And Susan deserves to know the truth."

"She already does. I told her that she had a half-sister named Solange."

"I mean the entire truth."

"For example?"

"That Jacques Fontaine is her father."

"He is. I think I ought to know who the father of my daughter is. But why are you so interested in our family history?"

"Because I love your daughter. And I believe she deserves to know the entire truth about her background."

"I told you. She already does."

"You'll have to do better than that, Madame Foster."

"What are you talking about?"

"Jacques Fontaine. I know that he is your brother."

The line went dead. But if Georges were correct, Madame Foster was already making a call to someone in Sauret. Susan's trip would not be in vain.

⌘

"Who was that on the phone?" asked Henri.

Anna remained silent, the phone still in her hand.

"Anna, are you all right?"

"I don't know. I just don't know."

"Sit, down, Anna. You're as white as a sheet."

Anna sat down on the sofa.

"You were right, Henri. I should have told Susan years ago about my past, my entire sordid past."

Henri laughed. "Anna, how many times do I have to tell you there is nothing sordid about your past? It's your friend, Isabelle, and that self-centered brother of yours who got you into all this. They are the ones with the sordid pasts."

"I know that. If only I'd had the sense to get the police involved when Isabelle poisoned Annemarie. All of this could have been avoided. And we would all know the whereabouts of Solange and Lili would still be alive."

Anna began to sob.

"Oh, my darling Anna, you were very young. You thought you were doing the best thing."

"But, don't you see, Henri. It wasn't the best thing. It was the worst. I should have gone to Annemarie's parents immediately and told them the truth."

"But their daughter was already dead."

"I know. But they would have insisted on a complete criminal investigation. Because of me, they never knew they had a granddaughter."

"And I, the village's only doctor, should have insisted on an investigation into Annemarie's death. Lili wanted me to get the police more involved. If I had, she would still be alive. Don't you think I relive that guilt every day of my life, Anna? But the past is over. We can't change it."

"When Susan found the birth certificate, I should have told her the truth. I can't believe I was so careless with those documents, at least with Susan's. I should have locked them up in a safety deposit box."

"You wanted them to be found, Anna. The compulsion to confess caught up with you. Why didn't you tell Susan everything?"

"She caught me by surprise. I wasn't prepared."

"What exactly did you tell her? It must have been quite a lot to send her running off to Dijon."

"Susan doesn't need much of an excuse to go to France. You know that. She so damned French. I never could exorcise her of her Frenchness. The memories of her early years in Dijon never left. They were always lurking around the periphery of our lives."

"So how much does she know?"

"That I gave birth to an illegitimate daughter in 1965 when I was only twenty and that I named the little girl Solange."

"Two lies. Oh Anna. Will it never end?"

"I didn't want her to start asking more questions. I needed more time to prepare my answers."

"Didn't she wonder why you decided to keep her?"

"I told her that times had changed. Damn it, Henri! How was I supposed to know that on the flight to Paris she'd meet someone from Dijon whose grandmother lived in Isabelle's old neighborhood."

"Was that who called?"

"Yes. His name is Georges Bonnard. He's a young man Susan met on the plane. He wanted to warn me."

"About what?"

"The fact that his grandmother knows that Jacques is my brother."

"How does she know that?"

"His grandmother has an old newspaper clipping with a picture of me with Jacques."

"Has he told Susan?"

"No. Thank God."

"He sounds like a decent sort."

"He says he's in love with her."

"Good. She'll need someone to help her absorb the shock of all these revelations."

"I'd better phone Michelle Dupré this weekend to let her know that Susan will be in Sauret on Monday. Michelle should be able to think of a solution."

"A solution to what?"

"Susan's curiosity."

"It's time for the truth, Anna."

"No! Not yet."

"You're being ridiculous."

Anna didn't respond. She paced the room, deep in thought.

"Solange!"

"What about Solange?"

"Susan's quest is to find Solange. Right?"

"Right."

"Well, that's it. It all makes sense."

"Anna! At the moment, nothing you say is making sense."

"Of course it does, Henri. Michelle can tell Susan that Solange left for boarding school in America when she was thirteen, went to college in the

States and decided to remain there permanently. That's the truth plain and simple. No lies included,"

"Anna! You know Solange's departure from France was not quite as benign as that. The girl's life was at stake. She didn't just leave France. She escaped."

"But Susan doesn't need to know that. All she needs to know is that Solange was sent to a Catholic girls' boarding school in the States. Susan will thank Michelle for the information and be on her way."

"Do you think that answer will satisfy Susan?"

"If it doesn't, Michelle can give her a little more information."

"Like what?"

"That the school is in the northern part of West Virginia. That will end Susan's snooping around in Sauret. She will fly home and phone the school to ask for Solange's updated address and phone number."

"Which the school will deny any knowledge of."

"With the donation I give them every year, that's exactly what they'd better do."

"Susan won't give up, Anna. You're simplifying."

"What do you mean simplifying, Henri?"

"I mean that you are not factoring in all the obvious variables."

"Such as?"

"Lili's death and the true circumstances of Susan's birth."

"I'm counting on Michelle Dupré to make sure those events don't come up."

"I hope you're right, Anna. I hope you're right."

⌘

Saturday was spent seeing the sights in Dijon. Georges was an excellent tour guide. They spent Saturday afternoon touring the Palais des Ducs de Bourgogne.

"How do you know so much about this place?" asked Jenna.

"My grandmother. She is a walking encyclopedia of everything in Dijon. From the time I was old enough to fly alone, my parents indulged me. They let me spend my summers here with my grandmother. That's why we're so close. On rainy days, she would bring me here to look at the paintings in the Musée des Beaux Arts, but it was the architecture that always fascinated me. The same architect who designed Versailles drew up the plans for the Palais."

"Jules Hardouin-Mansart?" asked Susan.

"You know him? You must know a lot about French architecture. His name is not all that familiar."

"Not really. But I love Versailles and have read lots of books and articles about its design and construction. And I've learned something today. I didn't realize he was the architect of this *palais.*"

"Good for you. It always seems so sad to me that an architect's masterpieces are revered for centuries but the genius behind them fades into oblivion."

"Does that bother you when you're designing something?" asked Jenna.

"Not really. My philosophy is that when the final product is admired the architect is receiving praise, even if his name is unknown to the admirer."

"That's a good way to look at it," said Jenna.

"It's the only way," continued Georges, "The only artists who receive fame personally nowadays are rock stars. Look at the Beatles. But they'll be forgotten long before the old masters. Writers leave books. Architects leave beautiful structures."

"And artists leave beautiful drawings and paintings," added Susan. "You're right about the rock stars, though. Who's going to remember them in a hundred years? They don't leave anything tangible. Nothing you can hum centuries from now like the great classical composers or Gershwin and Cole Porter."

The weather was cloudy and cool, but they ate lunch in an outdoor café to help satisfy Jenna's insatiable hunger for French culture. It was almost six before they finished their coffee. Georges dropped them at their hotel and left to spend the evening with his grandmother. Susan and Jenna decided to spend a quiet evening in their room watching a movie.

Around midnight, Susan reached for the phone.

"I'm going to call Scott."

"Why?" asked Jenna. "I thought you two were finished."

"We never broke up officially. And I sort of miss him."

"Sort of? You either do or you don't."

The phone rang several times before a giggly female voice answered.

"Hi. Who is it?"

"Susan. Scott's girlfriend."

"I don't think so."

"Who is it, Hon?" Scott asked from the background.

"Some wench who claims she's your girlfriend. Says her name's Susan. "

"Get rid of her," ordered Scott.

"Tell Scott to get on the phone immediately."

"Susan. How are you? I've really missed you."

"Like hell you have. Obviously your little friend turned on the speaker phone without you realizing it. I heard every word you said."

"Don't be silly. I was just kidding."

"Is this your version of when the cat's away, the mouse will play?"

"Well, what do you expect? You didn't even bother to let me know your were going to France."

"Yes, I did."

"You call a few words on my answering machine a personal message? I don't think so!"

"Who is she?"

"None of your damn business!"

"Well, I guess this really is goodbye, Scott."

"It doesn't have to be. We can still see each other when you get home."

"I don't think so, Scott."

"Have it your way."

"I will."

Susan slammed down the phone. Jenna ran around the room, clapping her hands and whooping for joy.

"It's finally happened," sighed Susan, "and the best part is I don't feel sad or upset."

"That's because you have Georges."

"He's just a friend."

"Not the way he looks at you. You two need time alone."

"Like that's going to happen with you around."

"I've got an idea."

"Oh, no. Not one of your loony tune plans."

"Well, it was one of my 'loony tune' plans that got you together with Georges in the first place. Admit it. Right?"

"Right. So what's the plan? I can hardly wait."

"It's simple. After our outing tomorrow afternoon, I'll say that I'm going to see a movie at the local theater, or *cine* as they say in this neck of the woods."

"But Georges knows you don't understand enough French to sit through an entire movie."

"Give me some credit, Susan. There's an old church in town that shows American movies with French sub-titles. That's where I'll go tomorrow night. That should keep me out of your hair for a few hours."

"I'd feel guilty if you did that. You could just say you have a headache and go back to the room."

"God, you are so thick sometimes. The idea is to leave the room free for your amusement. Why would you want me to be there?"

"Because nothing like what you're imagining is going to happen."

"But, if it does, the room will be Jenna-free. And I'm willing to bet you fifty euros that it will happen."

"Sounds like an easy way for me to make some money. Besides, how will you know if I'm telling the truth?"

"By the smile on your face."

"Okay. You're on."

Sunday was warmer than Saturday but just as cloudy. The three friends ate lunch at another outdoor café then headed to the Jardin de l'Arqueloise. Georges and Susan walked on ahead while Jenna purposely lagged behind. They had been strolling along one of the pathways for several minutes before Susan looked down and realized that she and Georges were holding hands. A quick glance over her shoulder showed Jenna smiling and holding up both hands with her fingers making the victory sign. Later, in the lady's room of a café, Jenna asked Susan if it was time for her disappearing act.

"If you insist," laughed Susan.

"I insist. And, Susan, you're blushing."

"It's the sun."

"We haven't seen a single ray all day."

When the two friends returned to their table, Jenna didn't even sit down.

"You two enjoy an evening alone together. You deserve it. I'm off to the movies, I mean *ciné.*"

"Are you going to the old church where they show the American flicks with sub-titles?" asked Georges.

"*Oui, monsieur.* The very one."

Georges started to stand up.

"Stay where you are, Georges. I can take a taxi."

"She's not too subtle, is she?" laughed Georges as they watched Jenna climb into a taxi at the main gate of the Jardin. When Susan didn't answer, he said, "I like Jenna, but I was hoping to spend some time alone with you."

"Me too," was all Susan could get out.

They ate dinner in a small restaurant then strolled hand in hand along the leafy avenue leading to the hotel. Susan was shaking like a leaf when Georges pulled her into the open doorway of an apartment building and kissed her full on the lips.

"I've wanted to do that ever since dinner at my grandmother's."

"What took you so long?"

"You. It was only today I believed you felt the same way. I didn't want to risk having you throw a fit like you did on the plane. That must have been some nightmare."

"It was."

"Well?"

"Well what?"

"What was the nightmare?"

"I'm too embarrassed to tell you."

Georges kissed her again when they arrived at the hotel.

"I don't want to leave," said George.

"Then don't."

"Are you propositioning me, Miss Foster?"

"Maybe," Susan giggled, pulling him by the arm towards her room door.

They made love and then lay in each other's arms in silence before drifting into a sound sleep.

The sudden noise of the door handle turning woke them both.

"Hey, Susan. Are you awake? Did you and Lover Boy finally make it? I want to hear all about it. What's that noise?"

"It's just me getting out of bed," said Georges.

"Oh, God! I am so sorry. I didn't know you were here, Georges."

Jenna opened the door to the hallway and fled in terror. Georges turned on the bedside lamp and looked at the clock. It was two a.m.

"I'd better get out of here," said Georges. "I had no idea how late it is. And you girls have a big day ahead of you tomorrow. Don't get up. I can let myself out."

He leaned over and gave Susan a long, lingering kiss. But before he opened the door and disappeared into the hall, Susan called out, "Georges?"

"What?"

"About the nightmare on the plane."

"What about it?"

"This was it."

Georges left without answering. But Susan knew he'd heard.

When Jenna returned to the room, she changed into her night clothes in the dark and slipped into bed.

"Are you asleep, Susan?"

"No."

"What are you doing?"

"Plotting your second assassination."

"That's okay. I don't mind. I just made fifty euros. The easiest bet I've ever won."

⌘

It was almost three o'clock when Georges slipped into bed. He was tired but found it impossible to sleep. He couldn't stop thinking about Susan. He couldn't remember the last time he'd felt this way about a girl. He liked to keep his personal life simple; but he couldn't stop thinking about her. If he weren't so attracted to her, he'd have written off last night as nothing more than a one-night stand. But his feelings for Susan went too deep for such trashy nonsense.

Georges got up and walked to his desk, being careful this time not to knock something over and awaken his grandmother in the next room. He pulled on his robe and sat at the desk with his head resting in his hands. He couldn't stop thinking about Susan's journey to Sauret tomorrow. Until his grandmother had mentioned the place, Susan had never even heard of it. He knew her mother had. The panic in her voice when Georges mentioned Sauret had given that away immediately. It was obvious she didn't want Susan to go there. But there was no turning back. Tomorrow afternoon, Susan and Jenna would be on their way there. Georges desperately wanted to help Susan, but he didn't know where to begin. He was beginning to regret having introduced her to his grandmother whose behavior had become increasingly enigmatic since their meeting. *Grandmèe* knew more about Susan's background than she was telling. That was evident from the way she clammed up when George questioned her.

Georges spent the rest of the night thinking about the facts as he knew them:

Susan had been raised as the only child of a single mother in Syracuse, New York. It took until the age of thirty for her to discover her real identity, and that discovery had been a fluke. One thing was evident; Anna Foster had never intended to have Susan find out her real identity. Why else would she have gone to such lengths to disguise her nationality and the details of Susan's birth, especially after Susan began studying French intensively and spent a year at the Sorbonne in Paris? None of it made sense. Two questions came to George's mind. The first was the identity of Susan's father. Was Susan really the product of an incestuous relationship? The second was the kidnapping theory. If Susan had been snatched from an unsuspecting mother, it made sense that Anna would have escaped from France and assumed a new identity. But what would her motive for kidnapping have been? The only explanation that seemed plausible was that Anna was so bereft after putting Solange up for adoption that she wanted a little girl to replace her. That made sense, but why had she waited for ten years? Wouldn't she have done that while still in the immediate throes of grief? The more George thought about the situation, the more bewildered he became. Susan's relationship with her mother was so odd that he'd be willing to bet that Susan was not aware that her mother was currently in San Francisco. Surely she would have mentioned that in casual conversation.

George made up his mind to ask Jenna in confidence if Susan was aware of her mother's current whereabouts. He'd do that before they left for Sauret. And Susan was convinced that there was no man in her mother's life. Georges had asked her that point blank. But a man had answered the phone at the number Molly Murdoch had given him in San Francisco. And his accent was definitely French. Georges hoped he was not Jacques Fontaine. Susan had said that a couple of times a year her mother traveled to San Francisco on business. God forbid that those two were currently enjoying a romantic liaison in the City by the Bay. It didn't bear thinking.

For over an hour Georges kept recreating the scene in his grandmother's living room when she first set eyes on Susan. She'd been clearly disturbed. She had told Susan that she looked exactly like her mother. That comment had surprised Susan who said that she looked nothing like her mother and produced a photograph of Anna to prove it. *Grandmère* had not responded. The color draining from her face had been her only response.

Georges began to think of another theory. Was it possible that Anna was not Susan's mother? Who knew? Maybe the kidnapping theory was the closest he'd come to the truth. But it was already five in the morning. He was too tired to think any more. He crawled back into bed and fell asleep instantly.

On the other side of Georges' bedroom wall, his grandmother lay wide awake. She'd found it difficult to sleep since she'd met Susan Foster. She knew she could clear up the mystery with only a few explanations, but she didn't want to see her grandson get hurt. She knew he was in love with Susan. Why ruin it with lurid details that might be construed as the senile ramblings of an old woman? There was no doubt in Madame Bonnard's mind about who the biological mother of Susan was. She looked just like her, but she'd let Susan find out her identity on her own. That's why she'd mentioned Sauret. If she found Solange, the half-sister she was searching for, all the rest would fall into place. Solange was ten years old when Susan was born, old enough to remember the village gossip surrounding the birth. Francoise Bonnard's gut feeling told her that Susan had been born in Sauret, not Dijon.

⌘

When Susan and Jenna walked into the hotel lobby at eleven forty-five, George was already there, pacing back and forth.

"Is it my imagination, Georges, or are you a little nervous?" asked Jenna.

"What makes you think I'm nervous?"

"The pacing!"

"Was I pacing?"

"Yes," responded Susan. "I'm the one who should be nervous. Not you."

"Hurry," said Georges, ushering them into the car. "You don't want to miss your train. Did you phone the convent to let them know you were coming?"

"Of course, I did. What do you take me for?"

"Who did you speak with?"

"I'm not exactly sure, but she acted as if she couldn't figure out who I was talking about. Do you think your grandmother could be mistaken?"

"Absolutely not. She's rarely wrong."

"It's just that sometimes old people's minds play tricks on them."

"I assure you, Susan, my grandmother's mind does not play tricks on her. Trust me!"

Up until his phone conversation with Anna, Georges had begun to feel dubious about his grandmother's memory. But he wasn't about to tell Susan that he'd spoken with her mother. *It's frightening,* thought Georges. *I've known this girl only a few days and already I know more about her background than she does.*

"Will that be all right?"

"What? Will what be all right?"

"If we call you to pick us up at the station this evening? We can always take a taxi."

"I'll be at the station when your train pulls in."

Susan stood on the platform with Georges while Jenna rushed onto the train on the pretext of finding their seats.

"She's not too discreet, is she? After all, you do have reserved seats and the train is practically empty."

Susan laughed in reply. Georges held her close until the final whistle blew.

"Georges, how can I ever thank you for all you've done for us?"

"You already did last night."

When Susan boarded the train and found her seat, she was still blushing. Jenna pretended to be engrossed in a magazine but tossed it aside.

"I watched the entire scene. It reminded me of an old black and white film, the ones where couples are always kissing each other goodbye before one of them boards a train."

"I keep thinking that Georges is too good to be true."

"That's because you're not accustomed to decent men."

"And you are?"

"Here's the proof. Take a look," said Jenna, tossing her phone to Susan. "Go ahead. Read the text message."

Miss u lots. Can't wait till we meet up in New York, Susan read aloud. "I'd say you made quite an impression on Bob."

"And the great thing is he lives in New York. The guys I usually meet turn out to be tourists."

"And you had to come all the way to France to meet someone who actually resides in New York."

"Right! I'm excited for both of us. Now we can go home happy."

"Not quite yet, my romantic friend. Let's not forget the reason we're here."

"How could I? I'm never allowed to change the subject. Believe it or not, I've never been so focused. But I would like to see some action, and I want to be a participant, not just an observer in this gig."

"I can't imagine what there is to do. All I'll be doing is talking to the mother superior, asking if she can help us find Solange."

"Is she the woman you spoke with on the phone?"

"No. The receptionist wouldn't let me speak to her. "

"Why?"

"I have no idea. But, at least she made an appointment for me to meet with her. I was afraid to argue with the woman in case she wouldn't let me get my foot in the door. I can't imagine what the mother superior in a remote convent would be doing that prevented her taking phone calls, but I didn't want to press my luck by asking questions."

"She probably spends the entire morning on her knees praying in the chapel. Did you tell the receptionist what you wanted?"

"Didn't get the chance. We were disconnected."

"You mean she hung up on you?"

"I hope not. If that's the case, finding out information on Solange will be harder than I thought."

The train pulled into the Sauret station at two-thirty on the dot. There were no signs of life anywhere. There was no one managing the station and no signs of a taxi. The station building itself was in a state of disrepair.

"This must have been what it felt like arriving in the middle of nowhere in the old West," laughed Jenna. "I hope the French version of the James Gang doesn't appear over that hill, pointing their pistols at us."

"God forbid, Jenna. But you're right. It's not the most attractive place I've ever been."

There was a sign post with two arrows pointing in opposite directions outside the rusted main gate of the station. The one pointing to the right said **VILLAGE**. The one pointing straight ahead said **COUVENT**. "

"Which way should we go, Jenna?"

"Well, I vote for the village. There's no way I'm tackling that hill without hiking boots. Good grief, there's no telling how long it is to the convent on the top."

"You're right. There's got to be a taxi in the village."

The sidewalk led around a bend right into the center of the village. There was an old car with a cracked plastic sign which said *Taxi* parked outside a café. Susan and Jenna stood beside the taxi. There was no sign of the driver, but, as soon as they started to walk away, a man came running out of the café. "*Attendez! Attendez!, mes mademoiselles. Je mange mon déjeuner.* Then, instead of getting into the taxi, he walked back into the café to finish his lunch, leaving Susan and Jenna waiting impatiently on the sidewalk. It was at least ten minutes before he reappeared.

"He'd never make it in New York," laughed Jenna.

"You're right, but he has us over a barrel. He's our only hope of getting up that hill to the convent."

"Where to?"

"The convent."

"Thank God you didn't try to walk up there. It's quite a hike, and the edge of the road is falling away. It is very dangerous."

The steep hill was a series of hairpin bends which their driver raced around at breakneck speed. "Thank God, we didn't walk up here," said Jenna, clutching the sleeve of Susan's coat. "If something had raced around one of those bends, we'd be road-kill by now."

"The view from the convent is very beautiful. There is a lovely lake below. You can see it from the back of the convent," said their driver. And he was right. At the very top of the hill was a majestic brick building with a gleaming gold cross in the center of the roof. Four ornate cupolas were placed on each corner. It was a breathtaking sight.

"I wish Georges could see this," said Susan, getting out of the taxi. "I'm sure he'd be inspired."

They barely had time to pay the driver before he took off again, hanging out the window and yelling, "When it is time to return, phone the café."

"What's the number?" yelled Jenna, but he'd disappeared over the crest of the first hill before the words were out of her mouth.

"Now what?" asked Jenna. "If we're never heard from again, it'll be your fault."

There was a bell with a long rope attached at the foot of the steps leading up to the entrance.

"Should I?" asked Jenna.

"Might as well."

Jenna pulled the rope. The sound from the clapper hitting the sides of the bell was so loud that it echoed throughout the surrounding hills long after the clapper was still. But no one appeared at the door.

"This is ridiculous," said Jenna. "That din was enough to wake the dead. Where's the welcoming committee?"

The front door was finally opened by a very short nun dressed in full habit. She was smiling, but the smile faded from her face as soon as she looked at Susan.

"May I help you?"

"I certainly hope so," said Susan. "I am Susan Foster. This is my friend, Jenna. We have come here from America to find out some information."

"What kind of information?" the nun asked curtly.

Susan ignored the question. "I have an appointment to speak with your mother superior."

"She is expecting you?"

"I believe so, although I was cut off before the appointment was finalized. I wouldn't have come unannounced."

The small woman motioned to Susan and Jenna to follow her. They walked along a dimly lit hallway. At the end of the hall there were several doorways identified by numbers. The nun pointed to a chair outside one of the doors and told Jenna to be seated. "You must stay here since your friend is the one with the appointment." Her tone was civil, but the smile never returned to her face.

Jenna sat down without a word.

The nun led Susan down another long hallway. Halfway down, she stopped at an unmarked door and knocked.

"*Entrez! Entrez!*" called an impatient voice.

The nun opened the door and ushered Susan inside.

"This young lady wishes to speak with you. She says she has an appointment."

Susan gasped audibly. Seated behind a desk at the far end of the room was an attractive middle-aged woman in a modern business suit. Her dark hair was streaked with blond frosting. She was wearing makeup. Not a lot, but enough to notice. She stood up and walked around the desk to shake hands with Susan.

"Welcome to our convent, Suzette. I am Sister Madeleine."

"You are?"

"Well, I was at this time yesterday."

"I'm sorry. It's just that......"

"It's just that you expected a carbon copy of Sister Ruth."

Susan nodded in reply.

"Don't worry. Most people react this way when they first meet me. Thank God times have changed. I've never worn a traditional habit. I don't think I'd have lasted very long in a job that required a uniform, especially such a dark and cumbersome one. The very thought of it makes my skin itch."

"I can understand that. But I'm a little confused. If the line went dead before I could make an appointment, how do you know my name?"

"Madame Dupré."

"Madame Dupré? I don't know anyone by that name."

"I don't either. But she phoned early this morning to say that a Suzette Fontaine would be paying us a visit this afternoon. She will be here shortly. Now what can I do for you?"

"I thought you might be able to give me some information, but now I'm not so sure."

"What sort of information?"

"Details of an adoption that may have been arranged here. It was a long time ago, 1965."

"I have been here for only three years, so I know nothing about what went on then."

"How many sisters live here? Surely someone would remember that time."

"Perhaps. But many of those sisters cling to the old ways. They are very tight-lipped when it comes to some issues."

"Is there a sister from Dijon?"

"Not that I know of. But that doesn't mean anything. The older sisters gave up their identities when they took their vows."

There was a tap on the door.

"Who's there?"

"Sister Alicia."

"Come in, Sister."

The door opened slowly. An elderly, stooped-over woman, hobbling on a cane entered the room.

"I'm glad you're here, Alicia. There is someone I want you to meet. This is Mademoiselle Suzette Fontaine. She has come all the way from America to find out about an adoption that may have been arranged here in 1965. You were here then, weren't you?"

"Of course. I have been here since 1950. But how do you know of this adoption?" asked Sister Alicia, looking up at Susan's face. But, before Susan could answer, the old woman's raised her hand to her mouth and gasped.

"What's wrong, Alicia?" asked Sister Madeleine. "You look like you've seen a ghost. You're white as a sheet."

"*Mon dieu! Mon dieu!*" were the only words that came out of Sister's Alicia's mouth.

"Get hold of yourself, Alicia. What's the matter?"

"I'm sorry. I don't know what came over me."

"Well, Mademoiselle Fontaine wants to know is if we have a sister here from Dijon."

"*Oui. Oui.* I mean, we did. She is no longer here. She's been gone for at least thirty years."

"You mean she died?" asked Susan.

Sister Alicia didn't answer. When the silence became uncomfortable, Susan asked, "Do you know anything about an adoption she might have arranged?"

111

"Madame Dupré is here. She can tell you everything."

The old woman walked back to the door and announced the arrival of the mysterious Madame Dupré. A well-dressed middle-aged woman walked into the room. Sister Madeleine first introduced herself and then Susan.

"Come, ladies, let us sit down and discuss this mysterious business which seems to have upset Sister Alicia enormously. Do you wish to join us, Alicia?"

The slamming of the door on her way out was Sister Alicia's only answer.

"Such odd behavior," said Madeleine. "I've never seen her like this before."

"If you had been here in those days, your reaction would be the same," said Madame Dupré. Then she took Susan's hand in hers and said, "It is so wonderful to meet you at long last, Suzette. Or, do you prefer your American name, Susan?"

"I don't understand any of this, Madame Dupré," replied Susan. "How do you know about me and my visit here? And please call me Susan. I'm not all that familiar with Suzette yet."

"All right. And you and Sister Madeleine must call me Michelle."

"All right, Michelle. But who in God's name are you?" asked Susan.

"I am Michelle Dupré, the adoptive mother of Solange."

"My God," yelled Susan jumping to her feet. "I never dreamed it would be so easy. When can I meet my sister?"

"I'm sorry, Susan, but I can't answer that."

"Why not?"

"Because Solange is in hiding."

"In hiding! Why? Where? Is she hiding from the law?"

"Of course not. The story is one of epic proportions, but you must hear it."

"I don't care how long it is. That's why I'm here."

Sister Madeleine rose to her feet and walked towards the door. "I have business to attend to in another part of the convent. Make yourselves comfortable, ladies. I will arrange for coffee to be sent in."

"We don't want to take over your office, Sister."

"I insist. Sit at the table by the windows overlooking the gardens and the lake. The effect of that view on even the saddest of tales can be magical."

Susan and Michelle sat down at the table by the windows.

"She's right. It is an enchanting view," said Michelle. "I haven't been here in years. It's almost like coming home."

"But what about Solange?" asked Susan impatiently. "I want to know all about my sister."

"First of all, Susan. Solange is not your sister."

"I know that. Half-sister then."

"No. Not even that," continued Michelle. "You are not related."

"How can that be?"

"You have different mothers and fathers."

"I don't understand."

"You will. But please be patient while I retell these events as unemotionally as possible."

For the better half of an hour, Michelle explained in detail the circumstances of Solange's birth. Susan was too stunned to interrupt. When Michelle finally stopped talking, Susan's first reaction was anger at her mother for having claimed to be Solange's mother.

"Why? Why in the name of God did she tell me she was Solange's mother? None of this makes sense."

Michelle quickly came to Anna's defense.

"It made sense then. We were desperate. The parents of Annemarie, Solange's birth mother, never knew she was pregnant, and Anna and I never suspected for a minute that Isabelle was as mad as a hatter. A little too religious maybe, but not homicidal. After we realized that Isabelle had induced Annemarie's labor, delivered the baby and calmly held her hand while she bled to death, Anna and I decided to keep the gory circumstances of her death from her parents, especially since Isabelle had already notified them that their daughter had perished in an automobile accident. And there was nothing Anna could do since Isabelle had purposely broken that news to them before Anna herself received the news of Annemarie's death."

"But what about the funeral?"

"Isabelle made sure that Annemarie was buried immediately. By the time her grief-stricken parents came to Sauret, they had only a grave to visit."

"But didn't they check the newspapers for accident reports?"

"Evidently not. They took Isabelle's word for everything."

"And you adopted little Solange?"

"Yes."

"But what about the *acte* my mother showed me?"

"I gave her that *acte* in case it was ever necessary to show it to the parents of Annemarie. It never was. She kept it."

"My mother is the most deceitful woman I can imagine."

"No. Your mother is a wonderful woman. She stood by Annemarie from day one and did not betray her, even in death. Your mother has never in her life turned her back on family or friends. It is important that you understand this."

"Why?"

"Because you may find out other strange things about your mother that will make you question her deeds."

Susan sat in silence.

"Promise me, Susan."

"Promise you what?"

"Not to judge your mother."

"You have my word. But what about Isabelle? What happened to her?"

"She continued to live here at the convent. But she never took her final vows. She grew stranger and stranger until ten years later the sisters had her committed to an asylum over the border in Switzerland."

"She was that far gone?"

"And then some. We all suffered because of Isabelle. If your mother and I had pressed charges at the time she committed her first crime, another death could have been prevented and Solange would not be in hiding."

"What happened?"

"Isabelle became enraged when she found out I was already pregnant at the time of Solange's birth."

"Why?"

"Because I'd had so much trouble conceiving, she'd convinced herself that she was the angel of God who'd been assigned the task of delivering Annemarie's baby into my hands."

"What did she do?"

"Nothing at the time. But, when Solange was ten years old, another event set her off and she threatened to kill Solange."

"Is that when she was committed?"

"No. But it was shortly after that. Unfortunately, she escaped from that institution three years later when Solange was thirteen. We knew that Solange was in danger, but it was only because of your mother's compassion that Solange was sent to a girls' boarding school in the States. We could never have afforded that expense. Your mother insisted on helping us. Anna shouldered the entire financial burden. That was in 1978, the same year that the two of you emigrated to America."

"Why do you think my mother was so generous to Solange?"

"She never got over her guilt about Annemarie's unnecessary death. She has always felt responsible for Solange's welfare."

"But why is Solange still in hiding?"

"Because from time to time we receive threats from Isabelle?"

"Where is Isabelle?"

"No one knows."

"And what about the second murder you mentioned?"

"It does not concern you, Susan."

"If you say so. But Sister Alicia's reaction to me does. I swear when she first looked at me she said, *'la soeur noire.'*"

"It's probably because you have dark hair and are about the same height as Isabelle. *La soeur noire*, the dark sister, is what they called Isabelle. Sister Alicia is an old woman. Her eyesight is very bad. I wouldn't give it a second thought."

"I'm sorry about Solange. You must miss her terribly."

"Of course, but she has ways of keeping in touch. That is all I am willing to tell you."

"Can you tell me just one more thing?"

"That depends on what it is you want to know."

"Where did she go to school in the United States? Can you tell me that?"

"Of course. It was in the rural state of West Virginia."

"West Virginia? Why such an out-of-the-way place? That seems odd."

"Not under the circumstances. It is a rural area and has a wonderful Catholic boarding school for girls. It was founded by the same Sisters of the Visitation who reside here. Sister Jane de Chantal founded the order. She was from Dijon. Solange always referred to it as the school on the hill. But I have told you enough. Can I offer you a lift to the station?"

"Yes. That would be great. But first I have to find my friend, Jenna. She's been waiting for me for ages."

"Where?"

"In the entrance hall. You must have seen her."

"She wasn't there when I came in. She probably got bored and went for a stroll around the grounds. They are beautiful."

The two women found Jenna pacing up and down outside the entrance.

"Jenna, this is Michelle Dupré, Solange's mother. She's going to drive us to the station."

"Thank God. The guy who drove us up here was a maniac."

"That would be Robert," laughed Michelle. "He thinks Sauret is Le Mans. What time is your train?"

"Seven o'clock."

"Then you must come to my house for a light meal. You must be starving. There is plenty of time to get to the station."

⌘

The Dupré house on the edge of the village was plain but charming. Susan and Jenna waited in the living room while Michelle busied herself in the kitchen.

"This is so stark," whispered Jenna.

"Typically French!" responded Susan.

The only splashes of color in the room were the photographs on the mantel. There was one of a pretty blond girl, probably in her late twenties or early to mid thirties. These days it was hard to tell. The other was of a young woman of approximately the same age, surrounded by a handsome young man, a young boy and girl, and two dogs."

"Which one do you think is Solange?" asked Jenna.

"The one with the kids. The blond looks like Michelle."

"Well, neither one looks like you or your mother. The three of you don't even look related."

"That's because we're not."

"Not what?"

"Related."

"What do you mean?"

"Exactly that. Michelle explained everything about Solange to me. Solange's birth mother was a friend of my mother's named Annemarie. When Annemarie died just hours after Solange was born, the Duprés adopted her."

"Solange's real mother died in childbirth in the 1960's! How Gothic!"

"Not exactly. She was murdered. Poisoned to be exact."

"Poisoned? That's even more Gothic! Who did it?"

"A crazy young novice named Isabelle who was a friend of my mother and Annemmarie from Dijon. The story is, and I am sure this is the real story, that Annemarie was expecting a baby out of wedlock. My mother came here to ask Isabelle to help out, find a place for Annemarie to stay until her baby was born. Isabelle found the Duprés who agreed that she could stay with them until her confinement. Isabelle wanted Annemmarie to allow the Duprés to adopt the child. At first Annemarie agreed, but later on she changed her mind. Isabelle was furious."

"Why?"

"Because, unknown to my mother or Michelle, Isabelle had convinced herself that it was God's will to have the baby adopted by the Duprés. She carefully planned the baby's birth and Annemarie's death at a time when Michelle would not be at home."

"How?"

"She asked Michelle to drive to another village to pick up some supplies for the convent and invited Annemarie to visit her while Michelle was gone. Annemarie was in her eighth month. Michelle is convinced that Isabelle gave Annemarie a drink laced with an herb that induced her labor. Annemarie returned to the Dupré's house long before Michelle. According to Isabelle, Annemarie phoned to tell her that she was in labor and to hurry to her with a doctor. Isabelle did hurry to the Dupré's, but the doctor never arrived."

"Why?"

"Isabelle claimed that she was unable to reach him, so she had to deliver the baby herself. When Michelle returned home, Annemarie was already dead. Michelle and my mother were convinced that she had murdered Annemarie because she'd had second thoughts about giving up the child."

"But why would this Isabelle have cared about that?"

"Because she had convinced herself that God wanted the baby placed with the Duprés."

"Is she still in prison?"

"No. She never was."

"Why not?"

"No one wanted to press charges or investigate further."

"That's right," said Michelle, walking into the living room. "Isabelle was a novice in the order of the Visitation. The mind set of the village in those days was that a nun could do no wrong."

"What about Annemarie's parents in Dijon?"

"Isabelle told them that their daughter had died in an automobile accident. Anna and I decided to hide the gory details from them. In retrospect, we ourselves committed a heinous deed. They died never knowing about the existence of Solange. I gave Anna an official copy of Solange's *acte* in case she ever decided to tell them. But she and the *acte* moved to the United States with Annemarie's parents being none the wiser."

"And you and your husband lived an idyllic life in Sauret with your little Solange," said Jenna.

"Unfortunately no. As is so often the case with women who have trouble conceiving, I found out I was pregnant before Solange was born. Isabelle was furious."

"Why would she care about that when she'd already gotten her way with Solange?" asked Jenna.

"Because it interfered with the messages she insisted came straight to her from God. She was convinced that she had blessed an infertile couple with a child. She wanted the entire scenario to be as biblical as possible. It was a lovely story, but my pregnancy destroyed its validity."

"What did she do?"

"Nothing for a few years, but when Solange was ten years old things came to a head. Isabelle had become so irrational that the sisters had her committed to a Swiss mental institution from which she escaped three years later. Just walked right out the front door and was never seen again. Shortly after her escape, we began receiving phone calls threatening Solange's life. We didn't take them seriously until they became more frequent. Anna was preparing to emigrate to America with Susan, so she offered to take Solange with her. She helped us find the safest, loveliest hiding place for Solange that anyone could imagine."

"Did you believe Solange was in real danger?" asked Jenna.

"Let's just say that we weren't taking any chances. Shortly after Solange left Sauret, the calls started coming on a daily basis. That was in 1978 . She is still out there somewhere, threatening to find Solange and Anna. We still receive the occasional call."

"No wonder my mother keeps a low profile. Which picture is the one of Solange?"

"The family group. Solange has found happiness with a wonderful young man. I have faith that they will return here some day. I miss seeing my grandchildren. They are quite grown up now. That is an old photograph but one of my favorites."

"Where is your other daughter?" asked Jenna.

"Babette lives near here. In a little village called Marain. She is a nurse."

"Is she married?"

"Not yet. Plenty of boyfriends, but she is not ready to commit. She and her sister are very close."

"This is like an Agatha Christie mystery," said Jenna.

"You'll have to forgive Jenna," laughed Susan. "She reads too many crime novels."

"Well, I'll bet she's never read one as perplexing as this," said Michelle. "And none of it is fiction."

Michelle dropped the two friends at the station at six-thirty.

"Tell me one thing, Michelle," said Susan before she got out of the car. "How did you know that I was coming to Sauret today?"

"Your mother phoned me."

"When?"

"In the middle of the night. I guess she was confused about the time . She forgot that there is an eight hour time difference between here and San Francisco."

"San Francisco? My mother never mentioned San Francisco. And she certainly didn't know about my plans to visit Sauret."

"Perhaps she had an emergency in San Francisco."

"Perhaps. But that doesn't explain how she knew I was coming here."

"Don't make your life more mysterious than it is. I'm sure there is an explanation."

There'd better be, thought Susan as she boarded the train. *This cloak and dagger nonsense is getting way out of hand.*

Before they boarded the train, Michelle kissed Susan and Jenna goodbye.

"*Adieu, mes amis.* I hope the details of Solange's birth did not upset you too much. Please do not think ill of your mother, Susan. She has spent her life doing good deeds."

Susan smiled in reply. She was at a loss for words. Thinking of Anna Foster as a saint would take some getting used to.

Jenna and Susan were the only two passengers in the carriage. They selected a booth with a table and sat across from each other. Jenna was the first to speak.

"What did you think of Madame Dupré?"

"I thought she was charming. How sad that she doesn't know where her daughter is."

"That's a crock of you-know-what," said Jenna.

"Why do you say that?"

"Because she must know where she is. I figured that out right away when she said that Babette and Solange are still very close."

"I don't get it?"

"That's because you don't spend five days a week drilling kids in grammar. Michelle said that Solange and Babette ARE very close."

"So?"

"She used the present tense. So, that means that if they are still very close they must be in touch with each other. I'd wager Babette could give you Solange's phone number in a second."

"So that's why you asked if Babette was married. You wanted to know if her name was still Dupré."

"Right. We can find out Babette's phone number from the Marain directory assistance and ask her for Solange's number."

"What if it's unlisted?"

"We'll call around to all the hospitals in the area. A nurse shouldn't be too difficult to track down. The villages and towns around here are quite small. We're not talking L.A. or New York."

"You're a genius, Jenna. But what if she won't give us Solange's number. I'll bet Michelle is on the phone to her right now telling her we may contact her."

"Even if she won't give us Solange's number, she might slip up and tell us where Solange lives. Do you still want to find Solange even though you know she isn't your sister?"

"Yes. More than ever. I want all these relationships out in the open. I'll bet Solange knows lots about this mystery, especially the Isabelle part. I want to know more about her."

"Why? She sounds creepy. A little too macabre for my taste. Not someone you'd want to meet in a dark alley when you weren't carrying a lead pipe."

"I guess I'm just curious. I've never felt such a close attachment to a murderer before."

"We can start calling as soon as we get back to the hotel. You've been through a lot today, Susan.

"It's not just today, Jenna. The past few weeks have been draining. First of all, I find out that my mother and I are French, not American, that I spent the first few years of my life in Dijon, and that my father is the French journalist, Jacques Fontaine. As if that's not enough, my mother leads me to believe that a girl named Solange is my half-sister. Why would she do that?"

"Because she wanted to make a very complex story as simple as possible."

"I don't believe that for a minute. I get the feeling that my mother is afraid of Isabelle, the insane woman who killed Annemarie, Solange's birth mother. There's a piece of the puzzle missing. Since Solange was thirteen when my mother helped her escape to the States, she must know a lot about her. She wasn't exactly a child when all this was going on. God, I hope we can find her."

"Even if we don't, I have a feeling that your mother will tell you everything now that you've met Michelle Dupré and know the real story of Solange. She didn't feel she had to tell you everything before because she had no way of knowing that a young man named Georges whose grandmother lives in Dijon and remembers your mother and her friends would materialize and send you to Sauret."

"Poor woman. She must feel awful. I need to phone her to apologize for my behavior. As Michelle said, she was a wonderful friend to Annemarie. That Isabelle must be a real bitch. I can't imagine how she managed to pull off poisoning Annemarie without harming the baby."

"She was an expert in the use of herbs for medicinal purposes."

"How do you know that?"

"I did some snooping while you were speaking with Sister Madeleine and Michelle."

"What kind of snooping?

"Surely you didn't expect me to sit on my ass for two hours, staring into space?"

"What did you do?"

"First of all, I got into a conversation with a Sister Agnes. She offered to give me a tour of the gardens when she saw me pacing back and forth in the entry hall. I think I was making her nervous. They're not used to visitors. When we were in the herb garden, she told me that the sisters used to sell herbs in the village market years ago but had to stop because there was a rumor in the village that a woman may have been poisoned after eating or drinking something flavored with them. She said that a novice named Isabelle puttered about in the greenhouse for hours every day, mixing potions with all kinds of herbs. She claimed they were for medicinal purposes only. The gendarmes could never prove that Isabelle had mixed the fatal potion that poisoned the young woman. But they forbade the sale of the herbs in the local market from that day on. I'm sure the young woman they were speaking about was Annemarie."

"So Isabelle got off Scot-free?"

"Not really. It seems that a Lili Villiers, the wife of the local doctor, was so incensed over Isabelle's claim that she could not find her husband in time for him to help at Annemarie's delivery that she hounded Isabelle for years, trying to force her to confess that she had lied about trying to contact him."

"Did Isabelle ever admit to that?"

"No. But the body of Lili Villiers was found in the lake just below the cliff behind the convent."

"Was it an accident?"

"I don't know. Sister Agnes didn't have a chance to finish her story. Another sister *of un certain âge*, as they say in France, walked by and glared at her. I have a feeling she was telling her to shut up. I suspect the older nuns who were there at the same time as Isabelle live in fear that she'll return and wreak revenge on them."

"If I'd been in the convent then, I'd be looking over my shoulder twenty-four seven. Lili Villiers must be the second murder Michelle alluded to. If so, she is convinced that Isabelle murdered her."

They continued the rest of their journey in silence. They were exhausted. It would take days for their brains to process all the information they'd unearthed today.

⌘

Georges was waiting for them on the platform when the train pulled into Dijon.

"You're early. That's odd!"

"Not when the train is empty," said Jenna. "We didn't stop for more than a few seconds at each station. Except for a school girl who got off at the last stop, we were the only two on the train."

"We can talk in the car," said Georges, pointing to where cousin Pierre's Citroen was parked across the street from the station. "Come on, tell me, how did it go?"

"Better than expected," replied Susan. "We found out all sorts of important things."

"How important?" asked Georges.

"Well, for one thing, I discovered that I really am an only child."

"You mean there is no Solange?" asked Georges, helping the two young women into the car.

"Oh, there is a Solange all right, but she isn't my half-sister."

"What do you mean?" asked Georges, starting the car.

"I'll tell you when we get to the hotel. Jenna and I are bushed."

"Surely you could both use a glass of wine and some dinner before you call it a day."

"The wine sounds great, Georges, but we ate at the Duprés before we caught the train."

"And who are the Duprés? I wasn't aware you knew anyone in Sauret."

"We do now. The Duprés are Solange's adoptive parents."

"Were they nice to you?"

"Michelle, her mom, was, but we didn't meet the father. We had to catch our train before he got home from work."

Georges let them out at the front door of the hotel. By the time he joined them in the bar, a waiter was pouring the wine into their glasses.

"A toast," said Georges. "To the success of Susan's mission to Dijon and Sauret."

"*Salud*," the three uttered in unison as they clinked their glasses.

"What did you mean when you said you know now that you really are an only child?"

"Exactly what I said. You see, my mother is not Solange's mother."

"You mean that after all those years Madame Dupré can't bear to think of anyone other than herself having given birth to Solange? Right?"

"Wrong! It seems that a girl named Annemarie Marceau was Solange's real mother."

"What do you mean was? I don't get it."

"You will, Georges. It's actually quite simple. In March of 1965, Annemarie Marceau, my mother's best friend, gave birth to an illegitimate child in Sauret."

"So my grandmother was correct in thinking that your mother went to the convent in Sauret to have her baby."

"Well, she was half-right. It wasn't my mother who had the baby. It was Annemarie. Their friend, Isabelle, the one your grandmother remembered entering the convent in Sauret, found a family to shelter Annemarie until her baby was born."

"But why did your mother have possession of the baby's birth certificate and pretend the child was hers?"

"Because everything went horribly wrong at the last minute. Part of the deal about finding a family for Annemarie was that she'd let the Duprés who'd taken her in keep the child. Annemarie agreed to the bargain but changed her mind towards the end of the pregnancy. She decided to keep the baby."

"That doesn't sound unusual," said Georges.

"Right. And the Duprés understood her change of heart. But Isabelle went ballistic."

"After what my grandmother told me about her, I'm not surprised."

"What did she tell you?" asked Jenna, refilling their glasses.

"Just that at the time the girl in the neighborhood went to the convent in Sauret, the word was that her parents sent her there because she was on the unstable side. I'm assuming she was the one named Isabelle."

"If that's true, it certainly explains a lot," said Susan.

"How?"

"Brace yourself, Georges. Go on. Tell him, Susan."

"Isabelle murdered Annemarie."

"She what?"

"You heard me. She was so pissed off about Annemarie's change of heart that she slipped her a Mickey to induce her labor."

"Where did all this take place?"

"At the Dupré's home in Sauret in broad daylight. But Isabelle had planned so well for the event that she made sure Michelle Dupré was out of town on the fateful day. By the time Michelle arrived home, Annemarie was dead, and the only option for the baby girl was adoption by the Duprés."

"It must have been hushed up because my grandmother and her friends would have known about it otherwise. She'd never have gotten away with that nowadays. The papparazzi would have swarmed to Sauret in a flash."

""Ain't that the truth!" exclaimed Jenna. "And Isabelle didn't even go to jail."

"What did happen to her? Is she still at the convent?"

"No. And she never did take her final vows. A few years later, the sisters had her committed to a mental hospital in Switzerland."

"Thank God!"

"Not so fast, Georges. Our mad woman of Sauret is as free as a bird."

"How? Where?"

"She escaped after three years of incarceration. No one seems to know where she is."

"Maybe she's dead."

"She's not," said Jenna.

"How do you know?"

"Because she's still making phone calls to the Duprés, threatening to kill Solange. The calls are anonymous, but Michelle and Gaston Dupré are convinced they are from Isabelle."

"But why would she want to harm Solange?"

"Because, unknown to Isabelle at the time of Solange's birth, Michelle Dupré was pregnant."

"So?"

"So, that threw Isabelle into a complete frenzy because she was convinced she had been told directly from God to bless the Duprés with a baby since Michelle and Gaston had been unable to conceive. She convinced herself that Solange had to be murdered in retaliation for the Dupré's interference with her heavenly messages."

"Sounds like a classic case of schizophrenia," said Georges. "Does Solange still live in Sauret?"

"Of course not," said Susan. "According to Michelle Dupré, my mother felt so guilty about arranging for Annemmarie to go to Sauret in the first place that she paid for Solange's expenses at a boarding school in the States."

Georges gave a short whistle before adding, "That must have been a whole lot of guilt. Those places aren't cheap. But where is Solange right now?"

"All Michelle told us is that she's happily married with two grown children. She claims she doesn't know where Solange is. Only that she's out of harm's way. Jenna is convinced she does know her whereabouts. But I don't blame her for not revealing Solange's hiding place to two complete strangers. Jenna thinks we should contact her sister, Babette."

"Why?"

"Because Michelle said her daughters are very close."

"Aren't you missing the obvious?" asked Georges.

"The obvious?" repeated Susan.

"Your mother, of course. If she supported Solange's schooling, she's most likely been in touch with her. I'll bet your mother knows where Solange is at this very minute."

""You're right, Georges. God! A month ago my mother was a boring accountant. Now she's an international woman of mystery."

"But all mysteries have logical explanations, usually simple ones," said Georges.

"I don't know about that. If mysteries are usually logical and simple, how do you explain the fact that my mother found out I was going to Sauret today?"

"That is simple," said Georges. "I phoned her in San Francisco last night."

"This is getting ridiculous. Pour me another wine, Jenna," said Susan.

"We're all out," said Jenna, holding up the empty bottle.

"Well, go to the bar and order another one!"

"What kind?"

"I don't give a damn what kind. Just as long at it's red, wet and has a high alcohol volume," Susan yelled at Jenna who was already heading towards the bar.

"Okay. Hold your horses. I'm on my way. Try to calm her down, Georges, but don't let her ask or answer any more questions until I get back."

Susan was furious. The thought that Georges had gone behind her back and spoken to her mother filled her with rage. But she didn't speak until Jenna returned to the table with the second bottle of wine and refilled their glasses.

"Okay, Georges. What gave you the right to go behind my back and contact my mother in San Francisco? And how did you know she was in San Francisco?"

"Her assistant."

"You mean Molly Murdoch?"

"Yes. Molly Murdoch."

"How did you find Molly?"

"I got on the internet in the middle of the night and Googled your mother. But it took me ages to find her business number. When the person on the other end answered, I almost hung up."

"Why?"

"I couldn't understand a word she said. Her accent certainly wasn't American and definitely not French."

"She's a Scot. Glaswegian, as Molly likes to remind one and all."

"When I finally managed to adjust my ears to her brogue, she became quite talkative. We had a lengthy conversation."

"I'm sure you did. Molly has informed me on several occasions that Glaswegians could talk the hind legs off a donkey."

"If Molly is an example, she's not exaggerating. But she wasn't about to give me any info on your mother until I convinced her it was a matter of prime importance concerning her daughter. She finally told me that she was in charge of the office until her employer returned from San Francisco."

"Did she say why my mother was in San Francisco?"

"No. But she did give me her number. Your mother wasn't exactly cordial when she answered the phone. When I told her you were going to Sauret, she hung up on me."

"Why?"

"I think she wanted to contact Michelle Dupré immediately to warn her that you were headed to Sauret."

Susan smiled at Georges.

"You're not mad at me any more?"

"No. Not at all. If you hadn't made that call, Michelle would never have known I'd be in town. You must have really shaken up my mother."

Georges smiled in reply. But he didn't tell her that a man, a Frenchman, had answered the phone in San Francisco. That piece of information would have to wait for another time.

"We'd better get some sleep," said Jenna. "We're booked on the six a.m. train for Paris. Our flight back to the States leaves Charles de Gaulle at eleven."

"What about phoning Babette?" asked Susan.

"I say that we put that idea on the back burner. We'll contact her if we can't find out where Solange is from your mother. Besides, I'm about to pass out. I'm too exhausted to talk anymore."

"I can take a hint," laughed Georges. "I'm out of here," he said, rising to his feet. "I'll pick you ladies up at five-fifteen."

Jenna walked down the hall to their room, leaving Susan and Georges alone.

"Will you call me when you get back to the States next month, Georges?"

"Do you want me to?"

"Yes. I really do."

Georges walked Susan as far as her room, kissed her gently on the lips, then turned and left.

⌘

"Achoo"

"Susan, is that you?"

"Yeah. It's me on the brink of death," answered Susan, speaking as clearly as she could through her stuffed up nose. "Hang on, Jenna. Here comes another one. *Achoo!*"

"Good God, Susan. You almost blew my head off. Want me to call back later?"

"No. I think I'm okay for a few minutes."

"What's that rustling noise?"

"I'm wiping my germs off the phone with a Clorox wipe."

"How long have you been like this?"

"Since we got back from Paris on Tuesday."

"You sounded fine at JFK."

"I know. But I woke up wheezing and sniffling on Wednesday morning. The air on the plane always has that effect on me. I've been working at home all week. I haven't put in a single appearance at the office."

"They'll be asking you to show I.D. the next time you show up in person."

"Don't be sarcastic."

"I'm not. Just jealous I can't do the same thing. You're lucky you don't have to walk around in these freezing-cold rain showers. Hard to believe it's almost May."

"I've kept the blinds closed all day so I don't have to look out on the gloom. The only problem with that is I can see all the dust on the slats."

"Serves you right for having black Venetian blinds. Black shows up everything."

"I know. Same with the swags over them. But they do go with the decor. And no one can see in from the street."

"Have you heard from Georges?"

"No. I guess I won't till he gets back from France in a few weeks. I get the impression he thinks I'm a little on the unstable side."

"What gives you that idea?"

"He does. Maybe I'm paranoid, but it's as if he's a little leery of my background. Can't say I blame him. Have you heard from Bob?"

"Thought you'd never ask. He called last night. He and his munchkins are due back Saturday afternoon. We have a date for dinner on Sunday evening. Keep your fingers crossed."

"For what?"

"Me, silly. I really want this relationship to work out."

"If it's meant to be, it will."

"I'm not as fatalistic as you. There's more to finding Mr. Right than just waiting it out."

"Well, just don't let him think you're chasing him. Wait a minute! I've got to sneeze again. *AaaaaaaChooooo*! That's better. Now, what were we talking about?"

"My dinner date with Bob on Sunday evening and the future of our relationship."

"Right. Where are you going for dinner?"

"Dunno. But I imagine somewhere casual."

"How casual?"

"How should I know? It's only Tuesday. We're not going out till Sunday."

"Okay. But can I make a suggestion?"

"Sure."

"No matter how casual the date, do not wear those ugly shoes you bought at Macys. Understand?"

"Not really. All the college kids are wearing them."

"You're not a college kid any more. There's a big difference between coeds and thirty year old spinsters desperate for a mate."

"How dare you call me by that horrid word and utter the words out loud that I am desperate for a mate. You're making my ears hurt. Apologize or I'll hang up."

"No, you won't," laughed Susan. "Because you know I'm right."

"But those shoes are so comfortable."

"That's exactly the point. Comfortable shoes do not come into play at the beginning of a relationship. It's stilettos and fish net hose for Sunday evening."

"When did you become so fashion and relationship savvy?"

"Ever since I've had this blasted cold. I'm so bored I've spent the past two evenings pouring over old copies of *Cosmo* and watching reruns of *Sex and the City*. So, promise me you'll wear your sexy red patent spikes."

"I promise. If it means that much to you."

"I assure you it does."

"Why?"

"You're my best friend. Just looking out for your welfare."

"I'll follow your advice on one condition."

"What's that?"

"You've got to promise not to read or watch any more of that trash?"

"Why?"

"Because your brain will turn to mush. At your age, it doesn't take long."

"Perish the thought. But you don't need to worry. I've been surfing the web about something a lot more serious."

"What?"

"The Visitation Order."

"The what?"

"The Order of the Visitation. You remember. The one the sisters in Sauret belong to."

"From stilettos and fish net hose to religious orders all in one conversation. That's certainly going from one extreme to the other. Don't tell me you're thinking of taking vows?"

"Of course not. But I've found some amazing info. The woman who started the Visitation order was from Dijon."

"That is a coincidence."

"Not really. It's more like an explanation for why Isabelle went to the convent in Sauret in the first place and why Solange was sent to St. Cecelia's Academy in Wheeling, West Virginia."

"Wait. You're getting ahead of me. I can understand Isabelle going to Sauret because of the Dijon connection, but I don't understand what it has to do with Solange's exile in West Virginia."

"St. Cecelia's was established in 1848 by the sisters of the Visitation."

"You mean a group of nuns from France just upped and went to West Virginia in 1848?"

"Not exactly. And, remember, West Virginia wasn't even a state then. In the late 1700's a Visitation foundation was established in Georgetown in D.C. In 1831, another was established in Baltimore. It was nuns from the Baltimore convent who high-tailed it to Wheeling to set up a school for girls."

"They must have been hardy souls. Can you imagine how filthy they must have felt after that long train journey?"

"The B&O Railroad only went as far as Harper's Ferry."

"How'd they get to Wheeling?"

"Stagecoach through the mountains."

"Makes me think of the old ballad, *She'll Be Comin' Round the Mountains When She Comes.*"

"Doesn't it just! Anyway, after reading all this, it makes sense that when the Dupré family was desperate for a place to hide Solange the nuns in Sauret must have suggested one of the Visitation academies over here. There are five of them altogether."

"But why Wheeling, West Virginia?"

"Location. It's off the beaten path, practically in the middle of nowhere. The perfect hiding place."

"And all this came about because of a holy roller from Dijon!"

"Bite your tongue, Jenna. That holy roller was a widow with four children. She even took one of them with her to her first convent."

"Talk about reinventing yourself! Just like your mother. Is the ability to do that an intrinsic part of the French DNA?"

"Don't know. But as soon as I get over this cold I'm going to fly down there. Wanna go?"

"They have an airport?"

"Pittsburgh's the nearest. We can rent a car and drive to Wheeling from there."

"I don't have the money to pay for a last-minute flight."

"I'll cover it. Not paying rent has its rewards. We'll leave a week from this Friday when you have a day off school and fly back Sunday night. Okay?"

"Sounds like you have it all planned."

"Will you go?"

"Sure. But you're taking the blame if my love life goes south."

"Don't be ridiculous, Jenna. If Bob has the hots for you, he'll still be here when you get back."

"I wish you wouldn't make me feel like a floozy in a cheap romance novel."

"Well, if the shoe fits."

"It does, but I'm not allowed to wear it. Remember?"

"Just as long as you do. So, you'll go?"

"Why not?"

"And I promise not to bother you again after the Wheeling jaunt."

"I don't believe that for a minute. After we meet up with Solange, you'll be hauling my ass off to Vietnam to look for your father."

"Hadn't thought that far ahead yet, but it sounds like a possibility for the future. But I don't expect to meet up with Solange in Wheeling. Most people aren't hanging around their *alma maters* twenty years plus after graduation day."

"Then why are we going there?"

"To see if we can find any clues leading to Solange'a current safe haven."

"What about your mom? Does she know what you're up to now?"

"No. At least, not yet. I tried to call her Sunday evening when we got back, but, according to Molly Murdoch, who appears to have become her *alter ego,* she's still in San Francisco. I will call her tonight. I'm anxious to talk to her. We didn't part on the best of terms when I was up in Syracuse a few weeks ago."

"Are you still mad at her?"

"More than ever. I'm furious that she didn't tell me the truth about Solange's birth instead of pretending to be her mother for God's sakes. That just doesn't make sense."

"I'm willing to bet there's a lot more to that story than you already know."

"I hope not, Jenna. I don't think I could take any more surprises. I feel as if my nerves are under attack."

"Not to mention your immune system."

"I'll survive, but I've got to hang up."

"Time to get some shut-eye?"

"Uh uh! It's almost time for *Sex and the City*."

"Promise me you won't do what you did two years ago?"

"Oh that. You blew it all out of proportion. All I did was watch reruns of *The Nanny* for a week."

"But you took a week off work to do it."

"That series was hilarious. It was addictive."

"Like your personality."

"What's that supposed to mean?"

"That you need a friend like me to keep you on the straight and narrow."

"If it will make you feel any better, I plan to go to work tomorrow."

"Thank God."

"And you don't need to phone the office to make sure I'm there."

"I won't, but let me know when to meet you at LaGuardia."

"You should turn on *Sex and the City*. It's really good."

"Can't. I've got to rummage through my closet to find the red high heels."

⌘

They landed in Pittsburgh a few minutes before noon.

"Tell you what, Jenna. You get the luggage while I check on the rental car," suggested Susan on the long walk from their gate to the escalator that would take them to the tram for the exit area.

"What about lunch?" snapped Jenna. "I'm hungry. Actually, I'm starving."

"Me too. Pretzels and a coke didn't quite fill the bill, did they?"

"Or the stomach," laughed Jenna.

"I promise we'll stop for something on our way to Wheeling."

"I opt for something here before we head into the boonies."

"Good point. But let's get our luggage first before it has time to disappear if we're not right at the carousel."

"Okay."

After they left the area where only ticketed passengers could enter, they ended up purchasing sandwiches at the only café outside the security area. A little after one, they began their drive to Wheeling.

"Didn't you just pass the entrance to the interstate, Susan?"

"On purpose, Jenna. We're going the back way."

"Why?"

"Because I want to stop at Wentworth College to look around the campus before we drive into Wheeling. When I Googled the College's web-site, I noticed they're looking for a French instructor."

"You already have a job. And why in God's name were you Googling a college in the middle of nowhere?"

"Boredom. The novelty of *Sex and the City* reruns got tedious after a few episodes."

"You're dodging the question, Susan."

"What question?"

"The one about the French teaching position."

"Oh that. Well, I just thought it would be fun to look around the campus. Something to do, I guess."

"Whatever. You're the driver. As usual, I'm just along for the ride."

"So sit back and enjoy it."

It was a gorgeous day. After the gloom of a dreary day in New York, the rolling green hills of western Pennsylvania were a delight. When they crossed into West Virginia, it was just as green, but the straight road gradually gave way to a series of curves.

"I hope it's not going to be this curvy all the way to Wheeling," said Susan, clutching the wheel and slowing down. "I can't believe how fast those people are driving. I'm obeying the speed limit, but everyone is passing me."

"Yeah! And they're giving you dirty looks and hand gestures."

"Tough," said Susan.

They finally reached the crest of a hill overlooking a village which resembled a picturesque Swiss hamlet. A WELCOME TO WENTWORTH sign greeted them at the bottom of the hill, but the reality of the town was as far from a picturesque Swiss hamlet as one could get. The village was no more than a long ridge with a strip of houses, a church that had been converted into the village municipal offices, and a small grocery store. The only up-to-date structure was the red brick post office. A patrol car, half-hidden at the side of the road forced Susan to drive slowly through the town, obeying the fifteen miles an hour speed limit The last thing she needed was locking horns with a local cop. The other end of the village was a little prettier with a school on one side of the road and a church on the other. A final curve leading to a straight stretch flanked by houses and a second church brought them to the entrance of Wentworth College.

"I wasn't expecting this," gasped Jenna. "Why would anyone build a college here? We're miles from anywhere. Talk about an oasis in the desert."

"Let's pull in and stretch our legs," said Susan. "I'd like to walk around the campus. It looks very pretty. Okay with you?"

"The one with her hands on the wheel calls the shots," laughed Jenna.

Susan drove through the main entrance gate and followed a sign marked VISITORS CIRCLE. But she'd no sooner pulled into an empty spot in the circle than a campus policeman appeared out of nowhere, signaling Susan to roll down her window. Before she could speak, he said in an extremely unpleasant tone, "What dya' think you're doin' lady?"

"We were passing through town and wanted to visit the campus."

"Where's your parking permit?"

"We just pulled in. Haven't had time to get one. You saw us drive in."

"Are you gettin' smart with me, lady?"

"No. I just want to know how to get a parking permit."

"In there. Jist like the sign sez," he half shouted, pointing to the main door of the building on Susan's right.

"Okay. I'll go get one."

"You cain't leave that ve-Hicle here while you go in there," he continued, stressing the H sound as if it added to his sense of importance. "I'll have to give you a ticket."

"Where might I legally leave the ve-Hicle while I go inside for a permit?"

"Not here."

"You're being ridiculous."

"Don't you sass me, lady."

"I wouldn't dream of it, officer."

Before he could utter another syllable, Susan rolled up her window, drove around the circle to the entrance, and took a right onto the road they'd just come from.

"Oh, God. How sickening!" said Jenna, looking back at the campus.

"What?" asked Susan.

"That idiot cop just spat on the sidewalk. Ugh!"

"Snuff," said Susan. "And s'nuff for me. What an idiot!"

"Why are we driving back the way we came? Wheeling is in the opposite direction."

"I know. But I just want to make sure we're headed the right way. I would have asked Robo Cop, but he'd probably have had us followed all the way to Wheeling to make sure we got out of town. I saw a post office on the left as we drove in. It's a federal building."

"So what?"

"So good chance it's not staffed with locals."

They parked and went into the post office.

"Hi," said a friendly female voice. "I'll be with you in just a second."

"You were right," said Jenna. "She sounds too intelligent to be from here."

A young blond woman whose badge identified her as Betty appeared behind the counter.

"Now, what can I do for you folks?"

"We're heading to Wheeling," answered Jenna. "Just want to make sure we're driving in the right direction. These roads are really curvy."

"You haven't seen anything yet. As soon as you leave Wentworth, it's like a roller coaster. And when you drive through the town here, go at a snail's pace. Our friendly village cop isn't so friendly when it comes to speedsters, especially if they're from out of state."

"Why doesn't that surprise me?" laughed Susan.

"We've already driven through once," said Jenna. "We wanted to tour the campus, but our welcome there was as cold as ice."

"Fred Connelly must be on duty. He's a real piece of work."

"Actually, you're the first friendly face we've seen since leaving the Airport," said Susan. "Are you a native?"

"Not even a resident. I live over in Pennsylvania. I'll admit Wentworth takes some getting used to. When college is in session, the students outnumber the townies. There's a lot of animosity between the two populations."

"I can't believe there's a college here," said Jenna.

"Oh, it's been here forever. It's the oldest state college in West Virginia. It dates back to the mid 1800's.

"It must have been quite a commute before they paved the road."

"You're right. They don't call it the Cow Path to Culture for nothing. It's a great school. It's up for university status."

"That is impressive," said Jenna. "Unbelievable, actually."

"You'll have to forgive us city slickers," said Susan. "We live right in the heart of New York City, so we're a bit out of our depth in the countryside. We probably seem as odd to the people here as they do to us."

"You're fine. I go to New York once a year just before Christmas to shop and see a couple of shows."

"What do you think of our hometown?" asked Jenna.

"Great for a visit. But…"

"I know," laughed Susan. "You wouldn't want to live there. Right?"

"Right."

"Everyone says that," laughed Susan.

"So, what brings you to this neck of the woods?"

"We're looking for a school referred to as The School on the Hill."

"That's it. Wentworth College. You were just there."

"No. This school on the hill is a girls' high school, St. Cecelia's Academy for Girls.

"Must be on another hill, and not one I've heard of."

"That is my school," came a heavily accented voice.

Jenna and Susan turned around and came face to face with a blonde teenager holding a stack of envelopes.

"What do you need, honey?"

"Air-mail stamps for Germany."

"Give 'em here. Let me weigh them."

"Do you really go to St. Cecelia's?" asked Susan.

"Yes. I'm staying with relatives here for a year."

"In Wentworth?"

"No. In Bethany. If you came here on the back-road you must have passed the edge of it."

"I was clutching the wheel too tightly to read any signs. Is there a school bus into Wheeling?"

"No. But four of us commute from Bethany. Our families take turns driving us back and forth to Wheeling every day."

"Are you enjoying your year at St. Cecelia's?" asked Jenna.

"Not really. The school's all right, but I have to get up at five-thirty every morning to get to school by seven-thirty."

"Sounds brutal," said Jenna. "What time do you get out?"

"Three. But I play soccer and tennis, so I never get home before eight o'clock. By the time I eat something and do my homework, it's time for bed. Why are you going to St. Cecelia's?"

"A family matter," said Susan. "I have an appointment with Dr. Anderson at three-thirty this afternoon. If you don't get out until three, what are you doing here now?"

"I'm a junior. We didn't have school this morning because of May party practice this afternoon. I'm on my way there now with two other juniors from Bethany."

"May party practice?" asked Jenna.

"Yes. It's a school tradition. All the classes put on a musical program to honor the seniors. The juniors are the sponsors, so we are very busy these days. The seniors wear long pastel-colored gowns for the occasion."

"Sounds like a big deal," said Betty.

140

"Yes. It is very different from Germany."

"Could we follow you to the school?" asked Susan.

"Sure. What are your names? Mine is Svenja. Everyone calls me Sveni."

"Nice to meet you, Sveni. I'm Susan."

"And I'm Jenna."

"Well, it looks like you girls came to the right place," said Betty.

"Thanks for being so nice, Betty," said Jenna.

"Any time. Good luck."

Sveni got into the passenger side of a car driven by another teenage girl but rolled down her window and yelled, "Be careful. Go slowly through town. The cop is not a nice man."

"We know!" said Susan and Jenna in unison. "We know!"

"And remember the number one rule of Route 88 when you leave Wentworth."

"What's that?"

"If there's nothing driving towards you, take the whole road."

"Don't you dare do that, Susan Foster," said Jenna with fear in her voice. "Don't you dare!"

⌘

Susan didn't have a chance to follow Sveni's advice about taking the whole road. The oncoming traffic, most of which veered over to Susan's side, threatened to knock her into the ditch.

"At this rate, we'll never have a chance to use the number one rule of the road for Route 88," said Susan through clenched teeth.

"You're not kidding. Right now, it's touch and go about where we'll end up."

"What do you mean?"

"I mean St. Cecelia's or the local morgue."

"Don't be gruesome, Jenna. Where's your sense of adventure? You're white as a sheet.

"And you're clutching the wheel so tightly your knuckles are the same."

"I'll take your word for that. I'm too scared to take my eyes off the road to even look down at my knuckles."

After what seemed an eternity, they drove around one last curve and headed down a hill that led to a straight stretch.

"Civilization ahead," said Jenna.

"How can you tell?"

"A Convenient Store on one side and a car dealership on the other."

"You're right," said Susan, releasing her strangle-hold on the steering wheel. "I'm surprised the wheel didn't come off in my hands."

"Me too," laughed Jenna.

They drove through a pretty residential area with beautifully maintained older homes on each side.

"Good. I don't think we're in Klan territory," said Jenna.

"What's that supposed to mean?"

"We just drove past a Jewish synagogue and there are lots of black kids running around the school playground to your left."

"Afro-American, Jenna."

"Whatever! But, considering that old coot Byrd is a former Klan member, this is quite amazing."

"Byrd?"

"You know, that old senator from West Virginia who's always on T.V. filibustering and waving around a copy of the Constitution."

"How in God's name do you know all this?"

"Did my homework. Bob's a history teacher. When I told him we were coming to West Virginia, he filled me in from the time West Virginia became a state in 1863. The poverty here is about the worst in the nation."

"Well, you could have fooled me. This place looks pretty upscale."

"Yeah. I think it's the southern part of the state that's really in bad shape. Bob says the state motto is Thank God for Mississippi."

"Meaning?"

"Use your imagination, Susan. It really means that I will never accompany you there. It's the only state with a lower standard of living than West Virginia."

"And how do you know all this?"

"Bob again. If there's one thing I've learned, it's never, and, I emphasize the word never, ask a social studies teacher a question about U.S. history or geography. They will go on forever. But look, we are in civilization. A Sheetz gas station. We can breathe easy. And there's a Hardees. And there's the Hampton Inn. Let's check in before we go to the school."

"No. I don't want to lose our lead car. We'll check in later."

They turned left off the main road and then right onto a ramp leading to the highway for a few minutes before taking another right and then a left.

"Wow! Look up there," said Jenna.

"Where?"

"Straight ahead. I'll bet that sprawling brick building is St. Cecelia's."

"How can you tell?"

"The cross on the roof, dummy. It's a dead giveaway."

Jenna was right. A few seconds later, they turned up a driveway on the left. Curving, of course. At the top, both girls gasped.

"Are we still in the twenty-first century?" asked Jenna.

"Dunno," replied Susan. "That building reminds me of the old St. Trinian movies."

"The what?"

"A series of movies about an English girls' boarding school. The only thing missing is the girls hanging out the windows."

"That's because they all seem to be congregated on the front porch."

Sveni signaled for them to turn right into a parking lot facing the building.

"Thanks, Sveni," called Susan. "We can go it alone from here."

"No. I want to go with you. The lady at the main desk is not so friendly. I will introduce you."

"Sveni's right," said the driver of the car they'd followed. "Her name is Mrs. Rothwell, but we call her the Rottweiler behind her back."

Susan and Jenna followed the two girls up the steps to the front porch and through the front door. The interior was magnificent, but, before they had a chance to admire it, a heavy-set, dark-haired woman appeared out of nowhere and barked, "You can't just walk in here out of the blue. Who are you? What do you want?"

"They have an appointment with Dr. Anderson," said Sveni.

"Who asked you? And where are you supposed to be?"

"May party practice."

"That's in the gym. Not here."

Sveni turned and fled back out the door they'd just entered.

"Don't be angry with her. She was just helping us find our way," said Susan. "I have an appointment with Dr. Anderson at three-thirty."

"You need to sign in and get a visitor's pass."

"Where do we sign in?" asked Susan.

The woman didn't answer. She just pointed to a blue sheet of paper in an open binder. When both Susan and Jenna had signed their names, she handed them each a sticky peel-off label marked visitor. "Print your names on these and wear them the entire time you're in the building."

Jenna and Susan stood on the opposite side of the counter from the unpleasant receptionist awaiting further orders. When none were forthcoming, Susan asked, "Where do we wait for Dr. Anderson?" The woman shrugged her shoulders but didn't speak, so Jenna pointed to a room across the hall. "Let's wait in here. If it's off limits, she'll let us know."

The room they entered was a replica of a late nineteenth century parlor. They sat down on a plush red velvet sofa, hoping that they were not upsetting protocol.

"I can't make up my mind whether I'm on display in a museum or taking part in the musical, *Meet Me in St. Louis,*" said Jenna.

"I know what you mean. Look at those furnishings and that chandelier. Can you imagine what they're worth?"

"Not really. But I wouldn't want to break anything. I doubt we could afford to replace a single item."

"I just hope Dr. Anderson is nicer than the Rottweiler," said Susan.

"Don't call her that," snapped Jenna.

"Why?"

"Because it's an insult to all Rottweilers,"

When Mrs. Rothwell appeared in the parlor to announce that Dr. Anderson was free, she found Susan and Jenna engulfed in a fit of the giggles. They followed her to the main office where she blocked their entrance.

"My book says the appointment is for Susan Foster, so that means….."

"I know what it means," said Jenna. "It means I have to stay out here to keep you company."

If Mrs. Rothwell heard Jenna's remark, she didn't let on. She just scowled at both of them and walked back to her desk behind the counter without as much as giving Susan directions to Dr. Anderson's office.

"I think it's down there to the right of the library," said Jenna. "I saw a sign."

"It is," whispered a girl tiptoeing down the hall. "Follow me. I'm not supposed to be in here, but I forgot my book-bag. She'll kill me if she sees me in here. Please don't tell her you saw me."

"Believe me, kid. Your secret is safe with me," whispered Susan.

⌘

Dr. Anderson's office door was ajar, but Susan tapped on one of its glass panels to gain her attention. She signaled Susan to enter without looking up from the document she was reading. Susan walked in and sat in a chair on the opposite side of the desk. She had plenty of time to give the room the once over before Dr. Anderson looked up. The outer wall was a set of French doors leading to a balcony with an intricately carved wrought iron railing. Susan guessed that the porch ran the entire length of that area of the building.

"Miss Foster," said Dr. Anderson, rising to her feet and extending her hand to Susan. "I'm Dr. Anderson as you've probably surmised. I can't tell you how excited I am that you're here."

"You are?"

"Why wouldn't I be? It's almost the end of the school year, and I haven't found a replacement for our French teacher. I always hate to have staffing issues unresolved before the school year ends. I'm glad you changed your mind."

"French teacher?" responded a puzzled Susan. "Changed my mind? I don't understand."

"Aren't you the person who applied for the French position and then decided to go public instead?"

"No. You have me mixed up with someone else. I am a qualified French teacher, but I'm here on an entirely different matter."

"When I read the name Foster on my agenda, I was ecstatic. What did you say your name is?"

"Susan Foster."

Dr. Anderson glanced down at the folder she'd been reading. "You're right. I do have you mixed up with someone else. It was Sarah Foster who applied for the position. She was supposed to come for an interview yesterday but called to say she'd taken a position in one of the public schools. Unfortunately, there's no way we can compete salary and benefits-wise with the public sector, so I don't even waste my breath trying to talk even the most qualified candidates into changing their minds. Supporting dirty habits like paying the rent and buying groceries will always take precedence over the prestige of teaching at an esteemed academy like St. C's. But you didn't come here to listen to me grouse about the state of the economy at St. Cecelia's. What are you here for, Susan Foster?"

"I was hoping you could give me some information on a former student, Solange Dupré."

"That name isn't the least bit familiar. When was she here?"

"She graduated in '83."

"Oh, that was quite a bit before my time. I've only been here for five years. You say she graduated from here?"

"Yes."

"Then, you're in luck. There's a stand in the main hallway with photographs of each graduating class from 1902 to the present."

"Great. I'll take a look. Can you check her records for me? Find out where she lives now?"

"Just a minute," she replied, lifting the phone and keying in an extension.

"Kate, I want you to check for the file of a Solange Durpré, a student from France who graduated in '83. A family friend is trying to locate her. Check the boarding records. Call me back as soon as you do."

When the secretary called back a few minutes later, an exasperated Dr. Anderson yelled into the phone, "What do you mean am I sure she boarded. Of course, I'm sure she boarded. She couldn't have commuted from France every day. If she didn't stay in the school dorm, she would have resided with a family."

Dr. Anderson put the phone back in the holder and looked at Susan. "If anyone can locate your friend, Kate can. She has access to all the records."

"Do you have any students from France now?"

"No. We have a very small boarding program these days. In the mid-seventies, the sisters believed the day of the boarding school had become passé, so they let the program fizzle out. Bad move on their part. With the rise of the two-parent career track, schools with good boarding facilities are more in demand than ever. There's one such school right across the creek."

"Another girls' school?"

"No. Coed. Used to be boys only, but in '88 it admitted its first female students. The transfer line from here to there gets longer every year."

The phone rang.

"Yeah, Kate. Are you sure? H'mm. I'll check with her to make sure she has the right year. Okay, thanks. I'll tell her."

"Kate can't find any record for the name Dupré in the 1983 folders. She also checked the files for '82 and '84. Nothing!"

"But I know she was here."

"You must be mistaken, Miss Foster. Kate checked thoroughly."

"How long has Kate worked in the office?"

"I'm not sure. She was here when I arrived."

"Could I speak with her?"

"Of course. But you're wasting your time. This is not a large school. Kate is an extremely competent record keeper."

"I didn't mean to imply she wasn't. I just thought that if she worked here in the early 80's she might remember Solange."

"She would have said so. I don't mean to be rude, Miss Foster, but, if you have no further business here, I do. The end of the term is a busy time for me. You must let me get back to work."

"Of course. Thank you for your time," said Susan, rising to her feet.

Dr. Anderson didn't answer. By the time Susan left her office, she'd already gone back to the stack of folders she'd been working on. But Susan wasn't convinced that her concentration was real. A backward glance through the glass door panel proved her correct. Dr. Anderson was already picking up the phone.

Jenna was waiting for her outside the library door. She grabbed Susan's arm and pulled her towards a large free-standing picture montage.

"Look, Susan. This stand has photographs of all the graduating classes since 1902. It's amazing. I checked out the class of '83. And guess what?"

"It's all right, Jenna. I apologize for dragging you here on a wild goose chase."

"But I don't think it is. Look what I found. Ta-dah!" she said with a flourish of her hand. "Allow me to present the class of 1983."

Susan looked a the montage in front of her. She stepped closer and read the name under each photograph."

"So? You found the class of '83, but there's no Solange Dupré."

"That there's a photograph of."

"What do you mean?"

"Look closely." Jenna placed her index finger on a slot devoid of a picture. "I swear a photograph was removed from there. See what I mean?"

Susan took a closer look at the blank slot.

"I think you're right, Jenna. And the name below the picture is all smudgy."

"Like someone tried to erase it. But how can we find out why the picture and name have been erased?"

"That might be the sixty-four thousand dollar question. Somehow I don't think we're going to get an answer from a rude receptionist, a secretive directress, or a record keeper who lies."

"Well, they're sure not trying to hide the records of one of their 1959 alums. They've dedicated an entire room to one of their grads who became a West Virginia state senator."

"I'll take your word for it, Jenna. Right now, I'm confused. Let's go back to the hotel. I need a glass of wine. The mystery of Solange is just as real here as it was in France."

By the time they arrived back at the Hampton Inn, Susan had reached a decision.

"Jenna, if I drive you to the Airport Sunday morning, would you mind flying back to New York alone?"

"Why? Where are you going?"

"Back to St. Cecelia's. There are secrets hidden there that span two continents."

"And how are you going to unravel them?"

"That's the easy part. They're desperate for a French teacher."

"And you're going to apply. Right?"

"I certainly am."

⌘

On Saturday morning, Jenna and Susan sat across from each other in the dining area of the Hampton Inn, reading the local paper and sipping their second cups of coffee as slowly as possible. They were killing time. The silence was deafening. Jenna was the first to speak.

"I just want you to know, Susan, that you're carrying this search for Solange too far. I can't believe you're actually planning to go back to St.

Cecilia's on Monday to apply for a job you didn't know existed until yesterday."

Susan let out a long sigh before answering.

"You're right, Jenna. I am being ridiculous."

"What did you say?"

"I said that you're right."

"Be still my heart. I can't believe I'm hearing correctly. You've never told me I'm right about anything in all the years I've known you. Do you think I could have that in writing?"

"Unless I change my mind by the end of the day."

"You won't, not after we've bored ourselves to tears by dinner time, trying to figure out what to do in this friggin' place to entertain ourselves. Thank God our plane back to New York leaves at noon tomorrow. We could always check out this morning and high-tail it back to New York today."

"Don't think that hasn't crossed my mind. But I don't think we should."

"Why not, for God's sakes!"

"Because, once we get back to the city, it'll be at least a month before we can escape the hustle and bustle of New York again."

"I'd rather be frazzled by life in the city on a daily basis than bored in Wheeling, West Virginia for a single day. Frazzled I can handle. Bored scares me. I'm already nervous about putting in the hours from now until lunch. No wonder there are so many fatties here. The only thing to do is eat."

"Remember that golf course and park we passed on our way here yesterday? It's called Oglebay Park. According to a brochure I picked up in reception, it's supposed to be very pretty. We can tour the Mansion, walk around the gardens and lake, and eat lunch at Wilson Lodge."

"What does that leave us to do in the afternoon?"

"We'll think about that when the afternoon comes. There's also a little shopping area up to the left as you start up the hill for Oglebay."

"Sounds thrilling!"

"Now! Now! Let's be positive."

"If you say so."

They drove out of the Hampton Inn's parking lot at ten-thirty. There was practically no traffic. But what amazed them the most was the silence.

"I can't believe we haven't even heard a police siren once since we arrived. I think I may be too much of a New Yorker to live without witnessing at least two muggings a day," said Jenna.

"Relax and enjoy it, Jenna. For me, the scariest thing about this place is maneuvering the curves on Route 88. Hold on. Here we go," she laughed as she turned left on to the straight stretch of the infamous road.

They'd just turned the first curve when Jenna yelled, "Slow down, Susan. Take a left."

"Why?"

"This is the area where the little shops are."

"How do you know?"

"I read the sign. How could you have missed it?"

"By looking straight ahead at the road for oncoming traffic. These curves are hell," said Susan, veering left and maneuvering the curve that served as the road.

Three curves later they arrived at the top of a hill overlooking the city below.

"Great scenery, Jenna, but where are the shops? This building is a restaurant."

"Drive around it. They must be on the other side."

When Susan turned the corner she almost slammed into a golf cart. The driver just smiled and waved.

"I do have to admit that the Wheeling reaction to impending doom sure beats the Bronx cheer," laughed Jenna.

They parked in front of a quaint little book shop and went inside. They were the only customers, so it was pleasant to browse without interruption.

"You ladies just visiting the area?" asked the obvious proprietor.

"Yes. We are definitely just visiting," said Jenna.

Susan laughed. "You'll have to excuse my friend. She gets nervous outside metropolitan areas."

The young man smiled. "That's what happens to suburbanites in reverse. We get nervous when we're stuck too long in your quote unquote metropolitan areas."

"Really?" responded Jenna. "I've always been led to believe that people in the sticks spend their days dreaming of life somewhere else."

"Don't pay any attention to her," laughed Susan. "This is an impressive selection of books."

"Just your regular book store fare."

"Do you have much of a clientele?" asked Jenna.

"Actually, we do. You'd be surprised how many of the residents here can read. They teach us in school."

Susan and Jenna's faces turned scarlet.

"I'm sorry," apologized Jenna. "I didn't mean to imply...

"That West Virginians are illiterate? That's all right. It's a common misconception. We're used to it. Just don't ruin our reputation with the New York set when you get home."

"I might not be going back," said Susan. "I might get a job teaching French at a private girls' school in the area."

"St. Cecilia's?"

"Yes."

"Good school. My sister graduated from there."

"She did?" Do you remember which year?"

"Sometime in the early nineties."

"I'm trying to locate someone who was around in the early eighties."

"Then you've come to the right place. See that little boutique on the corner called Tienda de Lola? The woman who runs it, Lola Mendez, graduated from there around that time. I just saw her car pull up a few minutes ago, so she's probably still there."

"Thank you so much......," said Susan.

"Alex. It's Alex."

"Thank you so much, Alex. I'm Susan and this is Jenna."

"Nice to meet you."

"We'll be back to pay for these books," said Susan, placing three on the counter. "Do you mind holding them for us? I don't want to miss Lola. You have no idea how important this quest is."

"Then hurry up. Lola's not one to stay in one spot for long."

Susan and Jenna literally ran out the door of the book-shop along the wooden porch to the boutique on the corner. The interior was small but seemed even smaller due to the large number of customers.

"Hey, ladies," said a tall, willowy blond, approaching them. "You must be new here? Just visiting?"

"Yes," said Jenna.

"I know you're busy," said Susan, "but we need to speak with Lola. Is she here?"

"You're looking at her. What can I do for you ladies?"

"It's about the place they call the school on the hill."

"St. Cecilia's?"

"Yes."

"Another fund raiser! This is getting out of hand."

"No. Nothing like that. It's just that Alex next door said you graduated from there. We're looking for information about a girl who was there in the eighties."

"Let's go into my office. I'm sure I can help you. I'm pretty active in the alumnae organization. Who are you looking for?"

"A French girl who graduated in 1983."

"Solange? Do you mean Solange?" asked Lola immediately.

Susan and Jenna were too stunned to answer. They just stared openmouthed at Lola.

"Ladies! What's wrong? Say something!"

"Yes! Yes! Solange! Her name is Solange. That's who we're looking for."

"Sure. I know, or did know, Solange Dupré."

By this time they were standing in the curtained-off area of the small shop which served as Lola's office.

"Sit down. What do you want to know and why?"

"God, it's such a long story that I don't know where to begin," said Susan. "The people at the school wouldn't give us the time of day."

"At St. Cecilia's?"

"Yes. What a place!" sighed Susan.

"While Susan was attempting in vein to get some info on Solange, I looked at the senior graduation pictures out in the hall," said Jenna. "It was plain to see that a photograph was missing from the 1983 montage."

"That was my class. I graduated with Solange."

"Then she really was here, at St. Cecelia's I mean?"

"Of course, she was. We all loved her. She was with us all four years until something strange happened spring semester of our senior year. Come to think of it, I don't remember Solange being at graduation. We all thought it was extremely odd. She just disappeared without a trace."

"Did anyone give you an explanation?"

"No. For some reason it was all hushed up. The day after final exams she just seemed to vanish. My mother was really hurt because Solange and several Mexican girls used to spend the weekends at our house. My mother always insisted on cooking a big breakfast before driving us back to St. Cecelia's on Monday mornings. She prayed she wouldn't get stopped for speeding on the way to school since she was usually in her bathrobe. She and Solange were very close. My mother has never gotten over the fact that Solange never called to say goodbye. None of us ever heard from her again."

"Someone must have known what happened to her."

"I'm sure the nuns did, but they can be very close-mouthed. And, in those days, we were petrified of the sisters. They were not a force to be reckoned with."

"You're telling me that the disappearance of a girl from France who'd been at your school night and day for four years was never questioned?"

"Oh, believe me, all the students, mainly the seniors, talked about nothing else. But, in the end, we just decided that she probably went to San Francisco."

"Why San Francisco?"

"That's where she spent her summers with a Dr. Villiers from her hometown in France. She said she'd rather have gone home but for some reason couldn't. A French lady from the East Coast would spend a couple of weeks with her in San Francisco, helping her shop for clothes and things every summer."

"How interesting," said a stunned Susan. "How bloody interesting."

"I'm sorry I can't be of more help, Susan. But I've got to get back to work. Promise to let me know if you find Solange. Here's my card if you need my help. I know it's difficult to solve problems long distance."

"I'm not planning on leaving Wheeling till I find out what happened to Solange."

"Is she a relative of yours?"

"Not exactly. Let's just say she's a very close friend of the family."

"Well, keep me informed."

"I will, and, if things work out the way I hope, I'll be coming back to shop. This is a neat place."

"Thanks. It's been quite a success. Come back any time."

Susan and Jenna retraced their steps across the porch to the book shop. They settled their bill and thanked Alex profusely for his help. Just as they were getting into their car, Lola opened her shop door and yelled, "Talk to Sister Gertrude. If anyone has any info on Solange, it'll be her. She's a walking encyclopedia on St. Cecelia's. We always kid her about being one of the original nuns from Baltimore who established the school. She probably was!"

As they drove back down the winding drive to Route 88, Susan said, "Wasn't it nice of the directress to tell me all that yesterday?"

"She did?"

"No, Jenna. She didn't even mention Sister Gertrude. I am definitely going to apply for the French teaching position. That's the first thing on my agenda for Monday morning. The second is finding and talking to Sister Gertrude."

They spent the afternoon exploring Oglebay Park after an enjoyable lunch in the dining room overlooking Schenk Lake. They liked it so much they made dinner reservations for later in the evening.

When they arrived back at the Hampton Inn around four, Susan was relieved when Jenna announced she was going to take a nap before dinner. On the pretext of not wanting to disturb her, Susan picked up her phone and headed for the reception area. Her gut feeling told her that the French woman from the East Coast who shopped with Solange every summer was her own mother, Anna Foster. There was only one way to find out. Confront her mother directly.

⌘

Susan curled up in an armchair in the reception area and keyed in her mother's home number. After five rings, Molly Murdoch's familiar burr answered.

"Foster Accounting. How may I help you?"

"Molly, is that you?"

"Aye. The one and only. Is this Susan?"

"Yes. Sorry to bother you. I thought I'd dialed the house. Silly me."

"You did. It's just that since Mrs. Foster's been in San Francisco the fifth ring at the house transfers to my line."

"Sounds like a pain in the ass to me if you have to take calls at home."

"Not at all! Makes me feel guy important. Now, what can I dae fer you? As you can tell, I speak only Glesca at home."

"Go right ahead. I love it. I really do. And it makes me feel better about confiding in you."

"About what? Oh, wait a wee minute. It must be about your fella, the lad who phoned looking for Mrs. Foster's number a few weeks back. He was very nice. Does he have any brothers?"

"You know, I'm not sure. Our relationship hasn't developed that far."

"Developed that far? You Americans are guy slow when it comes to the oddest things. He sounds like a keeper to me."

"I know. And he helped me out a lot."

"With what?"

"Would you believe a missing person's case?"

"Good God! Who did you lose?"

Molly was on the brink of asking Susan if the missing person was a tall, dark-haired woman with a strange sounding accent who kept turning up at the office demanding to see Anna Foster, but something stopped her. No need to worry Susan. The woman was highly annoying and persistent, but Molly, in true Glasgow spirit, knew she could out-persist the hag.

"Molly? Are you still there?"

"What? Sorry. My mind was wandering a wee bit. It must be the wine."

"How much have you had?"

"To be truthful, not a drop. I was only joking."

"I guess the real reason I'm calling is to get my mother's phone number in San Francisco. I can't believe she didn't tell me where she was when I spoke to her last week."

"She didn't? That seems odd."

"It certainly is. She phoned me when I got back from France just to make sure I'd arrived home safe and sound. I just assumed she was at home in Syracuse."

"Mibbe she didn't think being in San Francisco was all that important."

"Get real, Molly. You're just trying to make me feel better. Would your mother fly off somewhere and not tell you her destination?"

"Sometimes I wish she would. My Mum's too much of a control freak to do that, especially when it comes to me. She phones from Wegmans when she's grocery shopping just to let me know where she is. How pathetic is that?"

"I think it's sweet."

"That's because you're not the one on the short leash. Got a pen handy? Here's the number in San Francisco."

"And whose number is it? Surely, she hasn't been in a hotel for three weeks?"

"I honestly don't know, Susan. As long as I've worked for your mum, she's never mentioned exactly where the number is located, and, as her employee, I've never felt it was my business to pry."

"Haven't you ever been curious?"

"Of course, I have. I've even fantasized that she's shacked up with a secret lover."

"Come on, Molly. My mother's in her 60's. She'd never do that."

"That's what you think. Stranger things have happened. And your mother is a very well-preserved sixty-five."

"You make her sound like a figure in a wax museum."

"Sorry. Wrong choice of adjective. I meant to say attractive. Does that sound better?"

"Much."

"You know, Susan. I've been thinking while we're talking. You could do a reverse people check."

"How does that work?"

"Get on the internet and go to one of the free reverse directory search engines. I think you type in the phone number and it gives you the name and address of the number's owner."

"Molly, you are a genius. If this works out, I'll owe you one."

"Just promise you'll fill me in on all the juicy details if it does turn out to be a love nest."

"I promise. But only because that's as far removed from the truth as could be. Trust me. My mother and I may not seem as close as most mothers and daughters, but I am one hundred percent certain that she does not have a lover."

"You're wrong, Susan. I know you are."

"What makes you so sure I'm wrong?"

"I just have a gut feeling that......."

"I know what you're going to say, Molly."

"And what would that be?"

"That when Glasgow people have a gut feeling they're usually right."

"Well, they are. You'll see.

After the two women said their good-byes, Molly walked into the kitchen and poured herself a glass of wine, thinking how odd it was that Susan couldn't just ask her mother straight out where the hell she was when she answered the phone. *After all. That's what Glasgow folks would do.*

Susan didn't waste a minute keying in the San Francisco number. No one answered. She tried a second time. Not even an answering machine. She pressed the end-call button and sat staring into space for several minutes before walking over to the hotel computer to follow Molly's suggestion about the reverse directory. It worked. Immediately, two listings for the number appeared on the screen. One was for a Dr. Henri Villiers. He was the proprietor of a family clinic in the Haight district of San Francisco. The second was a Dr. David Villiers, same clinic, address and number. Only the office address and number were listed. The number Susan already had must be a residence.

Although it was a Saturday afternoon, Susan decided to phone the clinic. After six rings, a very mature male voice, unmistakably French, announced that she had reached Dr. Villiers who was unavailable at the moment but to press one if it was an emergency. Susan did not press one. She pressed disconnect and sat staring into space for several minutes before heading back to her room to shower before dinner. In the mirrored wall of the elevator, she caught sight of herself smiling.

Well, Molly. It looks as if you may be on the right track after all.

⌘

"You're chipper this morning for someone who's about to spend another day in the this dump," said Jenna as they drove along I-70 towards Washington, Pennsylvania and the turnoff for the Pittsburgh Airport. "I still think you're crazy to go back to that quote unquote School on the Hill to be insulted again by the Rottweiler. She'll never let you through the main door. Svenja's not going to be there to help you this time."

"You don't know that."

"Yes, I do. She'll be in class, so you'll be ripped to pieces and your remains disposed of before the bell rings for lunch."

"Don't be ridiculous. Besides, they don't have bells or buzzers."

"Oh, spare me the agony! You'll be telling me next that everyone there from administrators down to the custodial staff has built-in radar."

"Don't you remember? Sveni told us it was a type of honor system. The teacher just goes by the clock."

"Well, as a teacher, I'd rather have a bell go off. I can just imagine our school on a system like that. The first kid into the room would move the clock ahead twenty minutes. It would be bedlam in the halls at all times."

"I thought it was anyway."

"Very funny, Susan."

"I get the impression the only bedlam they know at St. Cecelia's is the paranoia they feel about getting kicked out of class for uniform violations."

""Who told you that? Sveni?"

"No. I saw it for myself. When I was leaving Dr. Anderson's office on Friday, a teacher was standing behind a student in the hall, holding her by the scruff of the neck and lecturing her about the importance of having all parts of the uniform in place at all times. As far as I could see, the only thing wrong with the kid's uniform was part of a shirt-tail hanging below the blazer."

"I certainly hope they threw the book at her," laughed Jenna. "Sounds like she's well on her way to a life of crime. It's a good thing the uniform police are there to keep her in line. At my school we're happy when the girls have shirts long enough to hang down over anything."

"It does seem a little odd for this day and age. Perhaps Solange was drawn and quartered for a uniform infraction. That would help explain why the administration or whoever is responsible extracted her picture from her class's graduation collage."

They arrived at the Airport a little before eleven o'clock.

"Want me to go in with you?"

"No. I'll be fine. It's you I'm worried about. I hate to think of you spending time alone in Wheeling."

"Don't be silly, Jenna. I think I'll stop at that Robinson Township Mall we passed on the way. Take a look around the stores before I go back."

"Suit yourself. I'll call when I get back to the City. Good luck on the interview."

"Thanks. It's the first time I've ever interviewed for a job I don't want."

"Then why are you doing it?"

"I'm hoping they'll give me a tour of the building. I can look for clues about Solange."

"What sort of clues?"

"Tangible evidence that she was there."

"Don't forget to talk to the sister Lola mentioned. What was her name again?"

"Can't remember, but it'll come to me."

Horns blared in the line of cars behind Susan in the departure lane.

"Look. I'd better go, Jenna. Safe trip. Call me tonight."

"Will do."

As Susan drove off, she took a fast peek in the rear-view mirror at Jenna entering the terminal. *I hate to lie to my best friend, but desperate times call for desperate measures. And this is one of those times.*

Susan had no intention of stopping at the Robinson Township Mall. She was anxious to get back to Wheeling as fast as possible to start tracking down her mother, the Anna Foster who had suddenly become a woman of mystery.

Susan parked her car outside the Hampton Inn and walked to the Bob Evans restaurant across the parking lot. While she waited in line for a table, she was amazed at the size of the people, especially the young men and women who came and went. She'd never seen so many rolls of bare midriff fat in her life. These young women weren't just a few pounds overweight. They were morbidly obese. They were disgusting. She'd often watched features on the news about the obesity epidemic. Seeing it first hand was a shocker. Some researchers said it was a glandular problem, but the only glandular problem evident here was the one from the hand to the mouth. These folks were really into their chow. It was enough to make Susan do the obvious, order a side salad and a bowl of fresh fruit.

"Sure you don't want something more substantial, honey? Fries or hash browns come as side orders," prodded her super-sized waitress.

"Positive."

"Well, surely you'll have room for some pie after that skimpy little meal," the waitress added before she brought the check. "The pies are so good here that most folks end up buying a whole one to take home."

"I thought that might be the case," said Susan. "Just bring me the check."

"Okay. But you don't know what you're missin'"

Susan walked back across the parking lot to the Hampton Inn. She grabbed an apple from the bowl on the reception counter then took the elevator to her room. Munching on the apple helped give her the nerve to call her mother in San Francisco. Nervously, she keyed in the number of the mysterious Dr. Villiers. It would be noon on the West Coast now, not too early for a Sunday call. The phone rang four times. On the fifth ring, a male voice, younger than the one on the voice mail at the clinic, answered.

"Hello."

"Hello. Is Dr. Villiers there?"

"This is Dr. Villiers, the younger that is. What can I do for you?"

It took all the courage Susan could muster to say in a steady voice, "I was wondering if I could speak with Anna Foster."

"Who is this?"

"Her daughter."

"Susan?"

"Yes."

"This is David."

"David?"

"Yes. David. Henri's son. Surely you know all about me?"

"Of course, I do," lied Susan. "Is my mother there?"

"Not at the moment. They left last night for Monterey. They should be back late tonight. I just stopped in to check on the cats and walk the dog. You might know Dad's dog sitter has this Sunday afternoon off. Just my luck."

"What kind of a dog?"

"Russian Wolfhound."

"That figures. My mother loves those dogs."

"I know. That's the only reason Dad has one here. It's actually hers. Dad claims that if she ever breaks down and marries him, he won't know if it's for love of him or the dog."

"What about you?"

"Me? Oh, I love the dog too. Just kidding. I'd love Anna and Dad to finally make it official. Then we could really be a family. I can't believe we've never met. Your mother talks about you all the time."

"She does?"

"Why not? You're her daughter. Any messages for Anna?"

"No. Don't even bother to tell her I called. Promise? She's obviously too involved with her California family to bother with me."

"That's not true. The only reason she wanted to go to Monterey was to have a get-together with Jacques. He doesn't get out of Vietnam that often."

"Jacques?"

"Yes. Jacques Fontaine. He's a great guy. He and Dad have become good friends. It certainly makes family matters a lot easier. Listen. I've got to take another call. Nice talking to you. And don't worry. I won't tell Anna you phoned."

"Thanks, David."

Susan snapped her phone shut and let it fall to the floor. She was beginning to wish she'd never phoned the Villiers' residence. Life was becoming way too complicated. Her mother was obviously involved romantically with Henri Villiers, so why would he agree to visit Jacques Fontaine, Susan's father? And was it possible that Susan had a brother she'd never met? The possibilities kept on growing. Susan was now more determined than ever to track down Solange. If she could fight her way past the Rottweiler tomorrow morning and get her tour of St. Cecelia's, she'd feel as if she was finally accomplishing something.

Susan slept the rest of the afternoon. It was still light when she awoke. She showered and then walked across the street to a sports' bar for an early dinner. Noise was what she wanted, and lots of it. She couldn't bear the thought of hearing herself think. The click of pool cues and the cacophony of several T.V. channels going full blast were just what the doctor ordered. When she got back to her room around nine o'clock, the message light on her phone was blinking. She picked up the receiver. The voice mail was from Jenna.

"Just called to let you know I got home okay. You're obviously not there. Call when you have a minute. I need to ask you something."

Susan smiled to herself. It felt good having someone to call. She was beginning to feel very lonely in Wheeling, West Virginia.

"Hi, Jenna. Just returning your call."

"Where were you?"

"At the sports' bar across the street."

"How was it?"

"Loud. Very loud. I spent most of the time nibbling on a hamburger and watching the locals enjoying themselves. The bellies on some of those guys, not to mention the facial hair, tattoos and wearing baseball caps indoors was a little freaky."

"So, we're in no danger of losing you to Wheeling, West Virginia?"

"I doubt it. What was the question you needed to ask me?"

"Oh, yeah. I almost forgot. It just suddenly occurred to me that if you know you're not related to Solange, why are you still pursuing her?" It seems rather unnecessary at this point."

When Susan didn't answer, Jenna asked, "Susan, are you still on the line?"

"Yes. Of course I am. You're right, Jenna. It doesn't make sense. I guess the only word to describe it would be obsession."

"Well, get over this obsession and get back to New York where you belong."

"You know it! I'll be back on Tuesday."

"That gives you one more night to be swept off your feet by one of the handsome locals you've been describing. Should I be concerned?"

"Of course not, silly."

"Good. Give me a buzz when you're back in the land of the living."

After the two friends said their good-nights, Susan went back downstairs to reception where she typed and printed out a one page resumé for Dr. Anderson. The girl at the reception desk Faxed it to the number Susan handed her. Susan hoped it would go directly to Dr. Anderson's machine. The last thing she did before turning in for the night was phone St. Cecelia's. She left a voice message for Dr. Anderson, saying that she'd Faxed her resume for the French teaching position and would be available all day tomorrow for an interview.

Susan was amazed that she hadn't told Jenna about her conversation with David Villiers. She'd wanted to. But something stopped her. She'd suddenly felt too embarrassed to share the new information about her mother with her best friend in the entire world.

⌘

Before Susan jumped into the shower at six -thirty on Monday morning, she plugged in the in-room coffee maker. She figured the best time to catch Dr. Anderson was at the start of the school day before she became ensnared in her Monday schedule of meetings and the other minutia that seemed to take up all the working hours of a school administrator. She gulped down a cup of coffee between blow-drying her hair and applying her makeup. At seven o'clock, she left the room and headed for the elevator. When it didn't arrive promptly, she headed for the exit door at the end of the hall and ran down the stairs to the main floor. The smell of sausage and eggs was enticing, but she didn't have time for the luxury of a sit-down breakfast this morning. She grabbed a Danish on her way past the buffet table, left the building and got into her car with the speed of a marathon runner.

Despite the heavier than usual traffic, it took only a few minutes to reach her destination. Susan pulled into St. Cecelia's main parking lot where she nibbled on her Danish and had a ring-side view of the parents dropping off their daughters. It was only seven-forty five. When did schools begin starting so early? Eastwood High had started at nine o'clock, and Susan remembered having to sprint up the hill to make it for that.

A tap on the window brought her back to reality. It was Sveni, the German student. Susan rolled down the window.

"Hi, Sveni. It's nice to see a smiling face."

"I didn't think you'd be here this morning."

"I didn't either. Can you keep a secret?"

"Sure."

"I have an interview with Dr. Anderson for the French teaching job for next year, but she may not know it yet."

"I don't understand."

"Well, I'm going to walk right through the front door with you and demand to see Dr. Anderson. I left a message on her voice mail yesterday, so she'll know I'm coming. But the Rottweiler might not know about it. I figure that with you as back-up I'll have an easier chance of getting in."

"I love it! But what would you have done if I hadn't turned up?"

"I'm resourceful. I'd have figured out something. But let's go. I don't want you to get into trouble for being late."

"I hope you get the job. Too bad I won't be here. I'd sign up for French just for the adventure."

"Can't face another year at the School on the Hill, huh?"

"No way! It's too different here. School is fun in Germany. We have a lot more freedom there."

"You mean that St. Cecelia's isn't living up to the Hollywood version of the American high school?"

"Right. And my friends at the public schools agree. Rules, rules, rules! We hate it. We all want to go home."

"Well, Sveni, it'll be over before you know it."

"Thank God."

Sveni and Susan climbed the steps to the front door together.

"Stay close behind me. Maybe the Rottweiler won't see you," whispered Sveni.

But within seconds of their entering the building, a loud voice that actually did resemble a bark yelled, "You can't go in there."

"Caught in the act, am I?" said Susan in what she hoped was her most pleasant voice as she came to a halt outside the Dutch door with the open top that separated the entrance hall from the main office. Sveni raced down the hall and disappeared through a doorway before being detected by Mrs. Rothwell.

"Oh. It's you again. What do you want?"

"I want to speak with Dr. Anderson."

"You can't."

"Why?"

"She's busy?"

"Until when?"

"What do you mean when? All day."

"Can you just slip her a message that Susan Foster would like to speak with her?"

"She'll probably be out of the office most of the day."

"Can I make an appointment?"

"It wouldn't be until next week."

"But I'm flying back to New York tomorrow."

"Then I guess you won't be speaking with Dr. Anderson."

Susan was having trouble controlling her temper. It took all her willpower to stop from leaning across the desk and grabbing the woman by the throat. Mrs. Rothwell was one of the most exasperating people Susan had ever encountered. People in New York could be rude. But they could usually be cajoled into being reasonable. Fortunately, the phone rang before Susan could put her bodily-harm plan into action.

"Good morning. St. Cecelia's Academy for Girls," said Mrs. Rothwell in a saccharine attempt to sound pleasant. "No. I haven't seen her this morning."

A gray-haired woman walked out of an inner office and stood behind Mrs. Rothwell. "Who's it for?" she asked.

"Sister Gertrude. Oh, I didn't realized you were already here, Sister. Should I tell this person to call back later?"

Without saying a word, Sister Gertrude grabbed the phone out of the receptionist's hand.

"Hi. Sister Gertrude here. Sorry about the mis-communication. Sure. I can change her after-school session to Wednesday afternoon. No problem."

Sister Gertrude replaced the receiver and turned to walk back into her office.

"Don't just stand there. Go away!" ordered Mrs. Rothwell.

"Who are you talking to?" asked Sister Gertrude, turning around.

"I think she's talking to me," said Susan.

"Can I help you?" asked Sister Gertrude.

"I certainly hope so. Lola, the lady who owns the boutique on the way to Oglebay Park, told me that you could answer any questions I have about St. Cecelia's."

"Then why didn't you ask to speak to her in the first place?" barked Mrs. Rothwell.

"Ignore her," said Sister Gertrude, smiling at Susan. "Come on back. Let's go into the Herndon Room where we can talk privately."

"She doesn't have a name tag!"

"Then make her one! What's your name?"

"Susan Foster."

"I know what it is," said Mrs. Rothwell. "She was here Friday. I'm not stupid."

Susan followed Sister Gertrude into the Herndon Room. A few seconds later the Rottweiler appeared at the door with Susan's name tag. She didn't leave the room until Susan had stuck it on the right lapel of her jacket.

"If you take your jacket off, make sure you put the tag on your shirt. It must be showing at all times."

"Gottcha," said Susan. "This is a lovely room, Sister Gertrude. My friend, Jenna, who was with me on Friday, told me about it. It's very impressive."

"It certainly is. At St. Cecelia's we feel that we've contributed greatly to the empowerment of women in West Virginia. Not an easy task by any means. Judy graduated in '59. She served in the West Virginia House of Delegates and then the state Senate. Brilliant young woman. Never lost an election. Was taken from us at such a young age. An early call, as some would say."

"What happened?"

"Cancer."

"Well, this room certainly keeps her memory alive."

"And her spirit. We have an annual speech contest in her honor each year."

"Area wide?"

"No. In-house only. But I have a feeling you didn't come here to talk about our alums. Am I correct?"

"Partly. I have come to get some information about one particular alum."

"Who?"

"Solange Dupré from Sauret, France."

Sister Gertrude flinched before answering coolly, "When did she graduate?"

"1983."

"Hmm. The name doesn't ring a bell. But our classes were so large in the early 80's that I didn't know each student personally."

"Do you teach?"

"Yes. Logic and philosophy."

"Are those subjects required?"

"Yes."

"Well, wouldn't Solange have been in your classes?"

"Not necessarily. If she was just learning English, she might have been placed in one of our ESL classes instead."

"English as a second language?"

"Yes. Logic and philosophy demand a high level of English. If this young woman did graduate from here, her photograph would be in the 1983 montage in the hall. You can check on your way out."

Susan ignored the innuendo in the last sentence. The topic of Solange was going nowhere, so Susan changed the subject.

"The main reason I came here today is to apply for the vacancy in the French department for next year."

"That is good news," said Sister Gertrude, instantly forgetting her discomfiture over the illusive Solange. "I'm surprised Dr. Anderson didn't mention it."

"That's because I left a voice mail message only late last night telling her I'd stop by this morning to discuss the position. She wouldn't have known until she listened to her messages this morning."

"What time is your interview?"

"That's what I'm trying to arrange with Mrs. Rothwell. She refuses to give me an appointment for today even though I told her I'm flying back to New York tomorrow."

"Oh dear. She can be a bit of a problem. But don't worry. I'll make sure Dr. Anderson meets with you. It won't be until after school at three. Is that all right?"

"Sure."

"Does she have your resumé?"

"I Faxed it to her private office last night."

"Does Mrs. Rothwell know that?"

"We never got that far. You know, Sister Gertrude, your receptionist has all the warmth of a guard dog."

"I know. We hear that all the time. The custodial staff refers to her as the pit bull."

"I was thinking of something larger. A Rottweiler, let's say."

"Oh no, dear. Pit bulls are small enough to grab you by the ankles to keep you at bay. But, let's see. Since you're not going to meet with Dr. Anderson until three o'clock, I'll have our admissions director take you on a tour of the building. You can eat lunch in the dining room then observe some classes in the afternoon. I'll give Nancy a call. Tell her to meet you here for a tour. I've got to get up to third floor for class," she said, glancing at her watch.

With a wave of her hand, Sister Gertrude left Susan alone, waiting for her tour guide. Susan felt dejected. Sister Gertrude hadn't been as helpful as Lola had led her to believe.

⌘

A young woman appeared at the door of the Herndon Room just minutes after Sister Gertrude's hasty retreat.

"Hi. I'm Nancy, the admissions director. You must be Susan. How are you?"

"Better, now that I'm looking at a friendly face. You're the most normal person I've met since I entered the building."

"Then you won't be surprised to learn that I hear that a lot. But let's get started. You'll be glad you wore comfortable shoes. This is an enormous building, as you'll soon find out," said Nancy, ushering Susan into the school's chapel.

Susan was speechless. The stained glass-dome above the altar was magnificent.

"Not quite what you expected for a high school. Right?"

"Right. Do the girls have to attend chapel every day?"

"No. Once a week there is an ecumenical service."

"How do they change those light bulbs surrounding the base of the dome?"

"They all get changed every ten years. A company that specializes in that sort of thing changes each bulb."

"What if one blows before the ten years is up?"

"I guess it would have to wait. But, according to the sisters, that has never happened. They aren't turned on very often."

When they walked out of the chapel, Susan stood in front of an enormous floor to ceiling mirror.

"If I get a job here, that has to go."

"Why? Don't you think it's beautiful?"

"Of course. But I don't need a constant reminder of the pounds I need to shed."

"Well, do what I do. Check yourself out in it once a day. Haven't gained an ounce since I've been here. It works for me. But follow me. We'll start with the music wing."

Susan followed Nancy around the corner to another long hallway flanked by enormous windows on either side. The spaces between the windows were covered with student art work.

"This is the art gallery, I take it."

"Part of it. We only use it for special exhibits. Wait till you see the studio upstairs. We'll go there next."

Strains of piano, violin and cello music came from the far end of the hall.

"I'm sure you get the drift of what this area is all about. I'd suggest looking in on one of the classrooms, but the instructors are a tad temperamental. I guess it goes with the territory."

"I get the picture," laughed Susan, looking out the window at a gravel-coated area filled with playground equipment.

"I thought this was a high-school," said Susan.

"In recent years, we've added an elementary school. It's co-ed here through sixth grade. The playground is for the Montessori kids. That program has been here for years. It's thriving."

"And the high school isn't?"

"Unfortunately, no. You'll get to know the Montessori kids if you end up teaching French here next year."

"How so?"

"The French teacher always teaches basic French down there at least three hours a week."

"No way! I'm only going to be teaching in the high school."

"That's what they all say. Don't say I didn't warn you."

"Okay. I'll remember."

They climbed upstairs to a second floor and then up to a third.

When they didn't stop on the third, Susan asked, "Why aren't we stopping here?"

"We can if you want," said Nancy, opening a door and switching on the light. To the right was a hallway with small, glass-enclosed rooms. In each one there was a piano surrounded by stacks of boxes. Only one room was set up as an office.

"These are the old piano practice rooms for the music students. Unfortunately, declining enrollment at St. Cecelia's over the past fifteen years or so has turned this area into a sort of dumping ground for anything not being used."

"What about the office? Whose is that? It's immaculate."

"That? Oh, that was the basketball coach's office. I think it's being kept as a shrine to our glory days as a basketball power."

"When was that?"

"Just a few years ago. The directress of the school before Dr. Anderson decided that St. Cecelia's needed a championship basketball team. She was convinced it would boost the enrollment."

"And did it?"

"Yes. With lots of tall Eastern and Western European, African and Australian scholarship students who got a great education and free rides to major basketball powers around the country."

"How good was the team?"

"It was fantastic. The only problem was that we were so good that none of the local teams wanted us on their schedules, so we ended up playing teams in other states. We even went to tournaments as far away as Arizona and Florida. The cost to the school was prohibitive. The lady responsible is no longer here. Too bad! She was very nice and obviously thought she was doing the best thing for the school. She had great ideas. I just wish she'd been able to put them all into action. I miss her."

"Did it help boost local enrollment?"

"Not really. The people in this area want their athletes to play in the Valley where a string of relatives can turn up for each game. They have no interest in a team that plays all over the map."

"You're painting a dismal picture of both the school and the area."

"As well as the fate of forward looking administrators," added Nancy with a shrug of her shoulders. "Come on. Just one more flight. If you thought the chapel was impressive, you'll flip out when you see the art studio."

Nancy was right. The art studio was a gigantic attic loft similar to the ones showcased in movies about famous artists. Light from the half-moon shaped windows illuminated the entire space. The studio was a hub of activity. Several girls stood painting at easels while others were bent over eclectic groupings of desks and tables, working on a variety of mediums."

"What do you think?" asked Nancy.

"It's incredible. I'd love to have been a student here."

"The fine arts department at St. Cecelia's has always had a sterling reputation. The girls can select a concentration in either art of music if they wish. It's quite a big deal. At least, it was. Unfortunately, the newer administrators and teachers aren't aware of that fact. And, if they are, they could care less."

"When do I get to see some regular classes?"

"Probably this afternoon. But let's hurry and get out of here before Miss Van Gogh sees us."

"Is that really the art teacher's name?"

"No. I'm joking."

"What's her problem?"

"Nothing. It's just that she's always so damned cheerful, and I don't feel like chit-chatting."

"That's not a very nice attitude. I guess you're not as friendly as I thought."

"You wouldn't be either if you'd just been told that your contract wasn't being renewed for next year."

"When were you told?"

"First thing this morning."

"I'm sorry."

"Me too. If they do hire you, don't get too cozy."

"I hear you. But I would only want to be here for one year."

"Good. You'd have to be a sadist to stay any longer."

Neither of the women spoke again until they reached the main floor. Susan broke the silence.

"Okay. Let me get the layout straight. The wing we just came from is the music and art area. What's the one on the other side?"

"The monastery. That's where the sisters live. It's very nice, like a college dormitory. Unfortunately, there are very few sisters. When one dies, there isn't exactly a line of young women standing in line to take her place. Women's lib really dealt these gals a blow. The students they taught to stand up and be heard in the world did just that. The only time they return is for class reunions. It's sad when you think about it."

They climbed another flight of stairs. Nancy opened a door at the top.

"What's up that other flight?" asked Susan, pointing to the right.

"More classrooms and the dance studio. But we're going in here. Forward!"

The sound of piano music drifted out from behind closed doors.

"I thought we'd left the music wing."

"There's a lower school recital going on in the music hall," said Nancy. "Let's go in," she said, opening the door to an enormous room dominated by a large, ornate crystal chandelier. The stage at one end was flanked on either side by a grand piano. A girl of about fifteen or sixteen was playing a Chopin Sonata on one of them. Susan was surprised that the audience was so large. There were very few vacant seats.

"I thought you said this was a lower school recital," whispered Susan.

"Wait till we get out in the hall," Nancy whispered back.

They managed to close the doors to the music hall without drawing attention to themselves.

"It is a lower school recital," said Nancy. "They always have a high school girl play a couple of pieces to encourage the young ones and keep the parents awake."

"I'm surprised there were so many adults in there, especially in the morning."

"Ohio Valley Syndrome. They travel in tribes, morning, noon and night. You'll find out if you come here next year."

As they walked on down the hall, the sounds of classes in English, math, science and history greeted them through half-open doorways. Susan spotted the uniform infraction teacher from yesterday in one of the classrooms.

"What's her story? She had one of the girls in tears over a shirt -tail hanging out yesterday."

"She's a real trip. The girls say she has an iron in her closet to take care of what she calls their 'pressing needs'. She's basically a nice person."

"What does she teach?"

"History. If you want to get on her good side, tell her you love Labrador retrievers. She has several."

"I'm making mental notes, Nancy. Sounds like I'll need all the help I can get."

"You will. Trust me!"

They passed one large classroom devoid of students.

"This is Mr. Garrett's room. It's a real hoot."

Susan followed Nancy into the room.

"I see what you mean. That rug's almost wall-to-wall. I've never been in a classroom with an Oriental carpet before."

"And you probably never will be again."

The wall areas between the chalk boards were decorated with postcards and colorful maps of England's literary heritage. But the pièce de résistance was a high-backed Windsor chair with a table at the side, set with a china cup and saucer and matching teapot.

"Does he also do costumes?"

"Wouldn't surprise me," laughed Nancy. "Mr. Garrett is a very nice man."

"No irons in the cupboard?"

"I asked him that once, and he replied, 'Only skeletons.'"

"Where are the language classrooms?"

"In the language wing, of course. Where else?"

They walked through another door and turned right onto a long corridor with lockers on either side. A little further down on the left there were two very messy rooms.

"Junior and senior lounges," explained Nancy. "You'll be given a dossier on these at the beginning of the school year. There's a complete litany of rules and regulations about who has and who hasn't lounge privileges. The list changes every week, so there's always a brouhaha going on between the students and teachers."

"Sounds like serious stuff."

"At St. Cecelia's it is. If there's one thing I've learned about this place, it's that you can do anything as long as you don't look like you're enjoying it."

"The girls in the art studio looked like they were enjoying it."

"Looks can be deceiving. The art teacher's been known to reduce some girls to tears by refusing to let them take certain classes."

"She can do that?"

"Evidently."

"You'd think since they're desperate for students they'd be a little more accommodating."

"You'd think! But, in this haven of lunacy, the old-maid brigade rules the roost. One of these days, some aspiring novelist will immortalize them."

"You think so?"

"It's inevitable."

Susan jumped when a loud siren went off.

"Fire drill. Follow me!" said Nancy, walking briskly through another door then down a few more steps to another long corridor with Susan following behind. Girls poured out of doorways on either side and headed towards a door being held open by a teacher at the far end of the hall.

"Be careful," warned Nancy. "The fire escape is pretty steep."

"And pretty scary," said Susan, peering through the round holes in the ornately designed narrow iron stairs on her way to safety on the ground below. The sound of the students' heavy shoes on the metal was frightening.

Once on the ground, the students and teachers stood silently in groups according to class. Susan watched as one teacher marched over to two girls who were whispering to each other. She placed herself between them until the siren stopped.

"Good. That means we're all clear," said Nancy.

"What's that all about?" asked Susan, pointing in the direction of the two students who were obviously being chastised by the angry-looking teacher.

"She probably caught them talking. You're not allowed to talk during fire drills."

"What will happen to them?"

"They'll have points taken off."

"I don't even want to go there," said Susan. "But what about the language wing?"

"What about it? That was it, the hallway on our way to the fire escape."

"But I want to see the French classroom. Meet the current teacher."

"Sorry," said Nancy, looking at her watch. "We're going back into the building through this back porch entrance into the science lab. It's a shortcut to the dining room."

"When do I get to see the French room?"

"I imagine if and when you turn up for new teacher orientation in August."

Susan was furious but decided not to argue. Instead, she followed Nancy into the chemistry lab where girls in safety goggles and mouth masks were busy dissecting the bodies of dead cats.

"Anatomy class," said Nancy. "Don't know how those girls can eat lunch right after. Yuck!"

Outside the classroom, Nancy pointed to another set of stairs.

"Those stairs lead to the language wing. It's right above us. It's the quickest way to get back and forth to the dining room."

"Okay," said Susan, trying to get her bearings. But, just as they started to walk towards the dining room, three students came clamoring down the stairs.

"Stop right there, you three. You sound like a herd of elephants. Where do you think you're going?"

"Lunch."

"Lunch isn't for ten more minutes."

"But Mr. Bolton said we could come down early," said the obvious leader of the trio. "Don't you believe me?"

"No. Of course I don't believe you."

"Why not?"

"Because it's you three. I'm guessing that Mr. Bolton told you to work quietly while he went to the rest room or the teacher's lounge to run off something. Am I correct?"

"Yes, ma'am."

"Are you going to take points away?" asked a second girl. "We're so low already that we won't be allowed to go to the dance Saturday night if we lose any more."

"Then why do you keep breaking rules?"

"Because they're stupid rules," said the third.

"Well, I guess this is your lucky day. Walk in an orderly fashion to the dining room and stand quietly outside the doors until it opens. Come to my office after school to help me unload some large boxes. I'll give each of you some points for that. Deal?"

"How many points?" asked the leader.

"As many as you need to make sure you get to the dance on Saturday. But you've got to promise me you'll behave the rest of the day and turn up at my office by three o'five at the latest."

"Thank you! Thank you! We'll be good," they yelled in unison. But they raced down the hall as noisily as ever.

Nancy laughed. "There are some people you just can't help."

"That was decent of you," said Susan.

"They're basically three good kids. Just high spirited. But let's get a move on. Upper school lunch is about to begin."

"Where is the cafeteria?"

"Bite your tongue, Susan. It is the dining room. Understand?"

"Gottcha!"

"Just follow me. I promise it isn't far."

They followed the clang of pots and pans down one more long corridor which ended at the doors to the dining room.

"Go on in, Susan. Dr. Anderson is already there. You'll be in good hands."

"You're not eating here?"

"No way. I have no desire to listen to the daily list of complaints about the length of the girls' skirts, the absence of a blazer or the height of the heels on their shoes. I'd rather pick fleas off my dog. Come to think of it, that's what I might be doing after the end of May. But anything's preferable to listening to the Old Maid Brigade. I shouldn't be such a stick-in-the-mud, but I'm in a real funk today. I hope I didn't ruin your school tour."

"Not in the least. Will I see you later?"

"I'll catch up with you by the end of the day. But you'd better hurry or you'll miss lunch. See you later."

⌘

Dr. Anderson stood up the minute Susan entered the dining room. "Over here, Susan," she said, pointing to an empty chair at the designated faculty table.

"Are you hungry?"

"A little."

"We'll get in line in a minute. Before we do, I want to introduce you to our faculty, at least the ones who are here."

It was clear from Dr. Anderson's tone that she was not satisfied with the size of the faculty attendance at lunch. The next few minutes were spent in introductions. Susan could tell from the forced smiles of the three women seated at the table that they were not happy about having their conversations interrupted. The male teachers were much more personable.

"Hi, I'm Bob Garrett. English."

"Oriental rug and china teapot?"

"You've seen my classroom? You remembered."

"That would be hard to forget," laughed Susan. "Very Mr. Chippsish."

The second man reached across the table to shake Susan's hand. "I'm Jonathan Bolton. Spanish."

"And is your room decorated to the same high standard as Bob's?"

"I like to think so. But it's a little homier."

"You mean it's a mess," said the sour looking history teacher.

"I do have some framed prints on the walls and curtains adapted from shower curtains. Some of the girls helped paint the room to jazz it up a bit."

"You'd think you could put class time to better use than spending it painting a wall," snapped the history teacher.

Susan expected a nasty confrontation, but the smile never left Jonathan's face.

"I'll have you know that those classes were great vocabulary and conversation practices."

The history teacher ignored his response and returned to her conversation with the other two women. They never did introduce themselves.

"Pay no attention to those two," said Bob. "They go at each other all the time."

"I'm surprised you didn't visit the language classes this morning," said Jonathan. "But that would have been too logical in this joint. Imagine showing a prospective French teacher the French classroom!"

"Jonathan! That's enough," said Dr. Anderson.

"Well, since we're constantly being scolded for gossiping and ordered not to, my new policy is to let it all out in public. But, it does take all the fun out of confabs in the halls or copy room. Anyway, Susan, when I heard that a candidate for the French teacher's position would be here, I assumed you'd be visiting the language wing." Before Susan could comment, a stern-looking Sister Gertrude walked through the door and handed Dr. Anderson a sheet of paper.

"That's Suzette's schedule for the afternoon." But the minute she said the name, Suzette, her hand flew to her mouth. "Sorry. I meant to say Susan."

"Why did you refer to me as Suzette?" asked an incredulous Susan.

"It was a mistake. Susan. Suzette. They're easy to confuse."

Jonathan looked at Susan and rolled his eyes. Then, looking at Sister Gertrude, he asked, "When do you have her scheduled for the language classes?"

"I don't."

"What?"

"I just thought it would be easier to have someone new visit the classes contained in one area rather than wandering from one end of the building to the other."

"I understand. You don't want her dazed and confused until after she signs on for regular duty. Right?"

Even the three women who'd ignored Susan laughed at Jonathan's latest barb. But Sister Gertrude didn't respond. She looked in the direction of the history teacher and said, "Hilda, would you make sure the girls in my class leave five minutes before lunch ends?. They're never on time."

"That's because they know she'll spend at least five minutes of class time ranting and raving about the importance of promptness," Jonathan whispered to Susan.

Sister Gertrude didn't hear the caustic remark. She was already out the door of the dining room before the words were uttered.

Susan stared at Jonathan in disbelief.

"Don't look so horrified, Susan," he continued. "Everyone's used to me."

"I'm not," said Hilda.

"You don't see me as a comedic diversion from the daily grind?"

"More like a huge annoyance that won't go away. Right ladies?"

Dr. Anderson didn't hear the latest bickering. She'd gone over to the cafeteria line to get Susan some lunch before the impatient catering staff packed up the left-overs.

While Susan munched on a sandwich, the room grew noisy with girlish chatter and laughter. Suddenly, one of the women jumped up and began ringing an old-fashioned school bell.

"Girls! Girls!"

There was a sudden silence.

"Keep it down, ladies," admonished the bell ringer. "We can't hear ourselves think."

The chatter and laughter resumed where it had left off but at a much lower volume. Girls began to wander up to the faculty table to ask for permission to go to the rest room, the library, their lockers or the computer lab. Some requests were granted; some were not.

"What's the decisive factor in granting or refusing permission?" asked Susan.

"Reputation plain and simple," said the primmest looking of the three women. "See those three at that table over there?"

Susan looked in the direction of the teacher's gaze. The three girls from the earlier encounter outside the science lab were starting to walk towards the faculty table.

"They're attached at the hip," said the teacher, pretending not to notice them. "They spell trouble in capital letters."

""What can I do for you ladies?" she asked when they reached the table.

"We were just wondering if we could go to the computer lab."

"Lunch is over in five minutes."

"But our next class is computer. We wanted to get a head start."

"Okay. But you'd better go directly to the computer lab. I don't want any bad reports."

"Thank you, Mrs. Rolston. We'll be good. We promise," they muttered in unison as they scurried out of the dining room.

Susan was having trouble imagining how much trouble they could get into on their way upstairs, but she kept her mouth shut.

"Here's your afternoon schedule, Susan," said Dr. Anderson. "You'll be in history with Hilda for two periods, so you can just follow her up to her classroom."

The look Hilda gave Dr. Anderson spoke volumes.

"I don't think she likes me," Susan whispered to Jonathan.

"She doesn't like anyone, so don't worry about it. But don't get too close to her on the way up the stairs. She might push you back down."

"Ignore him, Susan," said Dr. Anderson, drawing Jonathan a dirty look. But Susan could tell by the sound of her voice that she was trying her best not to laugh. "After Hilda's history classes, you'll be in one of Bob's English classes. When it ends at three, come to my office for your interview. Any questions, Susan? You look a little puzzled."

"I do have one big question, but you may not be able to answer it."

"Out with it fast, Susan, before Brunhilda runs off in an effort to lose you," quipped Jonathan.

Dr. Anderson ignored the interruption. "What's the question, Susan?"

"I was just baffled about why Sister Gertrude called me Suzette. That's all."

"I'm sure it wasn't intentional," said Dr. Anderson.

"Senility never is," added Jonathan.

"Isn't there somewhere you're supposed to be, Jonathan? A classroom with students perhaps," suggested Dr. Anderson.

"I'm on my way," said Jonathan, jumping up and heading towards a side door leading to the language wing stairs.

"Does he joke like that all the time?" asked Susan.

"Oh, he's not joking. All I can say in his defense is that it's a good thing he's proficient at what he teaches. But, back to Sister Gertrude, Susan. She appears to have taken a great interest in you. She arranged this afternoon's schedule for your convenience."

"But I'm not sitting in on any foreign language classes; not even French."

"There must be a reason for that. Nancy did show you the foreign language wing, didn't she?"

"Yes. But the fire alarm went off the minute we got there."

"That is odd. There wasn't a fire-drill scheduled for this morning. Sister Gertrude is in charge of the fire-drills. She must have forgotten to notify me about this one."

I'll bet! thought Susan, as she followed Hilda up the stairs to her classroom.

Despite Susan's annoyance over the omission of language classes in the afternoon's schedule, she had to admit she enjoyed the classes she did attend. Hilda's surliness and sarcasm worked to her advantage with her students. They appeared to be riveted to their seats with their eyes focused on her for the entire period although Susan couldn't decide if it was out of interest in the subject matter or fear of reprisal if they stepped out of line. Ending the afternoon in the Mr. Chips' atmosphere of Bob's English class provided a welcome degree of levity after the intensity of Hilda's history classes.

At three o'clock sharp, Susan headed back downstairs to the main office.

⌘

The biggest surprise of the day was the smile Mrs. Rothwell greeted Susan with when she walked into the office.

"Good. You're right on time. So is Dr. Anderson for once. She said to send you right down."

"Hi, Susan. Have a seat," said Dr. Anderson, hanging up the phone when Susan appeared at her office door. "How did the afternoon go?"

"Very well. I sat in on three classes, two in history and one in English."

"I know about the history classes," laughed Dr. Anderson. "That was Hilda on the phone, lecturing me about springing surprise visitors on her. She can be a real piece of work."

"But she is a good teacher. I was impressed."

"That's why we put up with her moods."

"Was Bob upset?"

"I don't think so. At least, he hasn't called to complain. He usually enjoys visitors. Anyway, I've been reading your resumé. Your credentials are stellar, but have you taught before?"

"Only student teaching during grad school. I quickly decided that I'd rather spend my time translating."

"A lot less stress and a lot more money, I'm guessing."

Susan felt her face redden but replied in the affirmative.

"As I told you on Friday, I didn't come here to apply for a job. I didn't even know you were looking for a French teacher. While I was waiting in the hall to speak with you, I helped three students practice for an oral French test When I was overheard speaking in French with them, someone assumed I was a candidate for the job. That's what caused the mix-up."

"I'm hoping that assumption turns into a good one for us although I can't imagine why you would give up a lucrative position with a translation company to teach here for a pittance. And it's probably going to be only a one year position."

"The money's no problem. I can still do my translations on-line. I'd be busier than usual, but I know I can handle both jobs."

Susan couldn't believe she was actually thinking about accepting the French teaching position at St. Cecelia's should it be offered. She didn't relish the thought of spending her days with the cast of characters she'd just met. And, for all she knew, there might be more of them waiting in the wings. But her determination to solve the mystery of the illusive Solange urged her on.

"Well, looks like the job is yours if you'll take it."

"Are you serious?"

"I am if you are."

"But I have to fly home to New York tomorrow morning."

"That's fine. We can do the paper work on-line. Salary negotiations et cetera."

"When does the fall semester begin?"

"Early in August," said Dr. Anderson, picking up a desk-top calendar and flipping ahead to August.

"Let's see," she said, running her index finger across the page. "Orientation for new faculty members is scheduled to begin on August fourteenth. Does that give you enough time for such a big move?"

"Plenty. I just have to find someone to live in my loft for the year. It shouldn't be a problem."

"The Wheeling realty companies are all on-line, so you should be able to find somewhere nice to live by then."

"And within walking distance," added Susan. "I'm not used to driving every day."

"You will need a car, though. It's a small place, but everything is spread out, and there is next to no public transportation."

"I've noticed. But I do intend to walk to work if possible. And one more thing. Could I please see the French room before I leave today?"

"Actually, no. Sister Gertrude informed me this afternoon that the French room is going to be her project this summer."

"Her project?"

"Yes. She claims that she's going to completely renovate it. Paint the walls, replace the furnishings and so on. If redecorating the French classroom occupies Gertrude all summer, it'll keep her out of my hair. But she did ask that you not be shown the room until the new term begins in August."

Susan couldn't believe that Dr. Anderson was honoring such an outrageous request. But she kept her mouth shut.

"If there's nothing else," said Dr. Anderson, "I guess we'll see you in August."

Suddenly, the sounds of a heated argument could be heard out in the hall.

"Not again," said Dr. Anderson. "I hate to cut this short, Susan, but I've got to referee the daily fray."

Dr. Anderson, with Susan at her heels, quickly left her office and headed down the hall towards the angry voices. At the entrance to the main office, the three girls from earlier in the day were arguing with Mrs. Rothwell.

"Girls! Girls! Will you keep it down to a mild roar," said Dr. Anderson. "You three again. What a surprise! What's the problem today?"

"Same as every day," replied Mrs. Rothwell. "They don't have May party practice until six, so they want permission to stay in the computer lab till then."

"Is Mr. Dennis in there?" asked Dr. Anderson.

"No. He left early," said the leader of the three.

"I caught them trying to sneak in," said Mrs. Rothwell with a look of triumph on her face.

"We weren't sneaking. The door was open."

"But you know the rules," said Mrs. Rothwell. "No one is allowed in the computer lab if there's no teacher present."

"We didn't know there wasn't a teacher until we went in."

"Perhaps I can help out," said Susan. "I have some computer work to do and absolutely nowhere to be. I could stay with the girls until six."

"Are you sure?" asked Dr. Anderson. "That would be great."

The three friends gave each other high fives and started running down the hall in the direction of the computer lab.

"Stop that running right now, you three," yelled Mrs. Rothwell; but the clatter of their shoes on the parquet floor showed they either hadn't heard the warning or were completely ignoring it.

"Be stern with them," warned Mrs. Rothwell, picking up her purse and heading to the front door. "They'll take advantage every chance they get."

"Thanks for the warning. I'll take care of them."

The three girls were already seated at computers when Susan walked into the room. They rose to their feet the minute they saw her. She walked to the instructor's desk and sat down, but the three girls remained at attention. When Susan didn't speak, the leader asked, "Can we sit down now?"

"Of course. Why are you standing?"

"It's the rules," said the shyest looking one. "We have to stand up when an adult enters the room."

"What happens if you don't?"

"Points off!" answered the leader.

"Well, I think it's a lovely rule," said Susan.

"It is," said a familiar voice.

Susan turned to see Nancy standing at the door. "I'm not coming in ladies, so you can remain seated. Are you behaving for Mademoiselle Foster?"

"Of course. We always behave," said the leader.

"Right!" laughed Nancy. "I see they've put you to work already." Susan laughed in reply.

"Well, I'm going home," said Nancy. "Will I see you again, Susan?"

"Probably not. I'm flying back to New York tomorrow morning."

"Take us with you," said the leader.

Ignoring her, Susan walked to the door and extended her hand to Nancy. "I guess this is goodbye, Nancy. Thanks for the tour. And good luck," she whispered

"Thanks."

Once Nancy had left, the three girls went back to their keyboards, but Susan could tell by their twitching that they would rather talk to her than work on the computers.

"Are you going to teach French here next year?" asked the shy one.

"Who told you that?"

"Sveni. She said you told her you might."

"Well, yes. I am. That's what I was talking to Dr. Anderson about when you three started arguing in the hallway with Mrs. Rothwell."

"We never argue with Mrs. Rothwell. It just sounds like arguing because she's so busy ordering us around that she doesn't listen to us when we ask her something quietly," said the third girl, speaking for the first time.

"Well, if I'm going to be teaching here next year, it's time we introduced ourselves," said Susan, in an effort to get off the subject of Mrs. Rothwell. "I am Mademoiselle Foster."

"I'm Heidi," said the leader.

"I'm Joni," said the second girl.

"And I'm Judy," said the third.

"It's nice to meet you, Heidi, Joni and Judy."

The three girls smiled and returned to their typing while Susan sat at the teacher's desk and devised a plan for getting back into the building after hours. To put the plan into action, she needed the help of these three students. She prayed that she could gain their confidence. But it had to be done before May party practice at six or it would never work.

"Do you have to lug those heavy backpacks all the way to the gym for May party practice at six?" asked Susan.

"No. We leave them in the library till after practice," said Heidi.

"Don't they lock the building before then?"

"Yes," replied Joni. "But we all have a code for the back door until after May Party on the twelfth."

"So you come back here after practice?"

The three heads nodded in unison.

"Why do you want to know?" asked Heidi. "Do you need to get back in later to sneak a peek at the French room?"

"Heidi!" said Joni. "I can't believe you said that."

"That's okay," laughed Susan. "But what made you ask me that?"

"Gertie. She's been a nervous wreck since you appeared on the scene today. I heard her telling Joe to pull the fire alarm for a drill at the time you got to the language wing. She told him she'd phone down to alert him when you and Nancy got there."

"Why would Gertie, I mean Sister Gertrude, not want me to see the French room?"

"I have no idea," said Heidi.

"I heard her tell Dr. Anderson this afternoon," continued Joni, "that she wants to totally redecorate the French room this summer. Even remove the big table and put in deskettes. That is so uncool."

"Why?" asked Susan.

"Because it's such a neat room. You'll love the long skinny table in there. In the olden days it was in the Sister's dining room. There are lots of those tables scattered around the building. There's a special name for them, but I can never remember it."

"Refectory," snapped Heidi. "How many times do I have to tell you that?"

"Don't argue, ladies. It doesn't matter what the table's called. I'm just curious about what's so special about that particular one that Sister Gertrude wants to remove it from the French classroom."

"She's probably trying to protect the table."

"Why?"

"Are you kidding?" said Heidi. "Every French class for years and years has ended the year with all the girls carving their initials on that table. They used to carve their names, both first and last, until they started to run out of space. Now they just do the initials."

"You know, girls, I think I would like to see that room, especially the table," said Susan. "You've aroused my curiosity." She could have hugged all three for providing her with a reason to see the French classroom with its famous table before anyone had a chance to remove it. But she curbed her enthusiasm and said calmly, "Ladies, I need your help."

"Will you give us points?"

"Can't. I'm not officially a faculty member. So, ladies, this will have to be a clandestine adventure."

"A what adventure?" asked Joni.

"A secret adventure, Stupid," snapped Heidi. "Don't you know anything?"

"Oh, I get it," said Joni, not the least bit non-plussed over the put-down.

"I need to sneak back into the building this evening to take a look around the French room."

"You can meet us after May party practice at the door just off the porch and go back into the building with us", said Heidi. "No one will pay any attention."

"What about teachers or sisters?"

"The teachers will be long-gone," said Judy. "And the sisters will be......."

"Praying in the chapel," said Susan.

"Are you kidding? More like watching *Lost* or *American Idol*," said Judy.

"Once we get into the building," said Heidi, "instead of going up the main stairs to the library to get my backpack, I'll take you up the back stairs to the French room."

"Are you sure you want to do that?" asked Susan. "Won't it be risky? I don't want to get you into trouble."

"It'll be dark up there in the language wing, so I can show you the way and lead you out if someone catches us."

"I get the feeling you've done this before."

"You mean gone up there in the dark?" asked Heidi, opening her purse and taking out a small flashlight."

"I guess you have," said Susan.

"She's crazy," said Joni. "Judy and I would be too nervous to go up there in the dark. It's creepy."

"Why *do* you go up there at night?"

"Just to look around and spook myself out. But tonight will be different. There's a reason for going."

"You girls remind me of The Silent Three," said Susan.

"Who are they?" asked Heidi.

"Three girls in an English boarding school who are always out late at night solving crimes."

"Never heard of them," said Joni.

"I'm not surprised. They were characters in an old English comic book. Long before your time, and mine for that matter. Anybody hungry?"

"Starved," said Heidi.

"Are you allowed off-campus before practice?"

"Sure. Just as long as we're back by six."

"For your help with getting into the French room, I'll treat you to dinner. Where do you want to go?"

"DiCarlo's Pizza in the Grove," they yelled in unison.

"Is it far?"

"No. We'll show you," said Heidi.

The three students followed Susan out to her rental. There was no question about the seating arrangement. Heidi immediately jumped into the front passenger seat, relegating her two friends to the back. As they pulled out of the parking lot onto the steep driveway, Heidi opened her window, stuck out her head and looked back at the school.

"Just as I suspected. Gertie's on the front porch looking our way. I wouldn't be surprised if she's on to us about tonight. We'll need to be careful. I can read that woman like a book. She's standing there thinking, 'what's the new French teacher doing with those three renegades?' Ladies, the password for this evening is definitely **SILENT.** If we're going to help Mademoiselle Foster tonight, we must become The Silent Three."

⌘

Susan dropped her Silent Three at the gym a little before six then headed back to the Hampton Inn. There was no need to hang around St. Cecelia's until eight-thirty. Once back in the room, she poured herself a glass of wine and turned on the T.V. She'd intended to watch the evening news before calling Jenna, but the local commentator's monotone made her so sleepy that she phoned Jenna to keep herself from dozing off.

"Hi Jenna. It's just me. Glad I caught you at home."

"Where else would I be at this hour on a Monday evening? I'm getting ready to start grading a stack of papers, so this is a welcome interruption. How'd it go today? Please don't tell me they offered you a job."

"They did."

"Then please don't tell me you accepted."

"I did."

"You can't be serious!"

"Never more so. And it might help you out."

"In what way?"

"I want you to move into my loft for the year I'll be in Wheeling. I don't want it vacant, and I don't want a stranger living in it."

"As if I could afford your pad! Dream on, Susan."

"I'm offering it rent-free. What do you say? You'll never get a better offer. Unless you're worried about having to give up your current apartment."

"No. I'll sub-let. That'll be easy."

"As long as you're willing to cover the utilities, it's all yours. You can move in on August first which is when I plan to move to Wheeling."

"I can feel that central air already."

"Right. You know what a bitch August can be in the concrete jungle."

"Well, now that the loft deal is settled, tell me all about today. I can't imagine why you would sign on the dotted line for what I'm sure is a disgustingly low salary."

"More like a pittance than a salary. But I can do my translations on-line. Think of it as my sabbatical."

"From what I've seen of Wheeling, West Virginia, I can't imagine anyone wanting to spend a sabbatical there. Did you ever get to meet Sister Gertrude?"

"I certainly did."

"Was she helpful?"

"Not in the least. She insists that the name Solange Dupré isn't the least bit familiar to her, and she made sure that during my entire first day at St. Cecelia's I didn't get near the French classroom."

"That's odd. What's she hiding?"

"Something. That's for sure. And Dr. Anderson told me that Sister Gertrude wants to totally renovate the French room before I see it."

"Weird."

"And get this. She slipped up and referred to me as Suzette in the dining room."

"That could be an honest mistake."

"Not the way her hand flew to her mouth the minute she uttered it."

"Too bad you won't get to see the classroom before any evidence of Solange's presence is removed."

"But I will. I've gotten to know three students fairly well. They're ornery as can be, always in trouble for breaking St. Cecelia's antiquated rules. I'm meeting them at a back door near the gym at eight-thirty when May Party practice ends. They're going to sneak me into the building when they go in to pick up their backpacks. I'll go up to the French room to look around."

"Be careful, Susan. I mean it."

"It's sweet of you to worry, Jenna, but I'll be all right."

"You'd better be. I don't want anything to screw up my only chance of living in a centrally air-conditioned loft in Manhattan."

"In that case, I'll be extra careful. I'll call back later this evening."

"If you haven't phoned by midnight, I'm phoning the Wheeling police."

"I'm sure you won't have to do that."

"You never can tell."

At eight o'clock, Susan drove back to St. Cecelia's. Parents waiting for their daughters to finish practice had parked their cars bumper to bumper on both sides of the road leading to the gym. Susan found an empty spot close to the back door of the main building and squeezed her small rental into an equally small space between two SUV's. Susan got out of the car and stood on the porch. She felt uneasy. But she might as well have been invisible. None of the women standing around talking to each other gave her as much as a passing glance. But it wasn't until the doors of the gym swung open and girls started spilling out onto the roadway that she let herself relax.

"Now! Follow me!" a voice from behind whispered in her ear.

Susan obeyed without even turning to look at the face of the speaker. She lost herself in the crowd of girls rushing into the building. They were too involved in their own affairs to notice the stranger in the crowd, and, even if they had noticed her, the hallway was too dark for them to identify her as one. A hand gripped her arm and pulled her away from the door where everyone was headed.

"Sh! Don't say anything. I'm taking you the short cut."

"Heidi? Is that you?"

"Yes."

"Where are we?" whispered Susan.

"On our way to the stairs at the foot of the science lab area where you ran into us this morning. Remember?"

"Vaguely."

"We'll climb the stairs outside the science lab. The language wing is at the top."

As they climbed the stairs to the language wing, Susan could feel her heart pounding. But she didn't utter a peep. The last rays of daylight filtering through the large hallway windows at the top of the stairs afforded them enough light to get their bearings before they started down the long dark hallway leading to the language classrooms. Heidi led the way. Susan followed behind, her right hand on the girl's shoulder. When Heidi came to a sudden stop, Susan almost tripped over her.

"In here," whispered Heidi, turning the handle of a door. The room was pitch black. Heidi turned on her flashlight.

"They were watching a movie in here today. That's why it's so dark. All the shades are pulled. But this little light is pretty strong," she said, waving it around the room.

"Wait, Heidi. Go back to the space between the windows. I want to see that picture."

Heidi did so. The picture was a framed photograph of the Visitation convent in Sauret.

"There are lots of photographs of that place around the room. I guess there was a girl from there who gave the photographs to the school, but that was a long time ago."

"Can I see some others?"

"Not now. We have to concentrate on the table," she said, shining the flashlight on the long skinny table that ran though the center of the room. They walked over to the table.

"Look closely," said Heidi. "There isn't a single smooth spot on the entire table top."

Heidi was right. The entire surface was etched with hundreds of initials.

"This is ridiculous," sighed Susan. "It's impossible to tell one set of initials from the other."

"Get under the table," ordered Heidi. "If the person you're looking for graduated in eighty-three, her entire name will be spelled out on the bottom of the table.

They crouched down and crawled underneath the table. There wasn't much head-room, but Susan was able to tilt her head back far enough to raise her eyes to the underside of the table top. Heidi was right. The names were listed in an orderly fashion according to the year of graduation. Heidi shone her torch on the list under 1983. Susan had just enough time to make out the name Solange Dupre before a loud cough came from a corner of the room.

Heidi turned off the flashlight and grabbed Susan's hand so tightly that her long fake nails dug into the flesh around her wrist. Without a word, they crawled out from under the table, rose to their feet and ran out of the room. They didn't stop running until they ended up at the side door leading to the outside of the building.

"Where have you been, Heidi? Mom's getting antsy," said an agitated Joni.

"I'm sorry, Joni. I forgot I was spending tonight at your house. I don't even have my backpack."

"It's in the car. I got it. What's the matter? You're both as white as a sheet."

"We're okay," said Susan, but the tremor in her voice said otherwise. "Thank you, Heidi. I owe you big time."

"How about points for next year?"

"As many as you want, but who do you think was watching us in that room?" asked Susan.

"Sister Gertrude. I know it was her. I'd know that cough anywhere. She's such a sneak."

Susan couldn't remember when or if ever she'd felt so frightened. Although she'd locked her car before going into the building, she checked the back seat before getting in. She wasn't taking any chances. Her heart was still pounding when she got back to her room at the Hampton Inn. She turned on every light in the room and poured herself a glass of wine. When the phone rang, she was shaking so badly that the receiver slipped out of her hand. By the time she picked it up, the caller had hung up. The message light started to blink. She was able to keep hold of the receiver this time. There was an irate message from Jenna.

"Where are you? I'm worried sick. Call the minute you get this."

The message snapped Susan back to reality. She keyed in Jenna's number.

"Hi. This better be you."

"It is."

"What took you so long? I was frantic. I've been sitting here imagining all sorts of scenarios, most of them dealing with a crazed nun coming at you in a dark room with a butcher knife."

"Well, you're partly right."

"Which part?"

"The dark room and the nun. I'm withholding the word crazed until further investigation. God, it was so scary, Jenna. Heidi and I were under the table in the pitch-black French classroom when someone coughed."

"What in God's name were you doing under a table?"

"I'll explain when I get back to New York."

"Did you dive under the table when you heard the cough?"

"No. We were already there when we heard it. I don't want to explain right now. I'll have nightmares if I do. I'm trying to push it to the back of my mind. I already told you I'll explain everything when I get back to New York."

"Which I hope will still be tomorrow?"

"It will be. Can you come over tomorrow night?"

"Sorry. Last PTA meeting of the year. I can't wait until you have all these obligations at St. Cecelia's next year. But I can come over on Wednesday night. Want me to bring Chinese?"

"Suit yourself. At the moment, my stomach is so tied up in knots I can't imagine ever eating again."

"Take a nice hot bath. It'll help you sleep. But, before you get into bed, make sure the door is bolted."

"I will. I promise."

⌘

When Susan awoke the next morning, she couldn't believe how stupid she'd been. She'd been so intent on bolting the door that she'd neglected to close the drapes or switch off the lights before getting into bed. So much for safety measures! She was appalled at her carelessness. She'd also forgotten to set her alarm or request a wake-up call. She looked at the bedside clock. It was just a little after eight. It was sheer luck that the sun shining into the room through the undraped windows had prevented her from oversleeping. She jumped out of bed and headed for the bathroom. If she left Wheeling by nine, there'd still be plenty of time to get to the Pittsburgh Airport, turn in her rental and check in for her twelve-thirty flight.

Susan took her suitcase with her when she went downstairs to breakfast at eight-thirty. By eight-forty five she was ready to check out. The desk clerk was clearly annoyed at having to end a personal phone call to take care of Susan's bill. She didn't smile or utter a word throughout the brief procedure.

"Can I make a reservation for August first?"

The clerk shrugged in reply.

"Is that a yes or a no?"

"Suit yourself."

"Well, I need a room for the evening of August first."

"This year?"

"Of course."

"We have to check. People make reservations way ahead of time."

"I'm moving to Wheeling to teach French," said Susan in an attempt to engage the surly young woman in conversation.

"How many nights?"

"Just one. Can I extend it if I need to?"

"Maybe; maybe not. Depends on the demand."

"Well, I'll try to move into my apartment on the second. I just thought it would be wiser to rest up for at least one night after driving all the way from New York."

"The rate will be ninety-eight dollars."

"I thought it was seventy-nine ninety-five per night."

"It was for the last four nights. It goes up in the summer."

"Oh, I see. You're talking about my August rate."

Without answering, the girl placed Susan's invoice on the counter top and turned around.

"Is that it? Am I all set for August first?"

The girl nodded without turning around.

Susan left her suitcase in the lobby and went to the ladies room. When she returned, the surly looking young woman had been replaced by an equally surly looking young man. He was seated at a desk, so Susan leaned over the counter and asked, "Is there a post-office around here?"

"If it's stamped, you can leave it here."

"I need to have some envelopes weighed," continued Susan. But the clerk had already returned to his paper-work at the desk.

"So is there?"

"Is there what?"

"A post-office."

"I'm not sure. Never been to one."

A man who'd just walked out of the elevator laughed.

"I think there's one in Elm Grove. Turn left onto National Road from here and keep going straight for a couple of miles. It's on the left."

"I don't have much spare time. I'm headed for the Pittsburgh Airport."

"It's on your way. Near the I-70 ramp."

"Thank you very much," said Susan, picking up a hotel service questionnaire on the way out. She rarely paid attention to those things, but the rudeness of the clerks deserved a few choice comments. She decided to mail it in rather than give the subjects of her complaints the opportunity to toss it into trash.

The two women in the post-office weren't much chattier than the hotel staff, but they were efficient. Susan waited until her large manila envelopes had been stamped and mailed before she said, "I'll be moving here permanently in August."

The woman waiting on her gave her a *what do you want me to do about it* look without uttering a word.

"Will I need to fill out a residence address card?"

No answer. The more alert of the two women handed Susan a sheet of paper. "Fill this out when you get here."

Before leaving, Susan decided to have another stab at conversation.

"You'll be seeing a lot of me after August first. I do French translations for an international company based in New York."

No reply, but at least the women nodded and smiled as Susan turned to leave. She decided that the first person she'd phone when she got back to New York was Molly Murdoch. Molly would talk to her. She'd talk to the devil himself if he walked through the door.

Susan was just about to get into her car when someone tapped her on the shoulder and said, "Good morning, Susan. Remember us? I'm Sister Alice and this is Sister Eleanor. We met you yesterday. We were very excited when Dr. Anderson announced that you'd be joining our faculty next year."

"She did? She made an announcement?"

"Oh, yes. Announcements are a big part of our tradition We have them every morning in the music hall before first period."

"Well, I guess I'll see you ladies in August."

"A move is always a lot of work," said Sister Eleanor.

"The good thing is that I'll be forced to clean out my closets. Lighten my load so to speak."

"Don't throw away any interesting clothes, like evening gowns or Halloween costumes."

"Why not?"

"I need them for the Play Box," said Sister Eleanor. "St. Cecelia's has a collection of costumes for all types of student performances."

"How many more do you have room for?"

"As many as you've got. There's no end to the space we have. We're up on the fourth floor, just off the dance studio. We'll show you when you get back in August."

"I'll look forward to it. And I promise to bring donations."

"Well, we won't keep you. You have a plane to catch. Drive carefully. See you in August."

When Susan drove out of the post office parking lot, she was smiling. Two sisters she'd met just briefly yesterday had recognized her. Hopefully, the rest of the area would warm up to her when she became a resident. *And, if I believe that, I'm crazier than I think*, she laughed as she drove onto the ramp leading to I-70.

⌘

The drive to the Airport, the flight home and the cab ride to her apartment went off so smoothly that it was only four o'clock when Susan walked into her building. She planned to phone Molly at six-thirty when her office duties would be over for the day. To kill time till then, she unpacked her suitcase and checked out the fridge. It was practically empty, so she walked to the corner deli and bought a Reuben and a salad for dinner. She stopped at the convenience mart next door to her building for bread, cereal and milk. She'd stock up tomorrow.

At six-thirty sharp, Susan keyed in Molly's number at home.

"Good evening, Miss Murdoch. Miss Foster here."

"Oh, hi, Susan. Nice to hear your voice. Your mum phoned today to ask if I'd heard from you recently. When I asked her to define recently, she changed the subject. I hope she didn't think I was rude."

"I'm sure she didn't. Did she give you any indication of when she's planning on returning to Syracuse?"

"Said she'd be home in a couple of weeks. Can you believe it?"

"Believe what?"

"That she'd stay away this long in May. It's one of our busiest times. I told her I'm getting a wee bit suspicious of this Dr. Villiers."

"You did? I'd be scared to death to broach that subject, and I'm her daughter."

"It's always easier for a stranger to ask personal questions."

"How do you know that?"

"Trust me. I just know."

"Well, for what it's worth, I'm back in New York, at least until August. I'm moving."

"Back here?"

"Not in a million years. No. I'm moving to Wheeling, West Virginia."

"You are? Well, send me all your gorgeous shoes."

"Why would I do that?"

"I hear they don't wear them there."

"That's a rumor. I didn't see a single person barefoot. Anyway, the next time my mother calls, don't tell her I'm moving to West Virginia. I want to tell her myself."

"I won't say a word. I swear you two are the oddest duo for a mother and daughter. If I didn't know better, I'd swear you weren't related."

"Believe me. We are."

"I'll believe you. Thousands wouldn't."

"Just one favor, Molly. Keep me posted on her plans about coming back to Syracuse."

"Will do. Anything else?"

"No. Just thanks for taking care of everything so well and for being such an understanding ear when I need to talk."

"Ach, it's a pleasure."

"My mother swears you could talk to the devil himself if he turned up."

"No more compliments or you'll be responsible for me getting above myself."

"I don't think there's much chance of that."

"High praise indeed, Susan."

Susan worked on some translations until the wee hours of the morning. She wished Georges would call. Now that she was back in New York she felt lonesome. She thought of Scott, but only for an instant. He was probably snuggled up with some bimbo from his office. She hoped that Georges wasn't with someone else. At least, he didn't have an office, but Jenna and Molly were right. A good-looking guy like Georges wasn't going to wait for her forever. She stared at the phone, wishing it to ring. At one point it did, but it went dead the minute she said hello. It was almost three before Susan fell asleep. She'd never felt so lonesome in her life. But her loneliness was short-lived. A banging on the door woke her out of a sound sleep.

"Who's there?" she asked, looking through the peephole of the hallway door.

"Who do you think?" came a familiar voice.

"Georges, is that you?"

"Who else would be banging down your door at four in the morning?"

"Why didn't you let me know you were coming?"

"We got cut off. I tried to call from the plane after we landed."

"That was you. By the time I got to the phone, you'd hung up. Why didn't you call from the terminal?"

"The battery on my cell phone went dead. I decided to surprise you. Are you surprised? Say something!"

"Come inside, for God's sake." Susan pulled George into her apartment and threw her arms around him.

"Does this mean you're happy to see me?"

Susan began to cry.

"What's the matter?"

"I was afraid I'd never see you again."

"Are you kidding? You're like reading a good book."

"There isn't an ending yet."

"I'm hoping it never ends."

⌘

Talk to the devil himself, thought Molly. *More like the devil herself.*

Ever since Anna had taken off for San Francisco, the aggressive woman who'd been so insistent about seeing her had started turning up at the office on a regular basis. Molly's reaction to her had run the gamut from angry to nervous to fed-up with the intrusion to feeling sorry for the woman. When she'd first started turning up at the office, she'd been well-dressed and immaculately groomed. But, after the third visit, it had been downhill in the appearance department. Her clothing was now sloppy and ill-matched. She tried to hide her disheveled hair under a series of poorly fitted wigs in a variety of colors. On one visit, she'd been a blond, the next a red head and last week a combination of the two colors. She wore bright red lipstick plastered on well above the lip line. It had been difficult not to laugh at her, but Molly's amusement had quickly turned to pity. The woman was clearly not all there. She refused to accept the fact that Mrs. Foster was neither in the office nor at home these days. She turned up on Tuesday and Thursday afternoons at four o'clock sharp and rambled on about the weather and the traffic on James Street. Molly gave her coffee and pretended to listen. She always ended the visit by demanding to know when Mrs. Foster would return.

"Are you daft, lassie?" Molly's mother had asked. "You shouldn't encourage her."

"But she's so pathetic, Mum. She likes to tell me about her childhood in France and how she ended up in a convent. And, you never know, she could be a long-lost relation of Mrs. Foster."

"I thought Mrs. Foster had no relations other than Susan."

"That's what she claims. Maybe she does have relatives but doesn't acknowledge them. If the woman who comes to the office is one, who could blame her?"

"What's the woman's name?"

"She won't tell me."

"Have you asked?"

"Of course I've asked. I'm not stupid."

"What does she say when you ask her?"

"She never answers the question."

"It's hard enough for me to believe that you're entertaining a crazy woman but downright preposterous that you don't know her name."

"But I really like her stories. They're quite intriguing."

"And you seem to be falling for them. If she's from Dijon, France and a convent out in the country, what the hell is she doing here? Syracuse is a long way from Dijon."

"So is Glasgow."

"But we live and work here. We don't just walk into local businesses and pull up a chair for a chat. We'd be arrested for harassment."

"But she has a lovely accent. I could listen to her for hours."

"Which you obviously do twice a week. Has she ever given as much as a hint about why she wants to speak to Mrs. Foster?"

"No."

"I know you speak to Susan from time to time. Have you mentioned the woman to her?"

"No."

"Well, if you ask me, Molly, the only odd part of this story is your refusal to mention it to either of the Fosters. Why haven't you?"

"I honestly don't know. She's sort of creepy. I'm almost afraid of her. That's why I don't turn her away."

"You're telling me you're afraid of her, but you have the coffee ready for her visits?"

"For some strange reason, I feel that I need to keep this woman calm. And you always tell me to go with my gut feeling."

"I do. But there's a limit. Promise me you'll be careful around this woman."

"I will."

"Do you have any idea where she lives?"

"She says she has a flat somewhere off James Street. Hixon Ave. That's where she said her apartment is. She says she's going to stay there until things get settled."

"What things?"

"I don't know. Evidently whatever business she has to settle with Mrs. Foster. She gets angry whenever Mrs. Foster's name comes up. I can't imagine anyone bearing a grudge against Mrs. Foster. Can you?"

"No. But you never know what happened in the past. I'll be glad when she returns from California and things get back to normal. It's downright weird, her just taking off like that and leaving you in charge."

"You don't think I'm capable?"

"It's not that. It's just so unlike her. And you've got to agree that the timing is strange. She leaves and a strange woman turns up on the doorstep. Mark my words, Molly. This is no coincidence."

"I never thought of it that way."

"Have you mentioned this woman to Susan? When did you speak to her last?"

"About an hour ago. She's getting ready to move to Wheeling, West Virginia at the end of the summer. She's going to teach French in a girls' high school there."

"I wonder what her mother thinks of that."

"She doesn't know yet. Aren't those two the oddest mother and daughter you've ever met? I can't imagine me going anywhere without you and Dad being aware of it."

"Some would say we're too clanish. But, then again, we're Scots. We're supposed to be."

"Right. And I like it the way it is. I can't figure out why Susan would move to an out-of-the-way place like West Virginia when she has a French boyfriend."

"How do you know that?"

"Talked to him on the phone when he called from France trying to get in touch with Mrs. Foster."

Her mother started to laugh.

"What's so funny?"

205

"For a minute I thought you were going to tell me that you've been having coffee with him twice a week at the office."

"Hardly. I promise you, Mum, the mysterious Tuesday and Thursday lady is my only mysterious visitor."

Before falling asleep that night, Fiona Murdoch prayed that Anna Foster would return soon. Something was not right. In the two and a half years her daughter had worked for Anna, Fiona had been suspicious of the woman's past. Her diction was a little too clipped for an American. And something was definitely off in the mothering department. Fiona had always thought she seemed more like a benevolent care-giver to Susan than a real mum. And her claim to having no relatives had to be bogus. Everyone had someone. Fiona was a good judge of character. She was rarely wrong in her assessments, but she'd never confided her suspicions to Molly "Still waters run deep," her own mother had always told her. Fiona could hear her mother's voice. "Those who claim to have no past are the ones who do. Take my word for it, lassie." Fiona had. She just hoped that Anna Foster returned to Syracuse before hers came back to haunt her.

⌘

Anna took the elevator to the ninth floor of the Medical Arts building where her gynecologist was located. The receptionist handed her a questionnaire attached to a clip board and asked her to fill it out. Since Anna appeared in the office only once a year, she was never a familiar face to Dr. Mercier's ever-changing lineup of clerical workers.

Anna took a seat and stared at the questionnaire for a minute before starting to fill it out.

Name _____

Home Address _____

Business Address _____

Telephone _____

E-mail _____

Fax _____

In the space for the address to send test results Anna wrote down Henri's home address. She wrote a 0 in the box for the number of child births and another 0 in the box for the number of pregnancies. She shivered at the thought of Susan's finding out that information. It would make the ever-growing rift between them complete. Jacques was right; big brothers usually are. She needed to tell Susan the truth. All of it. But she couldn't bear the thought of the child she'd raised from the time she drew her first breath looking at her with hatred in her eyes. And Susan would do that. She'd seen that look when she first told Susan about the existence of Solange. She had no desire to see it again. Suddenly, Anna burst into tears which gave way to loud sobs.

"Ma'am, are you all right? Would you like a glass of water?" asked the concerned receptionist.

Anna nodded.

While she sipped the water, the young woman tried to console her.

"Try not to worry. Dr. Mercier will see you in a few minutes. Perhaps things won't be as bad as you think. And, if they are, you've come to the right place."

Anna gave the girl a weak smile in reply.

The ten minutes Anna waited to see Dr. Mercier seemed like an eternity. But at least she'd managed to pull herself together by the time her name was called.

"Anna. How lovely to see you again," said the doctor, kissing her lightly on each cheek. "Any problems or just the routine tests?"

"Just the same tune-up."

"You do have a regular GYN on the east coast, don't you?"

"Of course," lied Anna.

"You should leave us a copy of her name in case we need to get in touch."

"There's no need for that. I'm planning a permanent move to San Francisco within the next year. You'll probably get tired of seeing me."

"I doubt that. I've always been flattered that you come all the way here for your annual physical. It gives my ego a boost."

Anna had never told Dr. Mercier that the real reason for her yearly checkup in San Francisco was to prevent anyone from finding out that she'd never given birth or ever been pregnant. She felt that her secret was safer with a doctor on the other side of the continent from Syracuse. She did have a general practitioner there, but his files contained nothing about her reproductive history.

"Do you still want all test results including your mammogram sent to Dr. Villiers' home address?" asked Dr. Mercier at the end of the exam.

"Yes."

"Well, I guess this is *au revoir*, as we say in France, till next year," said Dr. Mercier, shaking hands with Anna before she left the office.

"Right. You take care. I'll see you again next year if not before."

In the twenty-five years that Jeannine Mercier had been Anna Foster's physician, she'd never let on that she knew Anna was French or that she was Henri Villiers' mistress. Henri had told her Anna's story years ago but had begged her to keep it a secret. Out of a deep respect for Henri, Jeannine had never once revealed to Anna that she knew all about her past. *We French are good at keeping secrets. Perhaps too good. Anna will never be able to enjoy life until she admits everything to her daughter, the daughter she doesn't really have.*

That evening, Anna reached a decision. She would marry Henri before Christmas and turn over the business to Molly if she was interested in continuing it. But, most importantly, she'd explain to Susan the circumstances of her birth and how she came to be her surrogate mother. She was sixty-six years old. She wasn't getting any younger. She wanted to enjoy the years she had left, and she wanted to enjoy them with Henri. She owed him those years. And Susan deserved to know the truth about her past. How stupid she'd been to hide everything for so long under the pretense that the present was all that mattered.

As soon as she returned to Henri's, Anna phoned Molly to let her know she planned to return to Syracuse the first week of June.

"Think you can handle things just a little bit longer?"

"Of course I can, Mrs. Foster. Let me know your flight plans. I'll pick you up at the Airport."

"I can take a taxi."

"I insist."

"All right, Molly. I'll e-mail you the flight info as soon as I make the reservation."

⌘

Molly had decided to tell Anna about the mysterious visitor but not until after she returned home. Three weeks was a long time to spend listening to that woman babble incoherently every Tuesday and Thursday afternoon, but at least she restricted her visits to only an hour. The minute the clock said five, she up and left the office without as much as a "See you," "Good-bye," or "Thanks for putting up with me." Her mother now referred to her as Molly's new best friend.

In the end, Molly's problem solved itself. The visits ended as suddenly as they'd begun. When she failed to show up one Thursday at four o'clock, Molly was relieved but found it impossible to push her to the back of her mind. She drove slowly along James Street and Hixon Avenue looking for her, but after a few days of searching, Molly gave up. She never saw the woman again.

When Anna arrived home on June tenth, Molly met her at the Syracuse Airport.

"Good flight?"

"Yes. And, since you've been shouldering the business on your own for six weeks, I've decided that you need a vacation, a long one at my expense. This isn't the way to my house. Where are we going?"

"Mine. Mum wanted to have you for dinner. A welcome home gesture. Don't argue, Mrs. Foster. You deserve it. It'll be just you, Mum and me. Dad's away at the golf."

The real reason for the dinner at the Murdoch's was to tell Anna Foster about the mystery woman. Fiona Murdoch had been adamant that she should be told about the woman as soon as possible. Molly had argued against it, but her mother had won out in the end.

"You have to tell her, Molly. It's your duty."

"But she's stopped coming to the office."

"It doesn't matter. Always remember that keeping dark secrets never helps anyone."

"I will, Mum, but my brain's running out of space to store all the things you keep telling me to remember."

"Don't be daft, Molly. We Scots have a separate compartment for all that stuff. You should know that."

"If you say so."

"I do. I certainly do."

During a lull in the conversation towards the end of the meal, Mrs. Murdoch gave her daughter a quizzical look. When Molly didn't respond, she took the lead.

"Mrs. Foster?"

"Anna. Please call me Anna."

"Anna it is. Well, Anna, something a wee bit odd happened while you were away."

"Odd? I don't understand. Molly never mentioned anything."

"Well, Molly and I are hoping you can shed some light on a very strange situation. Go ahead, lass. Tell her."

"A couple of weeks after you left for California, a very strange woman with an accent which turned out to be French came to the office asking to see you. When I said you weren't there, she demanded that I give her your home address. Naturally, I didn't give it to her. I told her I didn't know where you lived. I'd never give anyone your address."

The color drained from Anna's face.

"Mrs. Foster. I mean Anna. Are you all right?" asked Mrs. Murdoch. "You're as white as a sheet. Molly, get Anna a glass of water. On second thought, forget the water. She needs a good stiff brandy."

It took Anna a few minutes and a few sips of the brandy to regain her composure.

"I'm all right. Please continue, Molly."

"Well, after two aggressive attempts to find you at the office, she changed completely."

"What do you mean?" asked Anna.

"Her manner. It was almost as if she suddenly realized that she could get further with me if she toned herself down. You know, the old adage

210

about it being a lot easier to attract flies with honey than vinegar."

"No. That's not it at all," said Anna. "I know who she is. She's manic-depressive. Has been for years."

"You know this woman?" gasped Molly.

"Unfortunately, yes. She can actually be quite dangerous."

"I told you, Molly," said Mrs. Murdoch. "You shouldn't have been so nice to her."

"Anyway," continued Molly. "She started turning up at the office twice a week."

"Why?"

"Just to chat. But it was all one-sided. She rambled on and on about nothing. And the change in her appearance from her initial visit was amazing."

"In what way?"

"Well, on the first two visits, she was meticulously dressed. After that, it was the complete reverse. She looked like a bag lady. I felt sorry for her, so, when she started coming to the office on a regular basis, I would give her a cup of coffee and let her ramble on. Fortunately, she never stayed more than an hour."

"How many visits are we talking about?"

"Six exactly. Seven if you count the first two when she'd been almost violent. Like clockwork, she'd turn up at the office at four on Tuesdays and Thursdays. Without so much as a glance at the clock, she'd get up and leave at five."

"That's part of her illness. She has an instinctive routine. But what did she talk about? Did she ask about me?"

"That was one of the oddest things about her. She never mentioned you after the first two visits. She just sat in a chair and babbled on and on. It was as if she was in a trance."

"But what did she say?" asked Anna.

"Nothing that made any sense. She just kept going on and on about her childhood in Dijon, France?"

"Are you sure?"

"Oh yes. She repeated that so many times I thought I'd go mad if she didn't shut up. Then, she'd up and leave without as much as a good-bye.

The visits stopped at the end of May just as suddenly as they'd begun. She did tell me that she had an apartment on Hixon Ave. I've cased that area several times, but without any luck. It's as if she's vanished into thin air. Who is she?"

"Someone I've known for many years."

"At first I thought she might be a relative," said Molly.

"Why?"

"The dark eyes. They're exactly like your Susan's."

When Anna didn't respond, Molly changed the subject.

"I've talked to Susan a few times. What do you think of her news, or perhaps I should say her career change?" asked Molly before remembering that she'd promised Susan she wouldn't mention that to Anna.

"Oh that! Yes. I am very pleased," replied Anna. Her refusal to admit her ignorance about Susan's plans in the presence of such a close-knit mother and daughter made Molly breathe a little easier. She hadn't revealed a confidence after all.

"I am very grateful to you, Molly, for the way you've handled everything in my absence. And I wasn't kidding about treating you to a nice long vacation before the end of the summer."

Anna looked at Molly and smiled. Little did the young woman realize that an all-expense paid holiday was small recompense for having saved Anna's life. There was no doubt in Anna's mind that Isabelle Duchamps had come to the office with murder on her mind. Molly was lucky to be alive

"Where do you think the woman has disappeared to?" asked Molly.

"I have no idea," said Anna.

"And she never even told me her name."

"Isabelle. It's Isabelle Duchamps. But promise me you won't reveal you know it if she turns up again."

"Why not?"

"Just promise me, Molly. Please?"

"Okay. I promise."

"Good. Now I need to go home. I'm feeling tired."

On the drive to her house, Anna made Molly promise once again that she wouldn't let Isabelle know she was aware of her identity should she put in another appearance at the office. That would be a big mistake. In her deranged mind, Isabelle would be convinced that Anna had told Molly all about her diabolical past. Anna would never be able to live with herself if Molly become one of Isabelle's victims.

⌘

It took Anna twenty-four hours to get up the courage to phone Susan.

"Would you answer the phone, Georges?"

"Sure. Hello."

"Is this Susan Foster's apartment?" asked the surprised voice on the other end.

"Yes, it is." He recognized Anna's voice from their brief conversation several weeks ago. "Hang on a minute. She's taking something out of the oven."

George walked into the kitchen and handed the phone to Susan.

"Who is it?"

"Your mother. I recognize her voice."

"Hi, Mom. Still in California?"

"No I'm back in Syracuse."

"Well, at least I don't have to hear it from Molly."

"I do wish you wouldn't be so sarcastic, Susan. After all, I had to hear it from Molly that you will be moving to West Virginia to teach French at St Cecelia's. You must have been impressed with the place."

"Intrigued would be more like it. And, yes, I'm moving there on August first. The orientation for St. Cecelia's new faculty members starts on the fourteenth. Thought I'd give myself a couple of weeks to familiarize myself with the area."

"Have you found a place to stay?"

"Actually, yes. I just found it on-line today. It's the top floor of a lovely old home that's been turned into two units."

"Where is it exactly?"

"National Road. Not too far from the intersection at Washington Avenue. It's not furnished, so I'll need to purchase some things when I get there. Thought I'd spend a couple of nights at the Hampton Inn on National Road while I shop for the necessities."

"There are some wonderful little antique shops at the Center Market. And the fish market is amazing."

"So, you do admit to having spent time in Wheeling, West Virginia?"

"A long time ago, Susan."

"Was that where you were when you left me with the family next door once a year?"

"You remember that?"

"Vaguely. They were the only times we were ever apart. Why didn't you take me with you?"

"I couldn't. Don't ask so many questions. I'm not in the mood for answering them. But why did you decide to take the French teaching job at St. Cecelia's?"

"Mainly curiosity."

"Don't forget it was curiosity that killed the cat. I'm serious, Susan. Be careful."

"I'll try. Will you visit me there?"

"Of course. It's been ages since I've been to Wheeling. We'll be busy at the office until the end of August, especially since I'm insisting on sending Molly on a well-deserved two week vacation."

"That's nice of you. And you're right. She does deserve it."

"I could come for a visit over Labor Day weekend."

"Are you serious?"

"Never more so."

"Great. I can pick you up at the Pittsburgh Airport. I just bought a cute little P.T. Cruiser this morning. The dealer is keeping it for me until the end of July. There's nowhere to park it around here."

"Sounds good. And it also sounds as if you and your friend, Georges, are getting along quite well. Won't he miss you when you leave for the hinterland?"

"He's leaving for Paris next week to work on an architectural design project for at least three months."

"Please tell him I wish him well and that I apologize for hanging up on him when he phoned from Dijon."

"I will. I promise. And tell Molly I send my regards."

Long after mother and daughter had said their good-byes, Anna sat on the couch, sipping a glass of wine. Labor Day weekend would be the time she'd tell Susan the entire truth about her background. It was time. The only fly in the ointment was Isabelle who had reappeared out of thin air. Surely she wouldn't think of tracking Susan to Wheeling. That was Solange territory. Isabelle would never believe that after what had happened at St. Cecelia's Susan would turn up there.

⌘

Anna drove Molly and her mother to the Airport for her flight to Barbados.

"How can I ever thank you, Mrs. Foster?"

"Anna. How many times do I have to tell you to call me by my first name? And you can thank me by enjoying yourself and returning with a healthy looking tan."

"I promise I will."

"Just don't go frying your northern European skin in the sun all day like those Brits in the Canaries."

"I won't. And I'll send you both cards and bring you back presents."

They accompanied Molly as far as the security gate.

"All right, you two. This it . No long drawn-out good-byes or I'll greet."

"You'll do what?" asked Anna.

"Greet. Cry!"

"Glasgow slang?"

"Of course. Now you two behave while I'm away."

"You're the one who'll need to behave, lassie. Enjoy yourself but not too much. And remember you've a good Scottish tongue in your head. Don't be afraid to use it."

"Well, that's her away," said Mrs. Murdoch, watching her daughter disappear into the departure area. "Now you can enjoy some peace and quiet in the office. At least for two weeks. I tell you, Anna, that lassie is on a constant high from the exuberance of her own verbosity."

"She is high-spirited," laughed Anna. "But she's a breath of fresh air. While she's gone, let's get together for a meal. And this time it will be at my house."

"Just tell me when."

Anna arrived back at the office a little after eleven, but it was so quiet without Molly that she found it difficult to concentrate on the lists of figures in front of her. By eleven-thirty, she was starting to yawn, so she picked up a pile of mail from the file Molly had labeled UNIMPOR-TANT (read only when dead bored). It was nothing but ads and requests for donations. She threw the first batch into the waste basket at the side of her desk and picked up another.

"What in the world have we here?" One of the envelopes was sticking to her fingers. She shook it off and stared at it in disbelief. The white business-size envelope was smeared with what looked like blood. But it was the handwriting that caught Anna's eye. The printing actually. Each letter had been meticulously formed in lower case. Anna knew only one person who wrote like that. Isabelle Duchamps. The postmark said Syracuse. The date was May twenty-sixth. Three weeks ago. With a pounding heart, Anna opened the envelope and withdrew and unfolded two sheets of paper . They were covered with printing in French, but Anna translated as she read.

My Dear Anna,

It as been a long time since we last met. Since then I have suffered greatly. I lay the blame for my misfortunes at your feet. You are an evil woman, Anna Fontaine. Through me, God will punish you.

Your brother, Jacques, was all I ever had. He loved me passionately, but you destroyed our love and our future when you stole our little daughter in such a diabolical way. You and your evil partner-in-crime, Henri Villiers. You took my baby and kept it for yourself. And you both believed that child of Satan, the young son of Dr. Villiers, who accused me of killing his mother and throwing her body into the lake below the Convent. Because of you, I was committed to an asylum instead of taking my final vows and spending my life in the service of God.

Do you have any idea what living in an asylum is like, Anna? No. Of course, you don't. The only good thing about it was having the time to plot revenge on you for ruining my life. God had big plans for me, Anna. You couldn't stand that! You were so jealous that you even ruined God's plan to bless a barren couple by giving them Annemarie's child. I have always known that you hired someone to impregnate Michelle so that I'd end up a laughing stock when Michelle gave birth to her own child. That is why I tried so hard to find and murder Solange. God did not want her to grow up in a household with someone's bastard. And don't tell me that Michelle's husband, Gaston, was the father of her child. I simply won't believe you.

You have won too often, Anna. After you stole my own flesh and blood, I knew that it was time to kill Solange. But you hid her and my little girl in America. And that little Villiers' savage disappeared at the same time. You think you are so clever, Anna. But your time is up.

Your Servant in God,
Isabelle Duchamps

Anna was shaking by the time she finished reading Isabelle's letter. But she had the presence of mind to reach for her Rolodex and flip through it for Emily Morrison's number. Her shaking fingers keyed in the number.

"Dr. Morrison's office."

"Is the doctor available?"

"She's with a patient. I can make an appointment for you."

"No. It's not about an appointment. This is Anna Foster from…"

"Foster Accounting. Our friendly and reliable bookie."

"Yes. That's right."

"Is there a problem with the account?"

"Sort of," lied Anna. "But it can be taken care of in a matter of minutes. Only I do need to speak with Dr. Morrison herself."

"She should be available at noon. Should she call the office?"

"Yes. Definitely."

"No problem."

The half hour until Dr. Morrison called back was one of the longest thirty minutes of Anna's life. Although she had taken the precaution of hanging the CLOSED FOR LUNCH sign on the door and locking it, she never took her eyes off the handle. Thank God she'd let Molly talk her out of replacing the paneled door with a glass one. Seeing Isabelle's face on the other side would have done her in.

Dr. Morrison phoned promptly at noon.

"What's wrong, Anna? Sounds like we're in trouble."

"No. I'm the one who's in trouble, Dr. Morrison."

"You sound nervous."

"I am. I just received a very threatening letter from a crazy woman."

"Is that a euphemism for disgruntled client?"

"If only. I need to see you immediately. This is serious. I want you to read the letter."

"Would it help if I stopped by the office in about an hour? I have rounds to make at the psychiatric clinic in East Syracuse. I don't have to be there until four."

"That would be wonderful."

Despite her fears of Isabelle appearing out of the shadows and stabbing her to death, Anna was able to pull herself together and walk to the local deli for a quick lunch. By the time Dr. Morrison arrived, she had her emotions under control.

Dr. Morrison read the letter.

"Do you have one of those plastic baggy thingies handy?"

"For what?"

"This envelope. It's going to a police lab we use to identify blood stains. It could just be blood from meat you buy in the grocery or it could be human. We need to make sure. If it is human, we'll find out the type. That could be helpful in identifying the sender if she shows up in person."

Anna opened Molly's supply cupboard and retrieved a baggy.

"Make that two while you're at it. We'll make a copy of the letter then place the original in the second baggy. The police should have a copy of this in case we have a real crazy on our hands."

"We do."

"Sounds like this woman's got it in for you big time."

"She does. But she's got her stories ass-backwards."

Dr. Morrison looked at her watch.

"If you can tell me the entire background of this case in one hour, I'm all ears. I'm afraid that's all the time I can offer you today."

Anna spilled out her entire life story in under forty-five minutes. She'd never talked so fast in her life in either French or English. When she finished, she gulped down a glass of water so quickly that her stomach ached.

"Well, Dr. Morrison? What do you think? Is Isabelle as crazy as she sounds?"

"Her rambling thought processes indicate that she's probably stopped taking medication recently."

"How can you tell?"

"The fact that Molly found her very calm on her visits to the office while you were gone. She must have been sedated. Now she's crashing, sort of a withdrawal."

"I'm wondering if she's still in town."

"It doesn't sound like it. The letter was mailed three weeks ago. As angry at you as this woman sounds, she'd have confronted you in person by now."

"But where would she have gone?"

"Into hiding. Let's hope she's back on her meds. Here's my personal card. Call if you need me, day or night. That's my home phone number."

Dr. Morrison placed the two plastic baggies in her brief case. "I'll take care of these. And don't be surprised if you get a call or visit from the police within twenty-four hours."

"Do we need to get them involved? Forget I said that. Of course we do. I'm being ridiculous. Thank you so much for your help."

"Just be careful, Anna. And don't hesitate to call if you need me."

Despite the fears for her safety, Anna decided not to unburden herself on Henri. For all she knew, Isabelle could have tapped into her phone line. According to her letter, she didn't know the whereabouts of David and Henri. Anna was determined not to help her find out.

Knowing that Emily Morrison, one of upstate New York's most esteemed psychiatrists, was aware of Isabelle's existence and that the police had been alerted gave Anna a degree of confidence about her safety, but that didn't stop her from placing the sharpest kitchen knife she possessed under her pillow when she went to bed.

⌘

Susan loved everything about her apartment on National Road except the woman who inhabited the downstairs flat. The upstairs where Susan now lived had been vacant for so long that the downstairs' tenant viewed Susan as an intrusion on her privacy. Whenever they met in the shared entry hall on the first floor, she did her best to avoid Susan. When Susan had asked her for directions to various places in town, she hadn't been the least bit helpful. She'd even refused to open the door to Susan's apartment when a furniture delivery was made a day earlier than expected and Susan wasn't at home although Susan had told her where she had hidden a spare key. That had forced Susan to extend her stay at the Hampton Inn by two days. But the bitch downstairs didn't faze Susan one bit. She could give as good as she got.

On August fourteenth, Susan walked the few blocks to St. Cecelia's. She was anxious to see what changes had been wrought in the French classroom by Sister Gertrude. She felt a lot more confident walking through the front door of the school as a faculty member than she had as a visitor in May. The Rottweiler was at her battle station but didn't utter a word, so Susan walked right in and headed for the stairs leading up to the language wing where she was greeted by Jonathan, the Spanish teacher.

"Well, well. You are a glutton for punishment. Welcome back."

"Thanks. Nice to see you. I'm almost afraid to open the door to the French room."

"It isn't that scary. If you're feeling energetic, you can repaint the walls and hang up some new pictures. That room is in drastic need of a make-over."

"Sister Gertrude had it completely redone over the vacation."

"No, she didn't. When I peeked in earlier, it was the same old decor. Early Cecelia. Nothing's changed."

Susan opened the door and gasped. Jonathan was right. It was exactly the same as the night she and Heidi had tiptoed around it in the dark.

"You're right, Jonathan. Nothing's changed although it was pitch dark the only time I saw it."

"What are you talking about?"

"This room. For some reason, Sister Gertrude didn't want me to see it. She even arranged for the fire alarm to be pulled when Nancy and I reached this area on the day of my tour in May. Remember? You commented at lunch that you were looking forward to showing me this area that afternoon."

"I do remember. Gertie jumped in with some convoluted reason you had to stay in the classrooms in the main hallway."

"Right. I was so ticked that I bribed three of your students to help me get back into the building after May Party practice."

"Is that when you named them The Silent Three?"

"They told you that?"

"They tell me everything."

"Did Heidi tell you that we were under the table in here in the dark when someone coughed?"

"No. She held out on me about that. All they really said was that they were changing their name from the Three Musketeers to the Silent Three. They think it makes them sound more mysterious."

"Well, the Three Musketeers isn't exactly original."

"I was the one who suggested it."

"Sorry."

"That's all right. I'm so used to being shot down, it never hurts anymore. It's difficult for a man to be witty around so many women."

"Well, thank God Heidi had a flashlight. She thinks of everything."

"I gave each of them one for their harmless nightly prowls."

"Now that is original!"

"It was a bit of an ego booster for them. They're constantly in trouble. Shirt-tails not tucked in. Skirts too short. Shoe heels too high."

"The Old Maid Brigade?"

"Right. This school is on the brink of closure and some teachers are more interested in the uniform than thinking up positive ways to retain the students. Their attitude has never made sense to me."

"If St. Cecelia's does close, they'll need psychological reconditioning. They wouldn't last five minutes in a public school in New York."

Their conversation was interrupted by the loud ringing of the phone at one end of the hall. Jonathan answered.

"Yes. She's already up here. I'll tell her. Yes. I'll tell her that too."

"Sounds like I've been tracked down."

"Indeed you have. There's a message for you at the front desk from someone named Lola."

"I'll get it at lunch time."

"No, Susan. You'll get it right now when you go to the main desk to pick up your official school name tag which can be worn on a ribbon around your neck or clipped to a pocket."

"I have to go all the way back down to the main desk then up again to the Music Hall for orientation?"

"Exactly!"

"Why can't that exasperating woman bring the tag up to the Music Hall? She's supposed to be at the opening meeting, isn't she?"

"Yes. But she needs to establish her authority over you. It makes more of a statement this way. And do be forewarned about wearing your I.D. The administration is holding a meeting this afternoon to figure out what to do with the teachers who refuse to wear the damned thing."

"Why would anyone refuse to wear it? Isn't that rather petty?"

"Of course it's petty. That's a great word to describe most of the faculty here. One of the teachers covers her own photograph with one of her dog. Not that there's much difference."

"Jonathan!"

"Just being truthful."

When the faculty divided into small discussion groups, Susan found herself at the same table as Sister Gertrude, Hilda, the history teacher and Jonathan.

"Welcome to St. Cecelia's, Susan," said Sister Gertrude. "I hope you found the French room to your liking."

"I certainly did, Sister. But why the change of heart?"

"I think you know the answer to that, Susan. What was the use of redoing the room when you'd seen all the evidence?"

"You almost gave me a heart attack that night. It was you, wasn't it?"

Sister Gertrude didn't answer.

"What are you two going on about?" asked Hilda.

"Mind your own business," barked Jonathan. "By the way Hilda, I heard an outrageous lie about you this morning."

"You did?"

"Yes. Someone told me that you cover up your I.D. picture with one of your dog."

"So?"

"Well, from the picture I'm looking at right now, he was obviously mistaken."

Hilda seethed with anger as the entire table burst into fits of laughter.

"Come on, Hilda," said Sister Gertrude. "Enjoy the humor. You can dish it out but can't take it, can you?"

For the remainder of the week-long orientation, Hilda ignored Jonathan. And, for weeks afterwards, whenever their paths crossed, Hilda would ask Susan, "Who told him that?"

"Told him what?"

"About me looking like my dog."

"I have absolutely no idea. But all he had to do was look at the picture to come up with the punch line. You left yourself wide open for that comment."

"Thanks a lot."

"Don't be so paranoid. He was only joking."

"You're on his side."

"Why do you say that? I hardly know the man."

"The two of you are thicker than thieves."

"If you say so, Hilda. If you say so."

⌘

The message Lola had left at the front desk was an invitation to attend her Soroptimist Club's annual wine and cheese membership soirée at a local restaurant. What the hell was that all about? Susan wasn't the least bit interested in joining a club, but, when she phoned Lola to decline the invitation, Lola informed her that she might have some information about Solange. Since she was in the midst of a series of style shows, the Soroptimist gathering was the earliest she could get together with Susan. Reluctantly, Susan accepted the invitation.

"You don't have to join. But it would be a good way for you to meet people. It's all women who work. We won't be offended if you don't join."

In the end, Susan was glad she'd accepted. It was a relief to be surrounded by so many friendly faces. Somewhere between the nibblies and dessert, Lola confided to Susan that for the past few weeks she'd seen a strange looking woman in Krogers on several occasions. The woman looked familiar, but she couldn't place her. Then, in Lola's own words, "The light bulb went on. Although it's been over twenty years and the woman's aged, not gracefully, I might add, I realized she was the nun in the habit who scared the hell out of us our senior year."

"What does that have to do with Solange?"

"The woman was French. She appeared at St. Cecelia's right after Christmas vacation that year. Sister Gertrude introduced her to the student body at announcements. We couldn't get over it. She was dressed in the traditional long black habit that our own sisters only dragged out from the Play Box on Halloween. Solange was mortified. She kept trying to ignore her, but she followed Solange around the school like a little puppy dog. We nicknamed her the evil sister. She was really scary."

"Why was she there?"

"Sister Gertrude said she was from a sister convent in France near Solange's hometown, but she never did explain what she was doing at our school."

"Did she teach?"

"No. She just wandered the halls all day and waited outside classrooms for Solange. Then she'd follow her to her next class and wait outside. We all made fun of her, but, in retrospect, I'm sure Solange was scared to death of her."

"How long did this go on?"

"The entire semester right up through exams. Then, a very nice lady, I think she must have been the one Solange met in San Francisco every summer, turned up."

"Did she get along with your evil sister?"

"That's just it! I remember that from the day that lady appeared, we never saw the evil sister again. And we never saw Solange after the last exam. Remember I told you it was as if she'd vanished into thin air? Well, now I'm thinking that the nice lady must have taken Solange somewhere to get her away from the evil sister."

"What happened to her?"

"The evil sister?"

"Yeah. Where do you think she went?"

"No idea. She disappeared as quickly as she'd appeared. We were all too upset about Solange's disappearance to give her a second thought, but seeing that woman in Krogers really jogged my memory. It all came rushing back. I could be mistaken, but I'm convinced the woman in Krogers and the evil sister are one and the same. The poor soul was so frail looking I was afraid to tap her on the shoulder and ask her who she was. And I thought it would sound ridiculous to say 'Excuse me, but were you once a Catholic nun who dressed in an old-fashioned black habit on a daily basis and stayed at St. Cecelia's Academy a few years back?' How lame would that have sounded?"

"You're right, Lola."

"So what do we do?"

"I guess the next time you see her in Krogers, if there is a next time, follow her to her car. You could write down her license number and check it out at the Motor Vehicle Department. Surely they'd give you her name."

"She may not have a car. She might come in one of those senior citizen vans. We could check that out. But we can't hang around Krogers every day waiting for this woman to turn up."

"I'll call Senior Services in the morning and ask them when their vans make Kroger stops."

"Good. And, if you can't get out of school during those times, I'll try to get there."

"I really appreciate your help, Lola. You must think I'm a real pain in the ass stirring up all this trouble."

"You're not. It's kind of fun when you think about it. Besides, you bought two tubs of butter for our fund-raiser and you've decided to join. You are going to join, aren't you?"

"Do I dare say no?"

Instead of answering Susan directly, Lola yelled to the crowd in general, "Hey, ladies. Listen up. We have a new member."

⌘

Susan phoned Senior Services during a mid-morning break in the orientation program. The woman she spoke with said that the van went to Krogers on Tuesday and Thursday mornings. It dropped off its passengers around ten and picked them up at eleven. Today was Wednesday. Since tomorrow's morning meetings were for the elementary teachers, Susan would be free to be at the store when the van arrived.

She phoned Lola to tell her the plan.

"Geez. I've got a style show over in Ferry at noon, so I can't be there."

"Well, try to describe her the best you can. What does she look like?"

"She's about your height but stooped over. She has a strange looking cane. It looks like a branch she picked up in the woods. Her hair was dark the first day I saw her but blond the next. She must do wigs. Promise not to get mad?"

"Why?"

"I couldn't help but think that her eyes were exactly the same color as yours. So dark blue they look almost black. I couldn't get over the similarity, and I'd seen you only twice. And both times she'd plastered on dark red lipstick on and way above the lip-line. She looked like Bette Davis in *Whatever Happened to Baby Jane.*"

"She sounds grotesque."

"Well, you can't miss her."

Susan made sure she arrived at Krogers at nine-forty five. When the Senior Citizen van pulled up, she pretended to be standing at the door reading the flier advertising the week's specials. There were only five passengers, three very well-dressed ladies with immaculately coifed hair and two men. Susan was disappointed but decided to pick up some odds and ends while she was there. Towards the middle of the store at the peanut butter section, she caught sight of Sister Gertrude assisting someone at the other end of the aisle. The woman she was helping was taller than Gertrude but too stooped over to reach the higher shelves. *My God*, gasped Susan as the woman turned her face in Susan's direction. *She looks just like the woman Lola described.*

Susan moved to another aisle before Sister Gertrude had a chance to recognize her. As soon as the two women headed for a check-out lane, she sneaked out the door and into her car which was parked close enough to the front door to afford her a good view of anyone leaving the store. After several minutes, Sister Gertrude emerged, wheeling the half-loaded shopping cart. The mystery woman, aided by her cane, hobbled along behind her. There was no need to copy down the license number. The car was Sister Gertrude's. She helped the woman into the passenger side then put the groceries in the trunk. Susan ducked down when Sister Gertrude walked by on her way to the cart drop-off lane. Then, she turned on the ignition and followed Sister Gertrude's car out of the lot and onto National Road. Traffic was light, so she was able to follow far enough behind without being recognized. When Sister Gertrude turned left at the light at the intersection of National Road and 88 North, Susan did likewise. *Where could those two be going? Obviously nowhere exciting with a trunk loaded with groceries.* Susan picked up her phone and keyed in Lola's cell.

"Hi. This is Lola. How may I help you?"

"It's Susan."

"Where are you? I can hardly hear you."

Susan realized she'd been whispering.

"Sorry about that. Is that better?"

"Much."

"I'm on 88. Just passing your entrance. I'm following Sister Gertrude's car. I just happened to see her in Krogers with the woman you described."

"You're kidding! Then she must be the right person if Gertie's involved."

"I'm going to follow them to see where they end up. Sister Gertrude obviously took her grocery shopping. God! I feel like a stalker. But I can't stop myself. My curiosity's gotten the better of me."

"Me too. Call me when you find out where they're going."

"Will do."

"And Susan," said Lola with a chuckle, "you don't need to whisper when you're following another car. The other driver can't hear you."

"I know," laughed Susan. "I'll call later."

"Wanna have lunch tomorrow?"

"Can't. A rep from the Diocese is speaking to us in the afternoon. But I'll take a rain check."

They drove past Oglebay Park. Susan guessed that Sister Gertrude's passenger probably lived in Wentworth. But, a few miles before the village, Gertrude turned on her right turn signal. There was nothing behind Susan, so she was able to slow down enough to watch the car pull into the secluded driveway of a small clapboard cottage. *Did the mystery woman live here by herself? And why was Sister Gertrude helping her?*

Susan had to drive quite a distance to find a safe place to turn around and head back towards Wheeling. Getting back to St. Cecelia's for a one o'clock meeting meant skipping lunch, but her discovery had been worth it. The meeting was just starting when Susan walked into the Music Hall. A few minutes later, Sister Gertrude strode in. She looked around the large room, spotted Susan, walked in her direction and sat down in the chair directly behind her. She tapped Susan on the shoulder.

"Did you find what you were looking for?" she whispered.

"What are you talking about?" Susan whispered back.

"You aren't exactly subtle, Susan. I was behind you all the way back to school. Talk to me at the break."

At the two o'clock recess, Gertrude signaled Susan to follow her into an empty classroom.

"Now, young lady. Explain yourself. Why were you following me? And don't say you weren't."

"All right. I admit I was following you. Someone told me that the lady you were with looked like someone who used to be a sister who lived at St. Cecelia's for a few months."

"Really? And would you by any chance have purchased the top you're wearing at your informant's boutique? It's got Lola Mendez written all over it."

"Okay. You win. I give up. But don't be mad at Lola. I'm the trouble maker. I got her roped into the Solange mystery."

"I'm not mad at anyone, Susan. I'm just frustrated. Is your mother planning to visit any time soon?"

"Labor Day weekend."

"Good. I'm sick of hiding your family's secrets."

"I assume you're referring to Solange."

"Right! And, as much as I like and admire your mother, I'm going to insist she tell you the truth."

"Does it involve the woman you were with today?"

"Yes. But don't ask me anything else. It's bad enough to have the worry of the school's enrollment decline on my hands without worrying about you stirring up trouble."

"I didn't mean to upset you."

"Well, just hang on until your mother gets here."

"I promise. But one more tiny question."

"What is it this time?"

"Why did you call me Suzette the first time we met?"

"It's your real name."

"How do you know?"

"Your mother told me."

⌘

The only problem with the first days of classes at St. Cecelia's was the intense heat in the un-air-conditioned building. It was so hot that Dr. Anderson decided that letting the students out at noon on the Friday of Labor Day weekend would improve everyone's temper including her own. Anna had decided to rent a car and drive to Wheeling but wasn't due to pull into town until well after three, so Susan decided to stick around the school to catch up on some paper work. She was happy that Sister Gertrude hadn't gone through with her plans to redecorate. The framed pictures of the convent outside Sauret and the table with Solange's signature etched underneath gave Susan a feeling of being at home. And Sister Gertrude had certainly done a three sixty in the attitude department. She was going to join Susan and her mother for dinner the following evening.

Susan raised one of the rickety windows in her room as far as it would go. She smiled as she breathed in the cool air that wafted in. Dr. Anderson had predicted that the minute she approved an early dismissal cooler weather would prevail. She was right. The temperature had dropped about ten degrees since noon and dark rain clouds hovered overhead. The building was so quiet without the students that Susan was having a hard time concentrating on lesson plans and grading the first quizzes of the semester. She grabbed the colorful shawl she'd brought in to brighten up an old stuffed arm-chair and wrapped it around her shoulders before wandering downstairs to the front porch. She followed the scent of freshly mown grass to one end of the building and found herself in the sisters' cemetery. The headstones were engraved with only the names of the deceased and their dates of birth and death. The graves were arranged chronologically from the late 1800's to the present. A sudden gust of wind made Susan shiver. Clutching her shawl tighter, she looked at the name on the headstone directly in front of her.

ISABELLE DUCHAMPS
1983

Isabelle Duchamps? Why was someone who wasn't a sister buried here? And was it merely coincidence that her name was French and that she'd died the same year Solange graduated? Could this Isabelle who was buried here be the nun from Sauret who'd threatened to kill Solange? Susan was so lost in thought that she wasn't aware of anyone approaching until she heard her mother's soft voice say her name.

Susan spun around to find Anna standing behind her.

"Mom. You're early. I thought you were going to the house."

"I did. Gave your horrid neighbor quite a start. She wasn't the least bit helpful when I asked if you were at home. She opened the front door and gave me my marching orders, but I just marched right on past her and up the stairs to your apartment."

"Good for you."

Susan embraced her mother then tightened the shawl around her shoulders. Then she started to guide her mother towards the building. "Let's go inside. It's getting chilly out here."

"No. Not just yet, Susan. There's something I have to tell you."

"Can't you tell me inside?"

"I'd rather do it out here."

Anna knelt down and touched Isabelle's headstone.

"Was Isabelle Duchamps you knew?"

"Yes. She was."

"Who? Who was she?"

"Your mother, Susan. Your real mother."

Susan didn't reply. She just stared at the headstone.

"Let's sit on the front porch, Susan. It's too cold out here, and the story I have to tell you will make it even colder."

They'd barely reached the steps of the front porch before the clouds opened up and showered the air with tiny, tear-shaped droplets. It was against this dreary backdrop that Anna revealed the circumstances of Susan's birth.

"I've suspected for some time that you weren't my birth mother."

"You have? For how long?"

"Since my trip to Dijon and Sauret. You don't have to be the brightest torch in the parade to figure out something's not quite right when people's hands fly to their mouths the first time they look at you. And it takes only a few people saying you look like your mother before you put two and two together. I don't look anything like you. Are you telling me that the same Isabelle who poisoned Annemarie is my mother?"

"Yes. That is the truth, but she isn't the woman buried over there."

"Who is?"

"I'm not sure. But that comes later in the story. You already understand the circumstances of Solange's birth. Right?"

"Right. Michelle told me the entire sordid tale. She also said that if those of you who knew the truth about Annemarie's death had gone to the police a second murder could have been prevented. But she wouldn't tell me the identity of the second victim."

"It was Lili Villiers, the wife of the village doctor. She was determined to clear her husband's name."

"The San Francisco Villiers I presume?"

"Yes. You see, Isabelle always insisted that she couldn't get in touch with Henri when Annemarie went into labor. To this day, Henri is convinced he was to blame for her death. I, likewise, bear a lot of guilt for Henri's wife's death. You see, unknown to me, Isabelle and my brother, Jacques, had continued a clandestine love affair even after she entered the convent."

"How did you find out?"

"Jacques confessed after Annemarie died. I was shocked, but Jacques thought it was funny. He kept insisting that even the most religious of women have hormones. I thought the affair ended when Jacques went to live in Vietnam. Obviously, I was wrong. It didn't take long to figure out why we saw so little of my brother on his periodic trips home."

"Then Jacques Fontaine really is my father?"

"Yes. No doubt about it. When Henri confirmed Isabelle's pregnancy, she was thrilled. She was convinced that Jacques would marry her. She was devastated when he told her he had no intentions of ever marrying her or anyone else. Henri confided to Lili that Isabelle was pregnant. Lili herself was pregnant with their second child. She used to take long walks up to the convent and around the walkway on the cliffs above the lake behind it. Sometimes, she would meet Isabelle on these outings."

"But didn't the nuns know she was pregnant?"

"She was able to hide her pregnancy under the long black robe the novices used to wear, but, of course, Lili knew. One day, Lili confronted her. She told her that if she didn't confess she'd never contacted Henri on the day of Annemarie's death, she'd reveal her pregnancy to the mother superior. Henri was concerned about Isabelle's reaction to Lili's threat and warned her to stay away from the convent area. Unfortunately, Lili ignored the warning. A few days later, she failed to return from one of her walks. Before nightfall, Lili's body was discovered in the lake by one of the locals out fishing. It was horrible."

"Was Isabelle arrested or even questioned?"

"No. Everyone, including the local police, was convinced that Lili had slipped on some loose rocks and fallen to her death. Isabelle was one of the witnesses. She told the police that she frequently saw Madame Villiers walking close to the edge of the cliffs."

"But what does all this have to do with my birth? And how did you end up with me?"

"A few days before Isabelle went into labor, she went to Henri for an examination. She started raving about how she was going to kill her baby if Jacques refused to marry her. Henri contacted Michelle who phoned and asked me to get to Sauret as soon as possible. On the pretext of needing to examine Isabelle again, Henri anaesthetized her while she was on the examining table. With me as his helper, he performed a Caesarian. Isabelle was too weak to put up a struggle when she woke up. The only thing she said as I carried you from the room was, "Suzette. Her name is Suzette.""

"Did she go back to the convent?"

"For a short time. But the sisters had her committed to an asylum."

"For giving birth to a child?"

"No. While she was recuperating at the Villiers' home, David, Henri's small son, told his father that he had seen Isabelle push his mother over the cliff. When Henri confronted Isabelle, she threatened to kill the little boy. That was the reason for her commitment. I am sure Michelle told you that Isabelle escaped from the asylum three years later. When the threats began against Solange, it was decided that she would come here to this beautiful school. You and I went to Syracuse. Henri and little David began a new life in San Francisco."

"But why is Isabelle buried here?"

"She isn't. In 1983, the year Solange was scheduled to graduate, Isabelle turned up here disguised as a nun. But I knew who she was. Just before graduation, I took Solange to San Francisco where she went to college. The sisters called me to say that Isabelle had become violent and was threatening bodily harm to all of them if they didn't tell her where Solange was. I returned to confront her. By this time, even the students were afraid of her. One evening, after I'd tried to calm her down, she jumped into one of the sister's cars and drove off this hill like a crazy lady. Later that evening, the superior here got a phone call saying that a young homeless woman who had done part-time work at the school had died in a car crash. The mother superior came up with the idea of burying the young woman here."

"Why does the headstone say Isabelle Duchamps?"

"To alleviate everyone's fears. Everyone was petrified of her."

"But where did she go?"

"We never found out. She just drove off into the night. But I never stopped being afraid that she would try to find and harm you. I did everything but barricade the house."

"Is that why you keep the front door locked year round?"

"Yes. I have lived in dread of her turning up at our house. She has been in Syracuse recently. But I don't know where she is at the moment."

"I do. She's here. I will take you both to her later this evening," said Sister Gertrude, walking onto the porch. "She is very ill. All we can do is make her comfortable. She will die soon."

"Do you hate me, Susan? I know now that I had no right to keep you from knowing about your real mother."

Susan walked over to Anna and put her arms around her. "You are my real mother. You always have been and always will be."

"Do you really mean that?"

"Of course. It's not often a girl has the same person as her mother and aunt."

"Do you want me to call you Suzette?"

"No. Susan. Susan will be just fine.

⌘

After her revelation about Isabelle's reappearance in Wheeling, Sister Gertrude was determined to arrange a meeting for the three women to make peace with each other. But she was too late. When she arrived at the house, Isabelle Duchamps was already dead. A note on the kitchen table directed Sister Gertrude to the pond behind the house.

Gertrude,

Thank you for your kindness. Although you knew I was an evil person, you helped me. You are the true servant of the Lord. Not me. I am an evil woman. Before the voices return and force me to harm my beautiful little Suzette, I must exit this world. You will find my body in the pond behind the house. Tell Anna that I am sorry for all my sins.

Isabelle Duchamps

The coroner's office issued a verdict of accidental drowning. Sister Gertrude saw no reason to show the authorities Isabelle's letter. Anna took care of the arrangements. Isabelle's body was cremated on Labor Day morning. By that evening, her ashes were on a plane headed for Dijon where they would be interred in the same plot as her mother and father.

"I'm going to stay here for a few more days, Susan. I need to take care of closing up Isabelle's cottage. It's not fair to put all this on Sister Gertrude. She has enough on her plate."

"I can take care of everything here. It's not as if my social calendar is overflowing," laughed Susan.

"No. I got us into this. It is my duty to finish it as painlessly as possible."

"You were on the phone for a long time last night. Henri?"

"Yes. He is as relieved as I am that Isabelle is out of our lives for good. He is very anxious to meet you."

"What about Solange?"

"Henri was going to phone her with the news. Let her know that she is finally safe."

"Where does she live?"

"Vancouver. Her husband is Canadian. You'll meet them soon. Henri and I have decided to get married the first week of December."

"That's wonderful news. I think I'm going to cry."

"I want you and Solange to be my maid and matron of honor."

Susan didn't respond. She walked over to her mother and threw herself into her arms.

"Will my father be there?"

"Yes. But don't be too hard on him. It was my idea to raise you. And he was the one who financed your education and purchased your Manhattan loft."

On Wednesday morning, as directed by Sister Gertrude, Anna met with Isabelle's attorney.

"You mean to tell me she actually had an attorney in Wheeling?" Anna had gasped in surprise.

"Yes. When she purchased the cottage last spring, she had to have one."

"But how could someone on a visitor's visa purchase property?"

"The house and two acres are in Susan's name. But her lawyer will explain everything."

When Susan arrived home after school on Wednesday afternoon, she found her mother going over a stack of official looking documents at the kitchen table.

"How did it go?"

"Very well. See those keys in the middle of the table?"

"Yes."

"They're yours."

"For what."

"Your cottage. Isabelle left you everything. According to her lawyer, she was left a tidy sum of money when her parents died. They were not rich people, but she was an only child, their sole heir. She named you hers."

"And you thought she wanted to kill me."

"According to a medical report she gave her lawyer, that was all part of the schizophrenia when she wasn't taking her medication. He said that her only desire was to see you face to face before she died."

"In a way, I wish she had," said Susan.

"But she did. According to some ridiculous story Sister Gertrude told me, she saw you one night while you and a student were prowling around the French classroom after dark."

"She was the person who coughed! All this time, I thought it was Sister Gertrude."

"Well, according to Gertrude, it was Isabelle. She followed you into the room with the intent of stabbing you to death. Only a fit of coughing stopped her from taking action before you ran out of the room."

"And I was afraid of Sister Gertrude!"

"Do you remember that night?"

"Ill never forget it. How did Sister Gertrude know she'd planned to kill me?"

"She confessed everything to her. That's why Sister Gertrude has been devoting so much time to her care, making sure she took her medication. Hopefully, the poor woman can get some rest now."

"Sister Gertrude or Isabelle?

"Both."

"This is a lot to digest. I keep thinking I'm going to wake up and it will all have been a nightmare."

"Well, at least it's over now."

"And you can concentrate on your wedding plans."

"Will you sell the cottage?"

"I'm not sure. Jenna's coming for Thanksgiving. She can help me decide."

"And Georges?"

"What about Georges?"

"Where does he fit in to all this?"

"I don't know. I keep thinking he's too good to be true. He doesn't keep in touch very often, but he said he'll visit me when he returns from France."

"Don't run from him, Susan."

"Do you ever regret raising me?"

"Not for a single moment. And, one more thing. I lied to you."

"About what?"

"The patter of one child's feet around the house being enough for a life-time. It's about time I became a grandmother. Neither of us is getting any younger."

⌘

Jenna glanced at the clock on the dash when she pulled off the Washington Avenue ramp on Interstate 70. The clock said four, but the dark November sky made it look more like five or six. The rain didn't do a thing to improve the bleakness of Washington Avenue. She already missed the lights of Manhattan. She'd never be able to understand how someone as worldly as Susan could live in such a dark and quiet place. No wonder she'd summoned Jenna to spend a few days with her at Thanksgiving. When Jenna had suggested the reverse, that Susan spend Thanksgiving in New York, she'd refused on the grounds that it would be too difficult to force herself to return to West Virginia. It started to pour just as Jenna turned right at the intersection of Washington Ave. and National Road. She pulled into the driveway of Susan's duplex and ran up the front steps. Thank God there was an overhang to protect her from the elements while she waited unsuccessfully for Susan to answer the doorbell. She must be at home. Her car was in the driveway, and a light was on in her living room which faced the front. She was on the verge of calling her on her cell phone when another car pulled into the driveway. A woman covered from head to toe in a rain poncho ran from the car to the small porch where Jenna stood frantically ringing the bell.

"What do you want?" the woman asked gruffly.

"I'm here to see Susan Foster, but she's not answering the doorbell."

"Maybe she's not in."

"Her car's here. I don't think she'd have walked anywhere in this downpour."

The woman put her key in the lock and opened the door.

"You must live here," said Jenna following her inside.

"Yes."

"You're on the first floor?"

"Yes."

"I just drove all the way from New York City to spend Thanksgiving with Susan," said Jenna, extending her hand. But the woman neither replied nor took Jenna up on the handshake. She pushed past Jenna, opened the door to her apartment and disappeared inside without a word.

"Well, a good-day to you to," murmured Jenna, unzipping her windbreaker and folding up her umbrella which dripped all the way up the stairs to Susan's door which she banged on with ferocity.

"Hold your horses. I'm coming,"

A few seconds later the door was opened by Susan draped in a terry cloth robe with a towel wrapped around her head. "How did you get in here?"

"Well, it wasn't with any help from you."

"Sorry about that. I was in the shower as you can see. I wasn't expecting you for another couple of hours.

"I got an early start. You sounded so desperate in your last e-mail that I left town as early as possible."

"Did you have any problem getting today off?"

"No. Our principal must have been in a good mood. She was actually concerned about me getting stuck in the day-before-the-holiday traffic. She just waved me out of her office and told me to have a good time and drive carefully."

"How did you get in here?"

"Your downstairs neighbor let me in. Actually, I ran in behind her. She's not exactly a chatty Cathy."

"Talked your ear off, did she?"

"Right! If I hadn't rushed through the door behind her, she'd have slammed it in my face."

"She's typical of the people in this area. Conversation isn't one of their strong suits."

"How do they communicate?"

"Must be by secret code. I've lived here for four months and haven't cracked it yet."

"No wonder it took you so long to find out the truth about Solange."

"You're not kidding. The folks who found her a school here knew what they were doing."

"What's the downstairs' neighbor's name?"

"Cathy."

"You're kidding."

"No. It really is. When I first moved in here, I tried to ask her several questions about the area. She gave me her em-ail address and told me to communicate with her over the internet."

"And she lives downstairs!"

"I know. It sounds comical telling you about her, but it's frustrating when you live here on a daily basis. But, come on in. Welcome to *Chez Susan*. What do you think?"

Jenna let out a long whistle before answering. "Sweet! Do you know what this place would go for in Manhattan? And it's so quiet," said Jenna, walking over to the wall of floor to ceiling windows facing the road. "I thought you said you were on the main road."

"I am. National Road! The original east-west route across the country before the interstates were built."

"When's rush hour?"

"We don't have rush hours in Wheeling. More like rush minutes."

"You're kidding!"

"No. Eight to nine in the morning. Four to five in the afternoon."

"I don't think I could stand the silence."

"It grows on you."

"No wonder you're bored. No noise. No conversation. What do you do for excitement?"

"Not much. But why don't you go into the kitchen and make us some tea while I dry my hair before it sticks to my scalp. If I wait any longer, I'll have to wash it again."

"Go ahead. I'll take care of the tea."

Jenna stepped into the large kitchen, filled the kettle and set it on the stove. While she waited for it to boil, she sat down at the table. A photograph on top of a stack of papers in the middle of the table caught her eye. She picked it up. It was a picture of a very tall, skinny dog covered in rough gray hair. It looked like a greyhound but wasn't. Jenna picked up the e-mail print-out which had been underneath the picture.

Dear Susan,

Thank you for filling out the background questionnaire. This is a picture of Kitty. Her puppies are due the middle of January. You should be able to pick yours up at the end of March or early April. Let me know if you're still interested.
Michelle

Puzzled, Jenna picked up another paper from the table. This one was an application from a kennel club in Ohio. None of this made any sense to Jenna. The whistling of the kettle broke her train of thought. She busied herself preparing two cups of African bush tea, the only kind she could find in Susan's cupboard. She'd never heard of the stuff before. It was bright red, but looked delicious.

"What's with the African bush tea?" she called to Susan.

"It's rooibos."

"Sure it is! Would you mind explaining to the uninitiated."

"It's the kind of tea Madame Ramotswe drank every day to calm her nerves."

"Madame who?"

"Ramotswe. She's the main character in McCall Smith's African series. I gave you a copy of *The Kalahari Typing School for Men* last Christmas. Don't tell me you haven't read it yet?"

"No. I haven't. Been too busy to do much reading."

"Spending all your time with Bob, the guy from Paris?"

"Yes."

"Sounds serious."

"I'll fill you in on my life if you fill me in on yours first."

"There's nothing to fill you in on."

"Well, could you explain these?" asked Jenna, reaching for the papers she'd just looked at and waving them in front of Susan.

"Jenna. I can't believe you've been reading my mail."

"Don't give me that. It was sitting here in plain view."

"Well, if you must know, I'm thinking of joining the St. Clairsville, Ohio Kennel Club."

"You can't be serious!"

"I certainly am."

"But you don't own a dog. Isn't that a prerequisite?"

"Unfortunately, yes."

"I don't understand."

"You would if you lived here," said Susan, bursting into tears. "It's horrible. I have no friends. No one talks to me."

"Well, you don't have to cry about it. Act your age for God's sake."

"I'll cry if I want to. I'm miserable," said Susan, drying her eyes between sobs. "When I go to the grocery store and see people I've met at school, they shift from one foot to the other and check their watches every few seconds when I try to engage them in conversation. They can't get away from me fast enough."

"Have you checked your deodorant and toothpaste? Maybe it's time for a change."

Susan picked up her tea spoon and threw it at Jenna. Then she burst out laughing.

"I know it sounds crazy. But I am miserable. That's why I invited you for Thanksgiving."

"Quit changing the subject, Susan. Call me stupid, but what does your misery have to do with a kennel club in Ohio?"

"Well, one evening I drove to the nearest shopping mall. It's in Ohio."

"That's the closest place with stores?"

"It's not as far as it sounds. It doesn't take that long to get there. When I was leaving the mall around eight-thirty one Tuesday evening, I bumped into a group of people coming out of the mall's community meeting room. I asked one of them what was going on in that room."

"Why?"

"Because the all looked so happy. They were laughing and chattering away to each other. That's all."

"That's all? I don't understand. What did this merry little band turn out to be?"

"The local kennel club. When the crowd dispersed, I looked at the notice board on the door of the meeting room. One poster said that the St. Clairsville Kennel Club met there on a regular basis the second Tuesday of each month."

"Then what?"

"I decided on the spot that if my social life hadn't picked up by the time of the next meeting I'd go along just for something to do."

"And it hadn't and you did. Right?"

"Right! And the people were very nice to me. They wanted to know all about me—in a way."

"In a way?"

"Well, they really wanted to know all about my dog."

"But you don't have a dog."

"I am aware of that fact, Jenna."

"So what did you tell them?"

"All about the Scottish deerhound named Angus that I planned to have by the summer."

"Have you lost your mind? How did you come up with that?"

"Molly Murdoch."

"Your mother's Scottish assistant? How did she get involved in this caper?"

"She didn't. I just remembered her talking about her family's deerhound back in Scotland."

"Named Angus?"

"I'm not sure about the name. She always referred to him as her big hairy beast. I had no idea how big they were till I got home from the meeting and Googled them. I take it you saw the photograph and letter from Michelle."

"They were hard to miss. So, who's this Michelle chick and why is she doing a background check on you?"

"She's the deerhound breeder, and the background check is strictly routine. Before you purchase one of her puppies, she needs information on you, rather a lot as it turns out."

"What sort of information?"

"Things like the size of the fenced in area you have available for the dog to exercise. It turns out that these beasties run like greyhounds. They need lots of room. But don't you think they're nice looking dogs?" asked Susan rhetorically, picking up the photograph and smiling at it. "Don't you agree?"

"Susan! Get serious. That dog's the size of a Shetland pony. Where do you plan to have it sleep?"

"I am serious. And Angus will sleep in the house. They don't make good kennel dogs."

"Are you allowed to have pets here?"

"Not here, silly. Did you think I was planning to let the dog run up and down National Road on a daily basis?"

"I haven't had time to think that far ahead."

"Well, as it turns out, I am now the sole owner of a cute little house in the country. A cottage. It's right in the middle of two acres which I intend to surround with a chain link fence."

"Wouldn't it be easier to join a local woman's club? At least you wouldn't need to own a pet to qualify for membership. And why in God's name did you buy property when you're planning on moving back to the City?"

"I can't leave here until June at the earliest when my teaching contract is up. And I didn't buy property. The house was an inheritance from my mother."

"Why did your mother have a house here when she already has one in Syracuse?"

"I mean my real mother."

"You mean Anna Foster is not your real mother? Then who the hell is?"

"Was. She was the evil sister who killed Annemarie."

"I have a feeling we're going to need something a lot stronger than your African bush tea for this story. Have you told Georges?"

"No. We're on a sort of sabbatical this year."

"He's crazy about you. And you're just plain crazy. Don't screw up this relationship, Susan. You'll regret it."

"I'll try not to. Do you and Bob have plans for spring break?"

"It's only Thanksgiving, Susan. But I do know that our breaks don't coincide."

"Good! I need you to go to Michigan with me."

"Why Michigan?"

"To pick up the big hairy beast. Please say you'll go."

"Do I have a choice?"

"Not if you're the friend I think you are."

"Okay. I'll go. But, hey, Thanksgiving is the day after tomorrow. Got the bird yet?"

"No. We can take care of all the food shopping tonight. And it will be so nice to shop with a friend. The people here are so tribal. You rarely see people out by themselves."

"Definitely not New York," laughed Jenna. "Definitely not! Anything on tap for tomorrow?"

"I thought we'd take a run out to my house."

"I still can't believe you're doing all this for a dog that hasn't been born yet."

"It's more than that. I need solitude to digest all this news about my real mother. I'll explain it all after dinner and at least one bottle of wine."

"So, it's house inspection tomorrow and cooking and eating on Thursday. What about Friday and Saturday?"

"Pittsburgh. You'll love the Warhol. We can stay in the city on Friday night. I've already reserved a room at the Hilton. We can shop till we drop on Saturday and drive home in the evening."

"Sounds like a plan to me."

"Too bad you won't be here on December 7th?"

"You're celebrating Pearl Harbor Day?"

"No. It's the kennel club Christmas party. And don't even think about coming up with a one-liner about that."

"Don't worry, Susan. I know when to keep my mouth shut."

⌘

Susan placed the large framed family portrait taken at her mother's wedding in San Francisco on the buffet in the living room. The wedding had been a true family affair in Henri Villiers' small garden at the rear of his house. This time last year Susan hadn't known any of these people other than her mother existed. Now their daily lives were inextricably intertwined. The bride and groom were flanked by their respective families. David and his wife stood to the right of Henri. Susan was squashed in between her father, Jacques, and Solange whose husband and grown son and daughter stood on the far left. Everyone was smiling. There were no more secrets. The wedding had been a happy affair. Solange and Susan had bonded immediately. Before Jacques flew back to Vietnam the day after the wedding, he made Susan promise that she would visit him there. The only person missing from the photograph was Georges. He'd been invited to the wedding but sent his regrets. No explanation. Just an e-mail saying that his schedule would not permit him to attend.

Susan wiped away the tears that had started to run down her face with the back of her hand. She wished she'd never met Georges. He obviously shared the same feeling about her. With a shrug of her shoulders, she sat down at the kitchen table and started to read her mail. There were three Christmas cards, all from friends in New York. She was so miserable living in Wheeling that she didn't even want to be reminded of New York. But Christmas always made Susan feel sad. Growing up in Syracuse, she and her mother had never had anyone to celebrate with. At least in New York there'd been a multitude of parties throughout December to take her mind off the lack of family gatherings. There was no sense in going to New York this year since Jenna was spending the holidays at Bob's parents. And she felt out of the loop with her colleagues at the translation center. Her mother and Henri had invited her to accompany them to Hawaii, but Susan had no desire to feel like a third wheel on someone's honeymoon. Next year she herself would arrange a huge family celebration on either the west or the east coast. Georges Bonnard would not be invited.

Before Susan opened the waste basket to toss in her junk mail, she gave each item the once over to make sure it really was junk. One large envelope with her name and address written in beautiful calligraphy caught her attention. There was no return address on either side of the envelope. She opened it and pulled out an engraved invitation inviting her to attend a Christmas celebration in the Ilenfeld dining room at Wilson Lodge on Friday, December twenty-first at eight p.m. The only strange part of the invitation was that there was no RSVP. She examined the envelope again. It was post-marked somewhere in Connecticut. The name of the town was too faint to read.

After announcements at school the next morning, Susan asked a few of the other teachers if they'd received an invitation to a party at Wilson Lodge on December twenty-first. No one had. Hilda's sarcastic response had been, "I couldn't go anyway. I loaned my sequined gown to my niece."

"You're just jealous," said Jonathan.

Susan fled down the hall to her classroom. She had no desire to get caught in another verbal cross-fire between Hilda and Jonathan. Not even the atmosphere of Christmas which pervaded the school could stop those two from firing zingers at each other at every opportunity.

Despite not knowing the source of her invitation for December twenty-first, Susan decided to attend. Her year of cloak and dagger work in searching for Solange had given her a taste for adventure. Besides, she had nothing planned for that particular evening. There were several planned festivities at St. Cecelia's before school closed for the holidays, but none of these events ever blossomed into invitations to events away from school over the holidays. There was a definite lack of camaraderie among the faculty members. Nevertheless, Susan enjoyed the Christmas concert held in the chapel, and the entire school seemed energized by the advent friend tradition which culminated in a grand feast in the music hall on the last day of the semester.

On the afternoon of the twenty-first, Susan got her hair and nails done at Kelly's, the salon on the lower level of Lola's and Alex's shops. Then she stopped in at Lola's to pick up the chiffon two-piece she'd ordered for the evening's event.

"I can't believe you're going to this do at Oglebay and you don't even know what it is or who'll be there. Are you nuts?"

"Bored and curious is more like it, Lola."

"You should have flown to Vancouver to spend the holidays with Solange and her crew. She told me in an e-mail that she'd invited you."

"I know, but with getting ready to move into the cottage in early January and a million and one other things, I didn't feel up to going."

"Well, just don't expect me to feel sorry for you for spending the holidays on your own. But isn't it great! Solange is planning on coming to our class reunion at St. Cecelia's at the end of April. I can hardly wait."

Susan turned to leave, but Lola placed a firm hand on her shoulder. "Slow down, girl. You're not leaving here until you tell me what shoes and accessories you plan to wear with this outfit."

An hour later Susan left Lola's clutching several black shopping bags embossed with the boutique's shiny silver logo. Tienda de Lola certainly was a unique boutique. And its owner had effortlessly talked Susan into purchasing a glitzy pair of shoes with matching evening bag and the longest pair of dangling earrings she'd ever owned.

Lola continued talking to Susan from the doorway while she placed her purchases in the car. "Give me a call tomorrow, Susan. Let me know how it went. In that outfit, you'll knock them dead. And don't forget to tell them where it all came from. We'll be having a sale right after the holidays."

⌘

Susan pulled into the parking lot of Wilson Lodge at seven forty-five. The spaces near the main door were all occupied, so she had to walk quite a distance in her sexy high heels. At least the sidewalk leading to the main door had been swept clear of the snow that had fallen in the late afternoon. Snow or ice would have spelled disaster. The thought of making herself conspicuous by sliding and falling face down on the sidewalk was mortifying; but she made it to the door without mishap and followed the sound of piano music up the stairs leading to the dining room. At the top, she had no idea where she was. A woman was playing Christmas music on a grand piano next to an enormous fireplace. Susan could swear she looked her way and smiled. She felt ill at ease until a waitress approached her and asked "Are you Susan Foster?"

"Yes. And who are you? You look familiar."

"You met me at St. Cecelia's turkey dinner. I'm Emma. My granddaughter goes to St. C's."

Susan and Emma shook hands.

"I'm feeling rather out of place, Emma. I received an invitation to dinner here, but I don't know who invited me."

"Don't worry. Just follow me," said Emma with a grin.

"But this isn't the dining room."

"Please do as I say. Okay?"

"Okay. You're the boss."

She followed Emma to one of the bistro tables set for two. One of the chairs was occupied by a man whose back was to Susan.

"Here she is, signed, sealed and delivered," said Emma before disappearing into the crowd of holiday makers.

The man stood up at turned to face Susan. It was Georges. Susan stumbled into her chair.

"I don't believe it. Georges Bonnard! What are you doing here?"

"Honoring the invitation I sent you last week."

"You sent the invitation?"

"Yes. I had a friend mail it from New Haven to throw you off the track."

"Why didn't you just phone?"

"I thought this was much more romantic."

Suddenly, the Christmas music stopped. The lady at the piano announced that she had a request for a special couple in the room. A hush fell over the room as she began singing, "You must remember this, a kiss is still a kiss......"

"I love you, Susan Foster," said George, reaching across the table for Susan's hand.

"And I love you, Georges Bonnard. I can't believe you planned all this."

"You haven't gotten to the best part yet," said Emma who'd reappeared with a bottle of champagne and two glasses. Susan took one of the glasses from her.

"Give that back. You got the wrong one," said Emma, handing her the other.

"Oh, my God," said Susan, reaching inside the champagne flute and retrieving a gold ring set with an exquisitely shaped diamond. Georges took the ring from her and held it at the tip of her ring finger.

"Will you marry me, Susan?"

When Susan didn't answer immediately, Emma broke the silence by blurting out, "For God's sakes say yes before I faint."

"Yes. Yes. Yes."

Georges slipped the ring on Susan's finger then leaned across the table to kiss her to the applause of everyone in the room. It took a few minutes for them both to realize that the music had stopped. The lady at the piano had vanished.

"When will she be back?" asked Georges.

"She's not coming back," said Emma, wiping a tear from her eye.

"But we need to thank her," said Susan.

"You already have," said Emma. "You already have."

Susan lay in that half-conscious stupor that frequently accompanies coming out of a deep sleep. It took her several minutes to screw up the courage to squint her left eye in the direction of her hand to see if the events of two night's ago at Oglebay Park had been real or the subjects of a Technicolor dream. But the proof that they'd been real was on the third finger of her left hand. Her next move was to gingerly slide her right hand over to the other side of the bed. It was only when she felt warm flesh beneath it that she knew she actually was lying next to Georges.

"Georges. Are you awake?"

"Have been for ages. Didn't want to wake you."

"Oh, God! I'd better get up. I'm supposed to meet another teacher at school at noon. She's going to help me with loading my final grades into the computer."

"Well, let's go. You take a shower. I'll start the coffee."

"Great. And get the paper from the bottom step in the hallway."

A few minutes later, Georges called out, "There isn't any newspaper."

"What did you say? I can't hear you for the water running."

"I just wanted to let you know," said Georges, pushing open the bathroom door, "that the paper isn't here. I'll go out and get one."

"Just call the number for the News Register office. It's on the kitchen bulletin board. Someone will bring one over."

"Are you sure?"

"Positive."

The doorbell rang about half an hour later.

"You were right," said Georges, walking into the bedroom, holding the Sunday paper.

"Was it a boy or girl?"

"Neither. It was a rather distinguished looking gentleman. Not your typical paper boy."

"Oh. That was Harry Hamilton, the editor himself."

"The editor?"

"Yeah. He just lives a few blocks from here. He and his wife have twelve kids who are kept busy delivering papers to subscribers left in the lurch. The tribe must be otherwise occupied this weekend if their dad himself came."

"Maybe they've gone on strike," laughed Georges. "I guess there are advantages to small-town life. I can't imagine service like this from the *New York Times* staff. Maybe I could get used to living here. Just as long as I can get my *Times* on a regular basis.'"

"Of course you can. I always pick it up at the super market. Did you mean that?"

"Mean what?"

"That you could get used to living here."

"Never thought about it. I just figured we'd live in New York after we get married. Didn't you?"

"Well, not exactly."

"What do you mean by not exactly?"

"My house."

"What house?"

"The one my mother left me."

"You mean the one in Syracuse?"

"House or mother?"

"Both. I just assumed that since your mother married Henri and moved to San Francisco that her Syracuse house was on the market."

"You assumed correctly."

"Then which house are you talking about?"

"The one my real mother left me right here in Wheeling."

"What are you talking about?"

"It seems that my real mother was the one of your grandmother's threesome who entered the convent in Sauret."

"You can't be serious."

"Never more so."

"What about your father?"

"What about him?"

"Who is he?"

"Jacques Fontaine. He is definitely my father."

"Then my grandmother was right all along, wasn't she?"

"It appears so."

"You know, she still feels guilty about the evening you and Jenna had dinner with us in Dijon."

"Why?"

"Because she lied about the newspaper clipping she claimed she couldn't find."

"Why?"

"Because it showed your father, Jacques, with his sister, Anna, the woman whose photo you'd shown her, claiming that she was your mother. My poor grandmother was convinced that you were the result of an incestuous relationship."

"Is that why she acted so cool towards me the rest of the evening?"

"Yes. But that was nothing compared to her state of mind after you'd left when I told her I was falling in love with you."

"That poor woman."

"Don't worry. I'll phone her tonight. She will be greatly relieved. But tell me the entire story."

"It'll have to be later this afternoon when I come back from St. Cecelia's. We'll drive out to my cottage in the country."

"But that's impossible."

"What's impossible? Georges, are you all right?"

"Look at this," said Georges, spreading out a section of the newspaper on the table.

"Why are you reading the obituaries?"

"It's her. The lady at Wilson Lodge who played and sang for us on Friday night. Look!"

The photograph staring back at them was definitely one of the pianist at Wilson Lodge.

"What happened to her? How can she be dead?"

"It says here that she gave her last performance at Wilson Lodge on Friday evening. She had been ill for several months," read George. "Now I get it. When I phoned to ask if anyone could sing that song for us, the person I was speaking to in the office said that it all depended on Barbara's schedule."

"I'll say it did. Now I know why Emma was crying. She knew that Barbara was definitely not coming back. She stayed just long enough to make sure our romantic evening went off without a hitch. Wow! Will we have something to tell our grandchildren!"

"She didn't even know who we were. You know, that woman's kind heartedness is going to go a long way in helping me make my decision about staying in Wheeling."

"It is? Well, just remember that when you see my lovely cottage. And it's got two acres of land, just perfect for adding on a studio for you."

"Well, hurry up and do what you have to at St. Cecelia's. I'm suddenly getting anxious to see my future home."

"Do you mean that?"

"Yes. I have a feeling there could be worse places to live than this neck of the woods. After all, we've got to live somewhere."

Printed in the United States
208119BV00002B/223/P

9 781607 030171